THE
DEADLINE

A NOVEL ABOUT PROJECT MANAGEMENT

Praise for THE DEADLINE

"Here's a management book which is just plain fun to read. *The Deadline* is an innovative and entertaining story with insightful business principles for team-based project management at the end of each chapter." — John Sculley

". . . it's a technological tour de force. It covers a wide range of topics, from project estimating to metrics, from conflict resolution to dealing with ambiguous specifications. . . . the bullet points alone are worth the price of the book. . . . *The Deadline* is almost as funny as a book full of Dilbert cartoons, but it's far less cynical. More important, it contains some profound wisdom and some practical, positive advice for improving the chances of meeting your next project deadline. I highly recommend it."
—**Ed Yourdon**, *American Programmer*

Also by TOM DEMARCO

Peopleware: Productive Projects and Teams, 2nd ed.
by Tom DeMarco and Timothy Lister
ISBN: 0-932633-43-9   Copyright ©1998   256 pages, softcover

Productive Teams: A Video
featuring Tom DeMarco and Timothy Lister
ISBN: 0-932633-30-7   Copyright ©1994   VHS or PAL   60 minutes

Software State-of-the-Art: Selected Papers
edited by Tom DeMarco and Timothy Lister
ISBN: 0-932633-14-5   Copyright ©1990   584 pages, hardcover

Why Does Software Cost So Much? And Other Puzzles of the Information Age   by Tom DeMarco
ISBN: 0-932633-34-X   Copyright ©1995   248 pages, softcover

Find Out More About These and Other DH Books

Contact us to request a Book & Video Catalog and a free issue of *The Dorset House Quarterly*, or to confirm price and shipping information.

DORSET HOUSE PUBLISHING
353 West 12th Street   New York, NY 10014   USA
1-800-342-6657   212-620-4053   fax: 212-727-1044
dhpubco@aol.com   www.dorsethouse.com

THE
DEADLINE

A NOVEL ABOUT PROJECT MANAGEMENT

TOM DeMARCO

DORSET HOUSE PUBLISHING
353 WEST 12TH STREET
NEW YORK, NEW YORK 10014

Library of Congress Cataloging in Publication Data

DeMarco, Tom.
    The deadline : a novel about project management / Tom DeMarco.
        p.   cm.
    ISBN 0-932633-39-0   (softcover)
    1. Industrial project management--Fiction.   I.   Title.
    PS3554.E449D42   1997
    813'.54--dc21   97-24716
                                                                            CIP

Cover Design: David McClintock
Cover Illustration: Tom DeMarco
Cover Photograph: Hein van Steenis

Copyright © 1997 by Tom DeMarco. Published by Dorset House Publishing, 353 West 12th Street, New York, NY 10014.

Distributed in the English language in Singapore, the Philippines, and Southeast Asia by Toppan Co., Ltd., Singapore; in the English language in India, Bangladesh, Sri Lanka, Nepal, and Mauritius by Prism Books Pvt., Ltd., Bangalore, India; and in the English language in Japan by Toppan Co., Ltd., Tokyo, Japan.

Printed in the United States of America

Library of Congress Catalog Number: 97-24716

ISBN: 0-932633-39-0   12   11

CONTENTS

CONTENTS

PREFACE

ঌ

$\mathcal{D}$uring the 1930's, the University of Colorado physicist George Gamow began writing a series of short stories about a certain Mr. Tompkins, a middle-aged bank clerk. Mr. Tompkins, the stories related, was interested in modern science. He would trundle off to evening lectures put on by a local university physics professor, and inevitably fall asleep partway through. When he awoke, he would find himself in some alternate universe where one or another of the basic physical constants was strikingly changed.

In one of these stories, for example, Mr. T. awoke in a universe where the speed of light was only fifteen miles per hour. That meant he could observe relativistic effects on his bicycle: The city blocks became shorter in the direction of travel as he accelerated, and time on the post office clock slowed down. In another story, Mr. Tompkins visited a world where Planck's Constant was 1.0, and there he could *see* quantum mechanics in action on a billiard table: The billiard balls refused to move smoothly across the table, but took up quantum positions in probabilistic fashion.

When I first came across the Gamow stories, I was just a teenager. Like Mr. Tompkins, I too had an interest in modern science. I had already read numerous descriptions of relativity and quantum mechanics, but it was only when I read *Mr. Tompkins in Wonderland* that I began to develop a visceral sense of what these matters were all about.

I have always admired Gamow's ingenious pedagogical device. It occurred to me that a similar device might be used to demonstrate some of the principles of project management. All I'd have to do is portray a veteran project manager sent off to some Wonderland where various of the rules governing project work could be instructively altered. Thus was born, with apologies to George Gamow, the idea of *The Deadline,* the story of a manager named Tompkins and his remarkable experiences running software projects in the ex-Soviet Republic of Morovia.

May 1997   T.D.M.
Camden, Maine

THE DEADLINE

A NOVEL ABOUT PROJECT MANAGEMENT

DEDICATION

To Sally-Oh

1

OPPORTUNITY KNOCKING

❧

$\mathcal{M}$r. Tompkins took his seat in the very last row of Baldrige-One, the main auditorium at the Big Telephone and Telecommunications Company's Penelope, New Jersey, facility. He'd spent a lot of time in this auditorium during the past few weeks, attending out-placement lectures. Mr. T., along with a few thousand other professional and middle management employees, was being given the boot. Oh, that wasn't the term they used. They preferred to call it "made redundant" or "downsized" or "right-sized" or "streamlined" or "managed down" or, best of all, "Released to Seek Opportunities Elsewhere." They'd even made an acronym out of that one: ReSOE. Tompkins was a ReSOE.

Today's event was yet another in the series called "Opportunity Knocking." This five-week program, according to the posted notice, was to be "more than 100 hours of inspirational training, skits, musical interludes, and celebration of ReSOE status." The still-employed Human Resources people who put on the various sessions seemed pretty convinced that ReSOE was a blessing in disguise. They made it clear that they would have dearly loved to be ReSOEs themselves. They really would. But no such luck. No sir, they would just have to soldier on, bearing the burdens of salary and benefits as best they could. Up on the stage now, they were trying to put on a brave front.

The last few rows of the auditorium were in what the acoustic engineers called a "null area." For some reason (no one had even a good theory about this), almost no sound from the stage could be heard in these rows. It made it a perfect place for a snooze. Tompkins always sat here.

He put down today's ton of handouts on the seat in front of him. Two fat loose-leaf notebooks and the usual assortment of favors were packed into a new canvas bag with its printed logo: "Our Company Is Thinning Down So the Rest of the World Can Fatten Up." At the top of the bag was a baseball cap embroidered "ReSOE and Proud of It!" Tompkins put the hat on, pulled it down over his face and, within a few minutes, drifted off to sleep.

A long chorus line of HR people on the stage was singing "Opportunity Knocking: Okay!" The audience was supposed to clap the rhythm and join in at the chorus, shouting out "Okay!" as loud as they could. At the left side of the stage was a man with a megaphone, exhorting the audience with cries of "Louder! Louder!" A few people in the crowd were clapping softly, but no one was shouting. Still, the noise, even the little bit that penetrated the null area, was enough to rouse Mr. T.

He yawned and straightened up in his chair. The first thing he noticed was that someone else was sitting there in the quiet zone, only one seat away. The second thing he noticed was that she was lovely. She seemed to be in her early thirties, dark and rather exotic-looking: mid-length black hair in a Dutch cut, very dark eyes. She was looking up at the muted stage act and smiling very slightly. It was not exactly a smile of approval. He thought he might have seen her somewhere before.

"Did I miss anything?" he asked.

She kept her eyes on the stage. "Only some very important stuff."

"Could you net it out for me?"

"They want you to go away but not change your long-distance account over to MCI."

"Anything else?"

"Um . . . let's see, you've been asleep for about an hour. Was there anything else during that hour? No, I guess not. Some songs."

"I see. A typically triumphant morning for HR."

"Ooooh. Mr. Tompkins has awakened, how shall we say it? in a slightly bilious mood."

"I see you have the advantage over me," Mr. T. said, offering his hand. "Tompkins."

"Hoolihan," she said, shaking his hand. Her eyes, as she turned to face him, were not just dark, but almost black. It felt good looking into them. Mr. Tompkins found himself blushing slightly.

"Umm . . . first name, Webster. Webster Tompkins."

"Lahksa."

"Funny name."

"It's an old Balkan name. From Morovia."

"But Hoolihan . . . ?"

"Mmm. A girlish indiscretion on my mother's part. He was Irish, a deckhand on a freighter. A rather cute deckhand, I understand. Mother always had a weakness for sailors." She smiled at him lopsidedly. Tompkins felt a sudden extra beat in his heart.

"Ah," he said, cleverly.

"Ah."

"We've met, I think." He meant it as a question.

"Yes." She didn't go on.

"I see." He still couldn't remember where it might have been. He looked around the auditorium. There wasn't another soul anywhere near enough to hear. They were sitting in a public auditorium and yet were able to have a private conversation. He turned back to his charming neighbor. "You're a ReSOE, I take it?"

"No."

"No? Staying on then?"

"Also no."

"I don't get it."

"Not an employee at all. The truth is that I'm a spy."

He laughed, thinking it a joke. "Do tell."

"An industrial spy. You've heard of such things?"

"Yes, I guess."

"You don't believe me."

"Well, . . . it's just that you don't look the part."

She smiled that maddening smile again. Of course, she did look the part. In fact, she looked like she was born for the part.

"Not exactly, I mean."

She shook her head. "I can give you proof." She unclipped her identity badge and passed it to him.

Tompkins looked down at the badge. It was imprinted HOOLIHAN, Lahksa, over her photo. "Wait a minute . . ." he said, looking more closely at the badge. On the surface it looked okay, but there was something wrong with the lamination. In fact, it wasn't a lamination at all; it was just plastic wrap. He peeled it back and the photo came away from the badge. He saw there was another photo underneath, this one of a middle-aged man. And now that he looked, her name was on a sticky label pasted on the front of the badge. He lifted the label and saw the name STORGEL, Walter, underneath. "Why, this is about the worst forgery I can imagine."

She sighed. "The resources available within the Morovian KVJ are not what you'd call 'sophisticated.'"

"You really are . . . ?"

"Mmm. Going to turn me in?"

"Uh . . ." A month ago, of course, he would have done just that. But a lot of things can happen in a month, things that change you. He thought about it for a moment. "No, I don't think so." He handed her back the pieces of her badge, which she tucked neatly into her purse.

"Wasn't Morovia some kind of a, well, a *Communist* country?" Tompkins asked her.

"Uh huh. Sort of."

"You worked for a Communist government?"

"I guess you could say that."

He shook his head. "What's the point? I mean, if the 1980's proved anything, it was that Communism is a bankrupt philosophy."

"Mmm. The 1990's, of course, are showing us that the alternative ain't too great either."

"Well, it is true that there have been a lot of layoffs."

"Only 3.3 million lost jobs in the last nine months. Yours among them."

A long pause as Mr. Tompkins digested that thought. Now it was he who said, "Mmm," and he thought, What a

5

heavy conversation. He switched gears, artfully, "Tell me, Ms. Hoolihan, what's it like to be a spy? I mean, I am in the market for a new job."

"Oh no, Webster, you're not the spy type," she snickered. "Not the type at all."

He felt a bit miffed. "Well, I don't know about that."

"You're a manager. A systems manager, and a good one."

"Some people don't seem to think so. I've, after all, been ReSOEd."

"Some people don't seem to think at all. Such people tend to become executives in large companies like this one."

"Yes, well. Anyway, just for my information, do tell me what's involved in being a spy. I mean, I never got to meet one before."

"As you might expect, stealing corporate secrets, the odd kidnapping, maybe occasionally bumping someone off."

"Really?!?"

"Oh, sure. All in a day's work."

"Well, that doesn't seem very respectable. You would actually kidnap people or even . . . you know, kill them, just to gain commercial advantage?"

She yawned. "I guess. Not just anybody, though. For bumping off, I mean. Whoever it was would have to deserve it."

"Well, even so. I'm not at all sure I approve. I mean, I'm quite sure I don't approve. What kind of a person would kidnap another human being—we just won't even talk about the other—what kind of a person would do that?"

"A pretty clever person, I guess."

"Clever?!? You have to be clever to do that?"

"Not the actual act of kidnapping. That's fairly mechanical. No, the trick is, knowing *whom* to kidnap." She bent down to her feet where there was a small refrigerator bag from which she took a canned soft drink and opened it. "Could I offer you a drink?"

"Um. No, thanks. I really don't drink anything but . . ."

". . . diet Dr. Pepper." She pulled out a cold can of diet Dr. Pepper.

"Oh. Well, since you have one . . ."

She pulled the tab and passed it to him. "Cheers," she said, clunking her drink against his.

"Cheers." He drank a mouthful. "What's so hard about knowing whom to kidnap?"

"Let me answer that question with a question. What's the hardest job in management?"

"People," Tompkins replied automatically. He knew exactly where he stood on this subject. "Getting the right people for the right job. That's what makes the difference between a good manager and a drone."

"Mmm."

Now he remembered where it was he had seen her before. It was in that corporate management class he'd taken almost half a year ago. She had been in the last row, only a few seats away when he had stood up to contest the seminar leader on this very point. Yes, now he remembered. They'd sent some guy named Kalbfuss, Edgar Kalbfuss, to teach the course, a guy who was probably about twenty-five and had obviously never managed anything or anyone. And he was there to teach management to people like Tompkins, who'd been managing for half their lives. And the worst of it was, he was prepared to teach a whole week with (judging from the agenda) not a single thing to say about people management. Tompkins stood, told him off, and then walked out. Life was too short for that kind of "training."

She'd heard it that day, but now he told her again what he'd said to Kalbfuss: "Get the right people. Then, no matter what all else you may do wrong after that, the people will save you. That's what management is all about."

"Mmm."

A long, significant silence.

"Oh." Tompkins caught on at last. "You're suggesting that figuring out the right people to kidnap is the same?"

"Sure. You have to pick the ones who will give your side a meaningful advantage, and whose loss will cripple your competitor. It's not easy knowing whom to pick."

"Well, I don't know. I suppose you could just pick the most *prominent* person within an organization. Wouldn't it be as simple as that?"

"Get serious. If I really wanted to harm this organization, for example, would I pick the most prominent person? The CEO, for example?"

"Oh. Well, certainly not in this case. I guess if you removed the CEO, the company's stock would probably go up about twenty points."

"Exactly. This is what I call the Roger Smith Effect, after the past chairman of General Motors. I was the one who decided to sabotage GM by not removing Smith."

"Oh. Good job."

"Now, if I did want to do some real damage to the Big Telephone and Telecommunications Company, I'd know exactly which managers to pick."

"You would?" Tompkins had some ideas of his own about who was really indispensable to the company.

"Sure. Want to see?" She took a pad out of her purse and wrote down three names. Then, she considered for a moment, and wrote down a fourth. She passed the pad to him.

He stared at the list. "Ugh," Tompkins said. "This would be like bombing the company back into the dark ages. You've picked exactly the four who . . . Wait a minute, these people are friends of mine. They have spouses and kids. You're not thinking of . . . ?"

"Oh, no. Don't worry about them. As long as the company keeps its present executive level, there is no need to sabotage it. Believe me, your soon-to-be-former employer is going nowhere, with these four good managers or without. It's not them I'm here for, Webster. It's you."

"Me?"

"Uh huh."

"For what? What use would the Morovian K–V– . . . whatever it is, have for me?"

"The KVJ. No, it's not the KVJ that needs you, but the Nation State of Morovia."

"Explain, please."

"Well, our Nation's Noble Leader, we call him NNL, for short, has proclaimed that Morovia will be first in the world in export of shrink-wrapped software by the year 2000. It's our grand plan for the future. We're building a world-class software factory. And we need someone to manage it. It's as simple as that."

"You're proposing to hire me?"

"Sort of."

"I'm flabbergasted."

"Also available."

"Well, that's true enough." Tompkins took another swig of his drink. He looked at her cagily. "Tell me what you're offering."

"Oh, we can discuss that later. When we're there."

He laughed, incredulously. "There? You think I'm going off to Morovia with you before we've even discussed terms."

"I do."

"I find that a very dubious proposition. I mean, given what I know about you and your inclination to use heavy-handed methods. Who knows what you might do to me if I decided not to accept your offer?"

"Who knows indeed?"

"I'd be a very foolish fellow to go with you. . . ." He stopped, wondering what he'd been going to say next. His tongue seemed a bit thick in his mouth, like a dry rag.

"Very foolish. Yes," she agreed.

"I, uh . . ." Tompkins looked down at the drink in his hand. "Say, you wouldn't have . . . ?"

"Mmm," she said, smiling her mysterious smile.

"Urghhhhh. . . ."

A moment later, Mr. Tompkins slid quietly down into his seat, quite unconscious.

2

STANDING UP TO KALBFUSS

ð

$\mathcal{M}$r. Tompkins was dreaming. He dreamed a very long dream. It seemed to go on for days.

The first part of the dream was of him walking with his eyes closed. There was someone on his right side, a firm hand under his right elbow, a warm presence against his arm. There was also a faint but very pleasant scent. The scent was light and distinctly feminine, with notes of rose and, perhaps, ginger. He felt rather content that the scent was there, also happy for the warmth. On his other side, there seemed to be a male presence, not nearly so warm and one that didn't smell all that great either. He thought it might be the guard, Morris—the one who had been on duty outside the auditorium. And it was definitely Morris's voice that said in his ear, "Here we go, Mr. T. Right this way. You're in good hands."

He was in good hands. Well, that was a relief. He was beginning to feel better and better. His tongue seemed thick and there was still an acrid taste in his mouth, but the whole rest of his being was pervaded by a sense of contentment. This must be what it's like to be on drugs, he thought. "Drugs," he said out loud. The sound of his own voice came back into his ears, echoing thickly. "Drookthe," it said.

"Yes, dear," a soft voice murmured beside him. "Drookthe. Only some very nice, little ones."

Then he was walking outside in the sun, with the warm presence beside him. Then he was riding. Then he was walking. Then he was sitting. Then he was lying down, and all this time he felt good.

The mysterious Ms. Hoolihan was near him much of the time. They were going somewhere together, somewhere rather naughty, he imagined. My goodness, he thought, almost as if he were a distant observer, Webster and Lahksa, running away together. Well, he could do a lot worse; he really could. She was murmuring again at his ear. A lot worse. He snuggled down next to her. Her marvelous scent was all around him.

Then, they were in a plane. The captain came by to say hello and the captain was Lahksa. The stewardess gave him a drink and she was Lahksa, too. She held the glass to his lips for him to drink. Then Lahksa was the captain again and had to be away, up front, flying the plane. She had bedded him down on his seat and hers together, with her sweater for a pillow. The sweater, too, was full of her scent.

A later part of the dream was different. At first, he thought it was a film. Oh good, he thought, a film. Nothing like a film when you're on a long flight and your new friend has to be up front, flying the plane. Wonder who's in the film?

To his surprise, the star of the film was Webster Tompkins. A familiar name, that, Webster Tompkins. Mr. T. tried to remember what other films the fellow might have made.

Hadn't he seen one or two of them? Sure enough, after the credits, there was a familiar scene; he'd definitely seen this one before. It was the corporate training room and there was a young man lecturing ponderously at the front. The part of the young man was played by Edgar Kalbfuss.

"We'll be doing GANNT charts," Kalbfuss was saying, "and PERT charts, status reporting, a section on interfaces to the human resources department, conduct of weekly meetings, use of e-mail, filling out time cards, progress tracking, project milestone reporting, and—this is a new section that we're *very* excited about—setting up a quality program. Yes, is that a question in the back?"

Mr. Tompkins stood. "Yes. My name is Tompkins. My question is, Is that it? Is that the whole agenda?"

"Yup, that's it," Kalbfuss answered confidently.

"That's your whole course on project management?"

"Uh huh. Um. Do you feel something is missing?"

"Nothing important. Just the matter of people."

"People?"

"Yes. We use people here to get the projects done."

"Of course."

"I might have thought you'd have something about people in your course."

"Such as?"

"Well, hiring, for example. Hiring is only the most important thing a manager does."

"Probably is," Kalbfuss allowed. "We're not saying you shouldn't be doing that. We're not saying it's not important to do it well either. And we're not saying . . ."

"Seems like you're not saying much of anything about it at all."

13

Kalbfuss looked down at his notes. "Um. No, I guess not. Well, you see, hiring is one of those *soft* matters that's not too easy to teach."

"Not easy, only essential. I notice you also don't seem to have anything in your course about matching people to their work."

"No. That too is important. However, . . ."

"However, you won't be saying anything about it."

"No."

"Nothing either about keeping people motivated."

"No. Again, that's a soft subject."

"Nothing either about team building."

"Well, I will be saying how *important* it is. How everybody should be thinking of himself, and here I might also say 'herself' . . . should think of himself or herself as a member of the team. We're all a team here, you know. Oh, yes. And I'm going to stress just how essential that is and how everybody should . . ."

"Yes, yes. But you won't be saying anything about how to build teams, how to keep them healthy, how to get them started, how to give them a chance of jelling, or any of that?"

"No. We'll be concentrating more on the hard science of management."

"You're going to teach us the hard science of management without even touching on people selection, task matching, motivation, or team formation—the four most essential ingredients of management?"

"Well, we're not going to talk about any of those. Does something about that bother you, Mr. . . ."

"Tompkins. Yes, something bothers me."

"What bothers you?"

"That you've got a course that leaves those four things out and you want to call the course 'Project Management.'"

"Oh. So, it's just the title that bothers you. Well, what should we call it then?"

"How about 'Administrivia'?"

There was a soft gasp in the room. Tompkins turned on his heel and walked out.

Rewind. The same scene was playing again: "How about 'Administrivia'?" Soft gasp. Tompkins turning on his heel and starting out of the room. One person looking after him. He turned to see who it was—a young woman, dark and pretty, black eyes, lopsided smile. Lahksa Hoolihan. "Administrivia," she mouthed the word silently to him, mouthed it appreciatively. He smiled. "Administrivia," her mouth formed the word. Her mouth was frozen on the syllable 'triv,' her lips arched, thick and dark pink.

Tompkins stirred in his airplane seat, pulling her sweater up to his cheek, inhaling the soft scent it exuded. Administrivia, he said to himself. He tried to remember Kalbfuss's expression when he had said that. He seemed to remember that the man had let his jaw drop. Yes, he had. Administrivia . . . jaw-drop from Kalbfuss . . . gasp in room . . . Tompkins striding out . . . Lahksa mouthing the word . . . Tompkins mouthing the same word . . . both their mouths arched at 'triv,' coming close together. Replay that from 'administrivia.' "Administrivia," he said, turned, looked at Lahksa, she formed her mouth around the syllable 'triv,' and he. . . . Rewind. Replay the scene from . . .

"Poor dear," Lahksa's voice said from above. She was bending down over him. "You're caught in a loop. It's the

15

'drookthe' that do that to you. Make you go over the same thing, again and again."

"Administrivia," Tompkins told her.

"Yes, I remember. You told him. I was impressed. I still am." She spread a blanket over him.

The film was starting over. The same film. The corporate training room with Ms. Hoolihan and Tompkins in the back row, Kalbfuss lecturing in front, "GANNT charts, PERT charts, status reporting, a section on interfaces to the human resources department, conduct of weekly meetings . . ."

3

SILIKON VALEJIT

ॐ

*M*r. Tompkins woke in his own bed. He was dressed in his familiar paisley pajamas, surrounded by an old set of worn blue and white sheets he'd had for years. His favorite molded pillow was tucked under his head. All these things smacked of home, but he definitely wasn't home. There was a wide window just to the left side of his bed where there had never been a window before. And outside that window was a palm tree, of all things. Imagine, a palm tree in New Jersey. Only, of course, he wasn't in New Jersey.

Opposite the bed in the far wall was another huge window. Tucked in beside the window was his grandmother's old rocker. It was rocking slowly back and forth. Seated in the rocker was Lahksa Hoolihan. She looked up from her book.

He still had that bitter taste in his mouth and his tongue still felt like a thick, dry washcloth. With not too much of a struggle, he raised himself to a sitting position in the bed. God, was he thirsty.

Lahksa pointed silently to the bedside table. He turned to find a large glass of water with ice cubes in it. He picked it up and drank thirstily.

There was also a pitcher on the table. When he'd drained the first glass, he filled it again and drank till his immediate need was past. A long silence as he struggled to understand what was going on. "So," he said at last. "You really did do it."

"Mmm."

He shook his head in wonder. "You people. Have you no shame? You would disrupt a person's life, tear him away from all he held dear. . . ."

She smiled at him. "Oh, Webster. It's not as bad as that. What did you hold so dear? Your job? The town where you lived? Sure, there were friends, but you were resigned to leaving them behind anyway when you found new work. So here you are. You've found new work, and plenty of it. What have we really torn you away from?"

There was some truth to that. Who would miss him, really? Who was there that wasn't going to be left behind soon anyway? "I had a cat," he said with sudden bitterness. "A poor little gray cat who had no one on earth to depend on except me! A cat named . . ."

"Seafood," Lahksa finished for him. "Yes, dear little Seafood. We've become great friends." She scratched the seat of the chair beside her leg. A little gray cat with white paws jumped up beside her.

"Seafood!" Tompkins exclaimed. "Stay away from that woman."

Seafood ignored him. He crawled onto Lahksa's lap and curled up. Lahksa scratched the top of his head, causing the little animal to purr happily.

"Traitor!" Tompkins sputtered.

ॐ

His clothes were laid out for him on the dresser, a pair of jeans and an old cotton shirt, socks and underwear. He looked pointedly at Ms. Hoolihan, giving her the broadest possible hint that he'd appreciate a little privacy. She smiled impishly. Tompkins gathered up the clothes and made his way into the bathroom. He shut and locked the door behind him.

The bathroom was huge. The open casement windows were at least six feet tall, set into a thick wall. He put his head outside to see that the exterior of the building was made of stone. Down below, only one story down, was an elaborate garden. The fixtures of the bathroom were old-fashioned, made of a handsome white porcelain with brass fittings. Everything was clean and elegant. He might have been in a fine old Swiss hotel.

"Got everything you need?" Lahksa's voice came through the closed door.

"Go away! Leave me alone."

"We can talk through the door."

"We don't have anything to talk about."

"Oh, but we do. We have to talk about your new job. I'm afraid you're already dreadfully behind."

"I just got here."

"The schedule is running. Isn't it always that way? I don't doubt you've met your match on this one. You'll never catch up."

That annoyed him. He came out of the bathroom, buttoning his shirt. "If that's true, if I took the job and indeed I never did catch up, it would only mean that the schedule was wrong from the beginning. Who set it anyway? Some nitwit, no doubt. Where do you have to go to get away from such idiots? I am sick to death of being given impossible schedules."

"You're cute when you get heated up."

19

That maddening smile again. She looked ravishing. "I don't find you the least bit amusing, young lady. Not at all. So just put that talk out of the way."

"Yes, sir." She looked contrite. Actually, she looked like a devilish woman pretending to look contrite.

Tompkins sat down on his grandmother's overstuffed ottoman, opposite Lahksa on the rocker. "Let's get down to brass tacks. What happens to me if I absolutely refuse to have anything to do with you and your stupid job? If I simply dig my heels in and say no. Do I end up at the bottom of some quarry?"

"Please, Webster. We're not at all that kind of operation. If you don't see this job as the opportunity of a lifetime and take it on willingly, we'll send you and Seafood and all your worldly goods back to Penelope, New Jersey, and wish you well. We'll pay you an honorarium for your time. We'll send you through Rome and put you up for a long weekend there to recuperate, all hotels and air fares first-class and on us. What could be fairer?"

"If I can believe you."

"If you can believe me. Why don't you try? I haven't told you even so much as one little fib. Have I? Think back. Have I ever said anything but the truth?"

He waved a hand dismissively. "Who knows? Suppose I take the job. What's in it for me?"

"The usual," she said. "Money. Oh, there's also the thrill of the thing, a sense of accomplishment, camaraderie, meaningful achievement, all that stuff."

"Right. Tell me about the money. How much?"

She pulled some papers out of the folder by her side. "We were thinking of a two-year contract." She passed him a letter. It was addressed to him on ornate letterhead, something about the Morovian National Bureau of Something or Other. He looked over the Terms of Employment section on the second page. They were proposing to pay him exactly twice what he'd been making, clear and tax-free, in American dollars. "Hmpf," he said.

"There is also a stock sweetener. And options," Lahksa told him.

He shrugged that off as hyperbole since he couldn't imagine what kind of stock the Nation State of Morovia might come up with.

Lahksa passed him another page. It was a deposit slip for his own Fidelity account. Written in the Total Deposit field was the full amount of the contract, two years' salary.

"How do I know you'll really pay when the time comes?"

She passed him one more item. It was a cashier's check on a New York bank made out to him in the full amount. "Payment in advance. You agree to take the job and we put the whole payment into your account immediately. You inform your lawyer and he calls you here when the deposit is clear. Fidelity sends a written confirmation. We can have all that in your hands within a week. Until then, you're our guest. Think of it as a holiday by the sea."

"I don't even know where Morovia is."

"By the sea. It's on the Ionian Sea, south and east of the heel of Italy. On a nice day, you can see the mountains of central Greece from your terrace." She gestured toward the French doors on the far side of the room.

Mr. Tompkins considered. "What's the job?" he said at last.

She batted her eyelashes at him becomingly. "I thought you'd never ask."

❧

"So let me get this straight," Tompkins said, looking up from the briefing papers. "You've actually got fifteen hundred fairly senior software engineers."

Lahksa nodded. "At last count. And they all work for you."

"And you say they're good."

"Certified as CMM Level 2 or higher by the Morovian Software Engineering Institute."

"This is extraordinary. How did that happen? How did you end up with all these highly trained engineers? I mean, a dinky little country like Morovia, one would never think . . ."

"Your biases are showing, my dear. What you're really wondering is how could there be so much skill available in a third-world post-Communist country."

"Well?"

"The Communist world did some things badly and some things well. What it did badly was to make the centrally planned markets work so goods and services could find their way to where they were needed. What it did well was education."

He had just been reading that somewhere. Where could that have been? "I seem to have seen that same idea just recently, and from a fairly respectable source, I might add."

"Yes, it was in Lester Thurow's new book. We found a copy open by the side of your bed. He was talking about the assets and liabilities of the former Soviet Union. Morovia is rather similar."

"And all my staff would speak and read and write English?"

"All of them. English-language skills are important here: Morovian is not exactly a global economy fast-track language."

"And the idea is to mold all this talent and good training into a world-class software industry."

"Yes. To begin with: six key development projects to produce six very carefully chosen software products. Our noble leader, NNL, has selected the products himself. You run the six projects and the rest of the organization. That's your job."

"Some job. I hope you're ready to pay the piper. I mean, this is going to take a huge investment in people and training and equipment."

"Webster, we don't propose to let you down in any way. When you look back on this from two years hence, you're not going to be able to say that the people weren't up to it or that there weren't enough of them or that you didn't have adequate support."

"Let's just talk about support for a minute."

"You have an experienced and resourceful personal assistant that I chose for you myself, a cadre of some two hundred excellent development managers, experts in dozens of key areas . . ."

"I'm going to want to bring in a few key people of my own. I'm going to pick them and you're going to deliver them. And I don't want them to be kidnapped either. I want them to come of their own volition."

"Sure." She evaded his eyes.

"No kidding, Lahksa."

"Oh, all right. You're no fun at all."

"And I may need some consultants, too, people with international reputations."

"As you like. Make up your list. We'll deliver them."

"Damn right, you will." He looked down at the notes he'd been taking. "I want everybody co-located, too. No fooling around with people in different locations. You never

23

get anything done if people are scattered off every which way. All together."

"That's already been done. We've moved the whole development community to the Flopczek Lowlands, an area that NNL has renamed 'Silikon Valejit.'"

They were seated in the living room of Tompkins' suite. This side of the building looked inland, away from the sea. Lahksa stood and led him to the opposite wall, out through the portals onto a wide balcony. The land fell away from them into a pretty little valley. "Silikon Valejit," she said, sweeping an arm across the valley. There were a half-dozen new-looking office buildings in a cluster just below. She pointed down toward them. "That is the Aidrivoli Campus, Webster, your new domain; it's just a ten-minute walk from here."

"Very pretty. If pretty valleys were all it took to make a success, I guess Morovia would have stood the world on its ear centuries ago." He looked down at his notes. "Oh, yes, I want final say on each and every schedule. This is a nonnegotiable demand."

She looked bored. "Okay," she said.

"And good network support. That means an up-to-date workstation on every desk, all networked together with ethernet or wider band connection. I want a full-time, network-savvy support staff and a full complement of hubs, routers, T1 or ISDN lines, the works."

Lahksa yawned. "Right."

"What else?" He knew he'd better think of everything he needed now. This was the time to lay down his demands. "What have I forgotten?"

"Only the most important things. Webster, has it occurred to you that we have an awful lot of staff for the mere half-dozen projects that NNL has sketched out?"

Tompkins looked down at the list of projects she'd given him. It was true that there wasn't an enormous amount of work there. There were six projects, six medium-sized software products to be built. He couldn't say yet exactly what each of them was, but there wasn't one of them that would require more than twenty people. "I see what you mean. Looks like we have work here for barely a hundred people."

"Right. And what are you going to do with the rest?"

"Beats me. Is that my problem? Let them take vacation."

"It's not your problem, Webster, but your opportunity. Haven't you ever in your life wanted to set up a controlled experiment in management? Have you never wondered what would happen if you ran not just one project to get a given piece of work done, but maybe three or four . . . ?"

Mr. Tompkins' eyes got a faraway glaze. "A controlled experiment . . . One project with lots of pressure and one with little and another project with almost none, all three charged with doing the exact same task. We could watch them to see which one finished first. I've always wanted to do something like that. We could set up one group with a staff that was too big, and another with a staff that was too small, and a third one that had just the right number as best I could guess it, just to see which one . . ."

Lahksa picked up for him: "One team with all senior people and another with some senior folk and some novices. . . ."

He was getting into it now. "One staffed by people that have worked together before, pitted against another team staffed with strangers. Why, if we could do that, Lahksa, we could begin to investigate some of the great mysteries of management. We could actually begin to understand what makes projects tick."

"It's all yours, Webster. You have got all of Morovia to play with." She nodded down toward Silikon Valejit. "It lies at your feet. The world's first Project Management Laboratory."

4
THE CD-ROM PLANT

ॐ

"*I* have a little present for you," Lahksa announced.

Mr. Tompkins looked at her closely. Here was something he had not seen in her outward appearance before: She seemed almost shy.

"A very little present, really." From her voluminous shoulder bag, she pulled out a handsome leatherbound book and handed it to him, her eyes down. He took the book in his hand. It was a lovely thing.

"Oh," he said, eloquently.

On the cover was inscribed in gold letters:

> **Personal Journal of**
> **Webster Tatterstall Tompkins**
> **❂ Manager ❂**

"Oh," he said again. He couldn't imagine where she had learned his middle name, which wasn't on any of his various

IDs. That was, of course, the sort of thing that Lahksa was good at, ferreting out odd bits of information.

"I thought you might profit from your experience here in Morovia by jotting down any lessons you learned. Who knows what you'll learn from running the management laboratory? Something useful, I expect."

Inside she had written a title page in her neat hand. It read "What I Learned," followed by his name and the year. She had also penned in an entry on the first numbered page:

Four Essentials of Good Management:

o   *Get the right people.*

o   *Match them to the right jobs.*

o   *Keep them motivated.*

o   *Help their teams to jell and stay jelled.*

(All the rest is Administrivia.)

At the bottom of the page was a date from earlier in the year. Mr. T. looked up. "That was the date of our Project Management seminar?"

Lahksa nodded. "Yes. Those were the points you made that day. I thought that they might be just the thing to get your journal started."

The personal assistant hand-picked for him by Lahksa was a young man named Waldo Montifiore. He had a sleepy, country-bumpkin appearance, with a thatch of yellow hair that stood up from the front of his head. His hair made him look rather like the Belgian cartoon character, Tin Tin. In fact, all he lacked to be a Tin Tin look-alike was a pair of knicker trousers and a little white dog.

He may have looked sleepy, but he was efficient enough at his job: "You have an appointment at ten o'clock," Waldo told him.

"I just got here. I haven't even sat down yet. I mean, I haven't even found my office yet."

"It's in there," Waldo gestured vaguely toward the door behind his own desk in the foyer. "It's very attractive. Ms. Hoolihan decorated it for you herself." He glanced down at his watch. "But maybe you can look in there later. I'm afraid you need to be directly on your way, or you'll be late." He gathered some papers together and stood up. "I'll walk you over to your appointment and explain along the way."

Out in front of the building, Waldo steered him along a wooded walking path toward a construction site on the far side of the campus.

"In order for this to make any sense, you have to think ahead all the way to the end of the current set of projects. If they do indeed deliver their six products and the products are as successful as we hope, and we are—as NNL has decreed—on the way to becoming first in world software exports by the year 2000, then we're going to need a pretty serious delivery capacity to get all the software out the door."

"Okay. So?"

"So, some of that will be possible to put in place much later, but there are certain capital projects that have to be begun now or they'll never be done in time." He pulled out a hand-drawn network diagram from his sheaf of papers. It looked like a PERT chart. "We'll need a pressing plant for CD-ROMs. Attached to the rear of the plant will be the packaging facility, shrink-wrapping, manual insertion, loading docks, and so on. As you can see," he put his finger on the box labeled CD Plant Complete, "the plant opening is directly on the critical path."

"That's a construction project."

"Right."

"What do I know about this stuff? I'm a software manager."

"Yes. Well, you are also the boss of the whole operation."

"I am? I mean, I guess I am."

"You are. Head of the Naczonal Byru av Data Schmertczung, that is."

"Uh huh. That would be the National Bureau of . . ."

". . . Data Schmertzing. Anyway, most of the work is specifically software-related. But there is also this little matter of the CD-ROM plant. I'm afraid the project is disastrously far behind already. And it all falls in our lap. I mean, *your* lap."

"Sorry to hear it."

"Mr. Mopoulka, the construction manager, is a very highly motivated man. He is bound to be, since he got his marching orders from Himself."

"Himself?"

"NNL, the Nation's Noble Leader. NNL can be quite persuasive. He can be particularly graphic when he lays out the consequences of failure."

"I see. One of those."

"Uh huh. Anyway, Mr. Mopoulka is certainly trying his hardest. But the project keeps falling behind."

Tompkins nodded glumly. "Well, we'll see what we'll see, I guess."

"It's just been the most disastrous possible luck." Mr. Mopoulka was wringing his hands. "Who could have foreseen it? In each of the other sites, we've encountered nothing but fine white sand. Who would have thought there would be this granite ledge right here? It's just terrible."

"So you plan to blast?"

"What else can we do? It will take weeks."

"How many weeks?"

The man evaded Tompkins' eyes. "Many, many weeks. But I don't know how many."

"Give me your best guess."

"It could be as many as . . ." he looked sharply back at Tompkins, reading his expression, ". . . as many as ten. Yes, ten."

"Ten weeks," Mr. T. repeated. He was wondering what different expressions he might have put on at the critical moment to have encouraged an answer of six, or eleven, or fifteen. He was also wondering what the real answer would turn out to be. His instinct told him he'd better open up a dialogue now if he was ever going to discover the truth. "When you say ten weeks, Mr. Mopoulka, I suppose there is at least some chance that it would be as much as . . . twenty," he offered.

Mopoulka looked like he wanted to kiss him. "Yes! Or even . . ."

"Thirty?"

"Well. . . . Probably not thirty, but twenty-five."

Mr. Tompkins changed tacks. "Look, Mr. Mopoulka, couldn't we move the plant site over to the west, just by far enough to avoid the ledge?"

"We couldn't do that!" Mopoulka moaned. "We couldn't."

"Why not? Is there granite over there, too?"

"No, it's clear. But the plan, you see, the one that NNL gave me, calls for the plant to be precisely here. Not over there. Here. I couldn't just change the plan."

31

"You couldn't?"

"Of course not. If I did, we'd lose time, we'd be late. And the lateness would be my fault, because I had decided to move the plant, don't you see? Whereas this way, if we're late, it's not really my fault at all. I hope you understand that. It's very important that you understand that. And suppose somebody doesn't like the plant's new position? Whose fault would that be? Mine." He looked thoroughly miserable.

"Uh huh. Listen, while we're talking about position, I note that the loading docks are at the rear of the building and that the land there is swampy. So, the trucks will have to come and go through all these wet lowlands, which are sure to be muddy in the rainy season. Is there a rainy season here?"

"Yes. In the spring. But what can we do about that?"

"Well, I'm thinking that we might shift the plant west just thirty feet or so, so the foundation is tucked right up against the granite ledge. Then we could reverse the plant floor plan entirely, build it as an exact mirror image of what the current plan calls for. That way, the docks would be on this end, directly over the ledge. We won't need any foundation under the docks at all, we can anchor them directly onto the granite. What do you think?"

Mopoulka was stunned. "You can't seriously be talking about facing the plant in the other direction."

"I can't? Why not?"

"It's just not what the plan calls for. The plan . . ."

"Yes, we'll have to get the plan redone. I'll take care of that. Count on me. In the meantime, just work to the exact mirror image of what you see here."

"But the schedule . . ."

"My problem, my friend. Don't worry about it. You work for me now. Build me a good plant. Keep your people working and keep them content and keep the work moving effectively. If you do those things, we're going to look at your effort as a success no matter when the project gets done."

He stormed back into the office, causing Waldo to look up, startled. Mr. Tompkins paused, red-faced, in front of the young man's desk.

"What the hell did NNL tell Mopoulka? The poor fellow was terrified. You told me that Himself could be 'persuasive.' I think you meant 'threatening.' What did he tell him, . . . that if the plant were late, Mopoulka would be sent off to the salt mines?"

Waldo swallowed uncomfortably. "Worse than that, I'm afraid. That he would be chopped up into little bits and fed to the fishes, more likely. Or that he would be hung from a meathook outside the castle wall. That one is rather a favorite for NNL."

"Meathook?!? You *must* be kidding. Can he really do that?"

"Well, this is, after all, Morovia. We don't exactly have a long tradition of civil liberties. Yes, I guess he could do whatever he wants. He never has, but he could. NNL is still getting used to his new role as an autocrat. The sky's the limit for 'persuasive' technique here. This is an excellent place for the study of negative reinforcement as a motivator."

"Well, I'm not the negative-reinforcement type. I figure the world has studied that one just about enough up through today. Write a letter over my signature to NNL telling him that all 'performance penalties' like the one dangled in front of Mopoulka are henceforth out of bounds. Tell him that I will take sole responsibility for motivation and reinforcement, both

positive and negative, of everyone who works for me. Tell him
he can take it or leave it. Tell him I am coming to see him
tomorrow . . ." Waldo was scribbling furiously on his pad, ". . .
and he can tell me *then* that he has agreed to all these terms or
that he is going to cut me up in little pieces and feed me to the
fishes, or whatever. He can do his damnedest."

"Um. . . . 'Sincerely Yours'?"

"No way. Sign it, 'Not to Be Trifled With, Webster T.
Tompkins.' Set up an appointment for me with NNL
tomorrow afternoon. Send the letter by fax so he's read it
before we meet."

"Yes, sir."

Within five minutes, Waldo had brought in the neatly
typed letter for his signature and it had been sent off by fax.

Well, he'd done some good things in his day. He'd brought
home an impossible project or two, pulled off some really big
system developments. He supposed he had achieved sufficient
prominence in the field so that there would be a little capsule
about him at the time of his death, published perhaps in *IEEE
Software* or in the *Annals of the History of Computing*. And
whichever it was, he imagined it would finish up on a somber
note like, "Died on Morovian meathook."

He was in a mood to put some order to his life, just in
case it was about to end precipitously. But more than that, he
was still angry. The memory of stupid, destructive "performance penalties" he'd come across in the past welled up in
him. Where did this "spare the rod" mentality come from in
some managers? Did they make such terrible parents as they
made terrible managers? Probably so.

The book that Lahksa had given him was there on his desk. He opened it to the first blank page and began to write.

From Mr. Tompkins' Journal:

Safety and Change

o   People can't embrace change unless they feel safe.

o   Change is essential to all success in project work (and in most other worthwhile endeavors).

o   A lack of safety makes people risk-averse.

o   Avoiding risk is fatal, since it causes you to miss out on the associated benefit as well.

o   People can be made to feel unsafe by direct threats, but also by the sense that power may be used against them abusively.

5

NNL

❧

*A*n early morning train took Mr. Tompkins from Varsjop up to the capital at Korsach. The little train followed the coast north as far as Lovradje, and then turned inland. In his lap was a booklet that Waldo had found for him called *Morovia for Travelers,* published in London. This was the first chance he'd had since his arrival to learn anything about Morovia. The book's copyright was in the name of Thomas Cook Ltd., and was dated 1907.

In between chapters, he put the book aside to concentrate on the scenery. The coast was lush and green, spotted with picturesque little fishing villages. There was vine growing most places, and thick, green fields of crops. Though he saw few cars, the villages seemed prosperous enough. The one that was pictured in his book, when he passed through it, looked pretty much the way it had in 1907.

He was feeling remarkably calm. The truth was that Morovia needed him. The demands he was making of NNL (no meathooks, and so on) were certainly not unreasonable. Coming on strong would not be a bad sign, he thought, in a new manager who was just taking charge. He ought to have some honeymoon capital coming. Finally, he suspected that Lahksa would not have let him go up to meet Himself if she judged he were destined for the hook. When she'd read his letter to NNL, she had merely shrugged.

There was an ample breakfast served on a starched white tablecloth that the porter laid over the table in front of Tompkins' seat. After the breakfast, he allowed himself a little nap.

Any remaining doubts about his likely reception by NNL evaporated as soon as Mr. Tompkins gave his name at the palace. The guards leapt to their feet, knuckling their hats in deference and bowing. "Mr. Tompkins! *The* Mr. Tompkins. Oh, yes, right this way, Mr. Tompkins. Sir." They led him through a massive reception hall, walled in stone overhung with wide tapestries, and then up a curving stone stairway that must have been twenty feet wide.

A young woman in a crisp blue suit met him at the top of the stairs. "Mr. Tompkins," she said. "Welcome. I am Miss Lane."

Everyone's English had been pretty competent, but Miss Lane's seemed particularly good. He had a hunch she was American. "I was wondering, you seem like you might come from ..."

"Providence," she finished for him. "Come right this way. Himself is expecting you." She took him along a balcony that opened out over a pleasant garden down below, through a large portal, and into an entry room. There was an arched door at the back that gave access to a huge office. Miss Lane left him at the door. The room was full of healthy, glistening plants, oriental rugs, and overstuffed furniture arranged into inviting seating areas. There was no light on in the room, all the light coming from three large windows that overlooked the garden. At first, he thought he was alone in the room. Then he saw a face at the very back, positioned behind a library table at the side of the main desk. The face was lit up by the glow of a computer screen. There was a faint tapping sound of fingers on keys.

Tompkins approached. "Um . . ." he said tentatively.

"Oh." The man stopped typing.

"I . . ."

"Uh . . ."

Tompkins opened his eyes slightly wider. Wait a minute. The face looking back at him was familiar. It was young, barely thirty or thirty-five, he thought, a plump, almost childish face. Wide-rimmed glasses giving a slightly owlish look, a mop of sandy hair.

"Say, you look like . . ."

The man waved a hand. "Now, don't jump to conclusions. I don't know you and you don't know me."

"No, but . . ."

"So, we'll just have to get to know each other. That's what I thought we would do during this meeting. Tompkins, isn't it?"

"Yes."

A soft handshake.

"And you are . . ."

"I am. Yes."

"The Nation's Noble Leader. Himself."

"Yes."

Tompkins realized he had no idea what to call the man. How does one address a sovereign ruler? He should have asked Waldo. "Um, I'm not sure how to . . . How do you like to be addressed?"

NNL thought a moment. "Sir, I think. Yes, I like that. Sir."

"Well, Sir, then." Tompkins put on his sternest look. "Listen, I sent you a letter."

"Oh, yes." Another dismissive wave of the hand.

"Well, are my conditions met? There's no use talking about anything else if not, you see. Those are my conditions."

"Let's don't sweat the small stuff."

"Small stuff?!? I don't think of it as small stuff. Well, do you agree to my terms? I have to know."

A sigh. "Sure. Whatever you like."

"That's what I like."

"Sure. Uh . . ." NNL seemed a bit lost. He looked back regretfully at the screen as if he would really rather get back to whatever he'd been doing. Now that Tompkins could see the screen, it seemed to have a page of program code on it, C++, he thought.

There was a sound behind them in the room, and Miss Lane arrived with a tray of soft drinks and snacks. NNL brightened appreciably. "Oh, good," he said. He helped himself to a kind of cream-filled cake, which he stuffed into his mouth.

"My god, is that a Twinkie?" Tompkins couldn't help asking.

"Yeshe," NNL responded, speaking around a mouthful of cake and cream filling. He helped himself to a Coke. Mr. Tompkins passed over the Snickers bars and canned drinks to take a few peanuts.

There was a long, uncomfortable silence after they both had swallowed. NNL spoke up at last: "Settling in okay, are you?"

"Oh, yes."

"Everything you need?"

"Uh huh."

"Just ask if you need anything."

"I will."

Another silence. Tompkins had what he'd come for. He supposed he might just excuse himself and leave. But that didn't seem quite right. He ought to show some interest in the man. "I gather you're somewhat new at this. At being . . . well, whatever it is that you are here."

"Tyrant. I always thought it might be nice to be a tyrant, and now I am. Yes, it hasn't been too long. I, too, am just set- tling in. I think I'm going to like it."

Tompkins went on in his line of inquiry. "If I could ask, how does one become a tyrant? How did you get the job?"

NNL leaned back in the plush executive's chair behind his mahogany desk. He put his feet up. "A coup," he said. "Well, that is the official story."

"It wasn't a coup then?"

"No, not exactly. It was more like a leveraged buy-out."

"Excuse me?"

"A buy-out. A deal. You know, a little cash, some stock, notes, that sort of thing."

"You bought Morovia?!?"

"I did."

"That is . . . extraordinary."

"Yes, well. I had a lot of stock in a large-ish company in the States. And I had some money, tons of it, actually. And, since I had always wanted . . ."

"You bought yourself a whole country? You just plunked down a pile of cash . . . ?"

"Mostly stock." NNL shook his head. "I had all this stock, but it wasn't as if I could just sell it or anything. It was unregistered. There is this awful department of the government that likes to torture poor executives who have made a bundle by forming new companies. And they really had it in for me. So, for instance, when I wanted to sell off a little stock, just enough to build a modest residence and buy a few paintings, they had a conniption." He put on a martyred expression.

"But, there is this loophole in the rules governing executives' stock," NNL went on. "It turns out, you can exchange your stock for similar stock in another company, and that escapes scrutiny. So I approached the former leaders here, the generals, and got them to incorporate Morovia. And then . . ."

"You did a stock switch," Tompkins finished for him.

"Exactly. The generals became very rich, and they went away to live on the Riviera—or wherever rich old Morovian generals go. And I got Morovia."

"You own the country, all the land and the buildings, and even the people." Tompkins could hardly believe it.

"Well, not the people. At least, I don't think so. But everything else. And just to make it all perfectly aboveboard, we had a plebiscite to confirm what we'd done. Passed by an overwhelming majority. Of course, we had to sweeten the deal by giving out stock and options to the citizens. It worked out well for everyone."

"But why would you do such a thing?"

"Well, the balance sheet, for one thing. My god, it's a better deal than has ever been done on Wall Street. All these natural resources, the beaches, the farms, the mountains.

Imagine the potential, just from dropping in a few resorts on this beautiful coast. And all of it undeveloped. I can tell you that Marriott and Intercontinental are very interested. So is Disney."

Tompkins just shook his head.

"Then, of course, there is all that marvelous, educated manpower, all those programmers and analysts and designers, software people. I didn't tell you, but I was in the software business back in the States."

"I see."

"I thought this could be the ultimate software factory."

"I see your point."

"And running it as Tyrant, rather than just as CEO, had some special advantages, at least I thought so."

"Special advantages such as?"

"Well, at my other company, when I tell people what I want—this or that product done by the end of the year, for example—I always have to cope with the nay-sayers."

"Nay-sayers?"

"I always seem to be surrounded by them," NNL said unhappily. "I say 'end of the year,' and they wrinkle up their brows and say, 'Oh, no, Bill. Oh, no. No, that won't be possible at all. Oh, no, Bill. Simply impossible.'" He was shaking his head sadly. "It's enough to make you puke."

Tompkins tried to look sympathetic.

"Whatever I wanted, it was always 'Oh, no, Bill.' Well, I thought, just once, I'd like to be in a position where people simply couldn't say 'Oh, no, Bill.' Where they wouldn't even dream of saying no."

"So, you thought that the position of Tyrant would give you certain managerial advantages."

"I did."

"And then I came along, and ruined it."

"Oh, even before you came, things were going sour. Awfully sour. Take this guy, Mopoulka, who's building the CD-ROM plant. When I gave him the job I told him, 'You'll have this plant built for me in eighteen months or I will have your head on a platter.' I actually said that. 'Head on a platter.' I'd always wanted to say that and I did say it, and it felt wonderful. I can tell you, he did not even *think* of saying 'Oh, no, Bill.' Not even a tiny little inclination. He just turned white and said, 'Yes, Sir.' It was glorious."

"But then it turned sour, you say?"

"He got behind anyway!" NNL moaned. "He got behind. He was going to be late, no matter what I had said, no matter what the penalties. And then what the hell am I supposed to do? Who would ever believe me again if I let him off. I'd have had to have his head on a platter."

"I see."

"I don't even know how the hell you do that. I mean, who does the dirty work? Do I have a Headsman who works for me? I don't even know. Maybe I'd have to do it myself. Damn. What a thankless task that would be. You chop off some guy's head, just to keep up discipline you know, and who ever appreciates what you've done? Nobody, I can assure you. Even though it may be quite necessary. What a mess." He put his head down on the desk like a schoolchild who'd been punished.

Mr. Tompkins waited a full minute for NNL to go on. Nothing. "So I kind of saved you," Mr. Tompkins ventured.

"Yes." The voice was muffled under his arms and against the desk.

"I let you off the hook, so to speak."

"You did."

಄

THE DEADLINE

NNL was feeling somewhat better after two more Twinkies and another Coke. "We should talk about the projects, Tompkins. About one of them at least. There is one that I have a particularly good feeling about."

"Which one is that?"

"Well, now think about this the way that I did when I first sketched the projects out. We want to be first in the world in software exports by the year 2000, so what do we do?"

"Think up some products and build them."

"No. We build them, but we don't think them up." He was tapping his head as though he just had an ingenious thought. "We don't have to think them up."

"We don't?" Mr. Tompkins asked.

"No. They've already been thought up. What the hell, why invent something new? We already know what the best-selling products are. We'll just rebuild them."

"Isn't that illegal?"

"Not exactly. It would be illegal to copy the code directly, that's what's copyrighted. But when you rebuild a product from scratch, there is no legal problem there. We may make one or two cosmetic changes, just so the thing is not identical. That should be sufficient. Then, nobody has the right to sue us. And, of course, there is no court to put the case in anyway, even if our competitors wanted to sue. This is the brave new world of global competition. Courts don't play much of a part."

"I see."

"So what do we build? What is the most successful software product of all time? In terms of copies sold, that is. Which one?"

"I have a hunch you're going to tell me."

"It's Quicken," he said.*

"Quicken."

"Yes. Made by Intuit. Millions of copies sold. Runs on PCs and Macs and Suns and Unix boxes. Everybody who's got a computer has a copy of it. People all over the world use it to balance their checkbooks or run their small companies or manage their investments."

"Well, not to be a nay-sayer, but if everybody has already got a copy of it, how are we going to sell ours?"

"That, of course, is the same problem that Intuit has. Since they've already sold a copy to just about everyone, you might wonder where their future revenue will come from. It's obviously expected to come from somewhere, or their stock would not be selling at such a large multiple of earnings."

"So, where does the future revenue come from?"

"New versions."

"We're going to sell our Quicken in direct competition with their upgrades? Why would anyone buy from us?"

"Price competition."

"How do we price-compete with a product that sells for about $29.95?"

"We're going to give ours away!"

"What? How do we make money doing that?"

NNL looked mysterious and exceedingly pleased with himself. "You build the product for me, and I'll make money with it. Tons and tons of money. That is a promise."

On the train back down the coast to Varsjop, Mr. T. pulled his journal out of his bag. He had resolved to write something in it every chance he had, every time he learned something. But

---

* Quicken is a registered trademark of Intuit, Inc.

what had he really learned today? He'd like to make an entry on 'How to make money giving your product away for free,' but he clearly wasn't ready for that one yet. He had yet to learn how the trick would be done. Curiously, though, he had no doubt that NNL would pull it off. The man seemed to have a certain knack for business.

Maybe there was something to learn from the matter of Mopoulka and the threat that NNL had originally used, hoping to get the plant built on a very tight schedule. After a few moments thought, he opened the journal and began to write.

From Mr. Tompkins' Journal:

<u>Negative Reinforcement</u>

    o   Threats are an imperfect way to moti-vate performance.

    o   No matter how serious the threat, the work still won't get done on time if the time originally allocated for it was not sufficient.

    o   Worse still, if the target doesn't get met, you may actually have to make good on your threats.

6

THE WORLD'S GREATEST
PROJECT MANAGER

ॐ

*I*n deciding if he should take the job, Mr. Tompkins had concentrated entirely on the question of whether or not the job deserved to be taken. He'd asked himself: Were the basic parameters workable? Could his immediate superiors—NNL and the Morovian government—be trusted? Was the undertaking sufficiently challenging? Would the effort be adequately rewarded? But now that he had made the decision and decided to stay, another kind of question began to bother him: Was he up to it?

The truth was, he had never managed this many people before. He had run a project with two hundred fifty once, and some thirty-five middle managers. But fifteen hundred! In Morovia, there would be nearly as many managerial staff reporting to him as he'd had in total staff on his largest project. And they were all unknown quantities. As Waldo kept reminding him, he needed to act now to staff and allocate the projects. NNL had laid out six projects to be the beginning of Morovia's powerful new presence in the software world. Six projects, that wasn't so bad, but he still wanted to avail himself of Lahksa's offer to run multiple teams doing the same work under different conditions, the Project Management Laboratory. Assuming he had three competing teams on each assignment, that meant he'd have to set up eighteen project teams and choose eighteen managers.

Waldo had required each of the two hundred working software managers to make up a resume, and now the two hundred resumes were sitting on his desk. He stared at them in dismay and they stared back at him, accusingly. He hadn't the foggiest idea of how to begin.

When he was sufficiently stressed (he'd noticed this years before), he had a terrible tendency to go blank, to drop out, and do something mindless rather than face the work. The mindless thing today was to read a book that Lahksa had packed up from the pile in his bedroom and put away here in the bookshelf of his office. The book was called *Structural Cybernetic Management*. He had always meant to read it. Before, though, he had always been too busy managing to have time to learn the theory behind it. Now he was determined to make time, at least to take a few hours before facing the horrible pile of resumes. He put his feet up on the desk and began to read.

The book was deadly. At the end of each chapter, he would put it down and open his journal to make some notes about what he had learned from the author. And, chapter after chapter, he had come up blank and not written down a single thing. "All the good stuff's probably at the end," he muttered to himself after Chapter 10. He pressed on into Chapter 11.

Waldo came in with a cup of strong Morovian coffee. He looked oddly at Mr. T. "The boss is in the dumps," he observed.

"Steeling myself for the task ahead," Tompkins told him, with a nod toward the massive pile of resumes.

"A bit daunting, isn't it?" Waldo said, sympathizing.

"It is. I'll get to it, though. Thought I'd just take a bit of time to get myself inspired before beginning. I'm learning 'structural cybernetic management,' which will no doubt be invaluable in sorting through the various managers on our staff and making my choices for which one to put where."

"Ah."

"Ah indeed."

"How did you make your people decisions in your old position, Boss? I mean, before learning the structural cybernetic approach? If I could ask."

Tompkins closed the book and sat up. "That was quite different. I didn't make any decisions alone. I had a trusted group of peers and subordinates that I had known for years. We'd sit around and hash over the possibilities."

"I see."

"I've got the 'sitting around' part pretty much under control...."

"Uh huh. It's the 'hashing over' part that isn't going so well. No one to hash with." Waldo observed.

Mr. Tompkins sighed. "Too true." There it was in a nutshell. He was utterly alone. Lahksa had said he could bring along some people of his own and import a few consultants. But it would be a long period of negotiation and arranging before anyone actually showed. Nobody jumps in an instant to take a new job in Morovia. (He was beginning to understand why Lahksa had opted for kidnapping.) No, there would be no familiar face on board for a long time, perhaps months. And during those months he'd have to make all of the key decisions alone, decisions that would set the projects irrevocably on their way.

49

"There is, perhaps, one possibility . . ." Waldo suggested.

"There is?"

"I mean, a possibility for a kind of instant 'peer,' someone who's had a long experience managing large efforts like this in American companies. His name is Binda."

"Oh, yes, NNL mentioned him. He was the guy who was originally picked for my job, wasn't he?"

"Yes. Lahksa brought him over, in the usual way . . ."

"And the fellow had the good sense to decline?"

"More or less."

"But then, didn't he go back?"

"No. For some reason he hung around. It was all very odd. None of us ever got to meet him. He arrived, moved into his suite—it's right adjacent to yours—and then went away. He comes back occasionally to get books or to drop things off. He doesn't stay the night. I don't even know what he looks like."

"And you're thinking he might be willing to sign on as a part-time consultant."

"Wouldn't hurt to ask." Waldo was looking coy. And he had something behind his back.

"Mmm. And what you're holding behind your back is, no doubt, Binda's resume. Give it here, Waldo."

"You're way ahead of me, Boss." Waldo handed over the four sheets.

Tompkins read the credentials out loud: "'B. Binda. Born, 1950. Education: U.C. Berkeley, summa cum laude, stroke of the varsity crew; MBA, Harvard. Professional experience: Xerox PARC, Apple, short stint at Tandem, eight years running major projects at Hewlett-Packard, and ten at Computer Sciences.' Wow, and look at these projects, not a loser among them. I'd always wondered who'd been in charge of some of these."

"I don't know if he would be willing, of course."

"But it wouldn't hurt to ask, as you said. What the hell—I think I'll do it. Who knows, maybe the guy will come on board as a second." He was feeling better already. With someone like Binda at his side, he would feel a good deal less daunted by the task ahead. "How do I find him?"

"You had best ask Lahksa about that." Waldo picked up Tompkins' empty cup and disappeared.

Tompkins headed down the corridor to Lahksa's office. Since there was not much desk work in her trade, her office didn't even have a desk. What it had instead was a comfortable couch by the window. He found her there, curled up with a paperback.

"Lahksa, where do I find this B. Binda? Any idea where he hangs out?"

"She."

"What?"

"She. She's a woman, Webster. You remember women."

He stared at her blankly. "Oh. I just thought ..."

"Your biases are showing, dear. Women can be managers, too."

"I'm not the least bit biased." He dumped the image of himself and his new male colleague Binda, working through the resumes over a few beers and telling war stories from their not-too-dissimilar pasts. And, in its place, he tried to imagine himself and ... He didn't even know her name. "What's her name?"

"Belinda."

Himself and Belinda Binda. "Not the least bit biased," he told her. "Waldo says she elected to stay on in Morovia, at least for a bit. Any idea where I can find her?"

Lahksa closed her book and sat up. "You know her story, I guess."

"She turned you down. Smart woman."

"No, it wasn't quite like that. She had burned out a few years ago. If you look closely at her resume, you see it has nothing after 1995. She just walked off the job one day and never went back. The resume in your hands was compiled by myself. I got a copy of her earlier resume from CSC and filled in a summary from their records of what she had done while she was there."

"Does Computer Sciences know they gave this information to you?"

"Of course not," she put on her impish look. "Anyway, then I set out to track her down. I found her living in San Jose."

"Plenty of good high-tech companies there. She was probably . . ."

"She was a bag lady."

"What?"

"A bag lady, complete with a shopping cart full of old stuff. I remember, she was distinctly grimy."

"I can't believe this. You tried to hire a bag lady for this job?"

"She was the world's greatest project manager in her day. She never missed a deadline, never brought in a project that was less than a success. And there are about a thousand people in the industry who would work for her again in a minute, who would follow her into battle."

"But a bag lady, living in the streets!"

"She was still sharp, the best. We talked for an hour about managing large efforts. I never heard anyone make more sense on the subject. Anyway, I thought I'd see if she might not be ready to come in from the cold. After an hour, I made my offer."

"You offered her the job."

"No, a sugar cube with two cc's of secobarbital and a drop of LSD. It's my usual formula, the same one I used on you."

"The 'drookthe.'"

"Yes. She popped it into her mouth. Said her body was sadly low on mind-altering substances."

"So, you brought her back here, and then told her about the job?"

"I did. She said 'thank you,' very politely. Said she'd always wanted to travel, and why not Morovia? She asked me if the weather was nice. I said it was, and she stood up and left. She walked down to the docks by the harbor. She's been there ever since."

"She's become a Morovian bag lady."

Lahksa sighed. "Yes, that's about it."

She wasn't hard to spot. Given that she'd been on the Berkeley women's crew, Tompkins knew she'd have to be tall, and she was. Even seated there on the grass in the harbor park, she looked long and lithe. And there was something magnetic about her—either magnetic or a little crazy; it was in her eyes.

"I think you're Belinda Binda."

"Not a bad thought. And who do you think you are?"

"Tompkins. Webster Tompkins."

"Pull up some grass." She glanced down at the spot beside her, and Tompkins sat himself down.

Belinda was sorting cans and bottles. All of the bottles and some of the cans, it appeared, had value (NNL had instituted deposit containers as a way to clean up the mess on the streets). Some of the cans, however, had no deposit markings on them. The ones that were redeemable she would place in a huge potato sack at her side and the others she would toss into the wire trash container under the palm tree. Tompkins watched in wonder. The trash container was a good thirty feet away, but she never missed. Every single can she threw landed exactly in the container.

"Wow," he said after the first few tosses. "You're good."

"Concentration," she said. "You just have to *not* think about it. Keep your mind disengaged. As it turns out, I don't have anything else on my mind anyway."

"I see. The value of an uncluttered mind."

"Uncluttered, or maybe just empty."

"I've brought you something—maybe it will engage your mind a bit. A gift." He handed her his copy of *Structural Cybernetic Management.*

She thumbed through a few pages and then began to skim rapidly, pausing only to pick up a few words here and there and some of the figures. Then she closed the book. "Sweet of you, Webster, to bring me a gift. Sweet. But, uh . . ."

"Not your cup of tea?"

"No." Belinda tossed the book in a long arch ending in the trash can. "Pure schlock."

"Mmm. You don't mince words, do you?"

"Has to do with being a bag lady. You should try it. Really. Tends to free you of your constraints."

"I imagine. Well, in the case of *Structural Cybernetic Management,* I had come to approximately the same opinion as you. It just took me longer. Somehow, the book misses the point on what management is all about. I mean, it's entirely too . . ."

"Heady. It's full of head-stuff. Management is not exactly a cerebral science."

"No, I suppose not."

"If you think about which of your organs is active as you manage, the head doesn't come into it much at all. Management is in the gut, in the heart, and in the soul."

"It is?"

"It is. The manager has to learn to trust her gut, lead from the heart, and build soul into the team and into the organization."

"Trust her gut . . ."

"That's for people decisions. You consider someone for a key position and he or she looks fine on paper, but something tells you to keep on looking. That something is your gut. And then someone else comes along, and a little voice inside you sings out, 'This is the guy!' or 'She's the one! Grab her and put her in charge of the whole works and leave her alone.' That's the gut speaking. The best managers are the ones with the best guts. The key brain function a manager has to master is to learn when to trust her gut."

"Uh huh." Tompkins pondered. "That's the gut. And the heart?"

"It's your heart that people respond to. They don't follow you because you're clever or because you're always right, but because they love you. I know that sounds very nutsy-granola, but it's the truth. I look back at the managers that I admired and they all had hearts as big as houses. Somehow, it's the heart that is the essence of leadership. The heady 'leader' can lead, but people won't follow."

Mr. Tompkins chewed that over for a moment. "It's an impossible formula, of course. Because you can't do much about the heart you've got. Your take on management doesn't provide any way for people to learn to be good managers."

"Maybe not. Maybe you have to be born to it."

He shook his head. "I haven't figured that one out completely. Maybe you do have to be born to it. And yet people grow into management, too; they start out awkward and become confident and eventually make wonderful managers. Is it that they're growing hearts as big as houses?"

"I think they are."

"Maybe so. And the soul? How does that figure in?" he asked her.

"That's a bit more complicated. It has to do with the fact that projects prosper to the extent that people learn to work together effectively. If they worked entirely apart, a bunch of piece workers in different places who didn't even know each other, then soul wouldn't matter. Management would be a simple matter of coordinating their efforts. It would be an entirely mechanical process."

"Maybe the structural cybernetic approach would work in such cases."

"It might. But the real world requires close, warm, and almost intimate interconnections between team members, and easy, effective, interaction through the whole organization."

"So, how do you make that happen?"

"Well, you don't *make* it happen at all. You *let* it happen. You create an atmosphere where it *can* happen. And then, if you're lucky, it *does* happen."

"The role of the manager in all of this is . . . ?"

". . . is creating the atmosphere where healthy interactions have their best chance to happen. That's what I call building soul into the organization. You do that in various ways, but you have to do it. Maybe you make a cult of quality work, or you instill in people the sense that the group is, in some sense at least, an elite, the best in the world. You get them to think about *integrity* and all the baggage that word carries. Whatever it is, there has to be some shared vision. It's that shared vision that unifies the group. I think of it as soul."

"Sounds complicated."

"Not terribly. You see, the group so desperately wants to be unified. The human creature has—built into its firmware—a need to be part of a community. And, in today's rather sterile modern world, there isn't much community to be had. In particular, the bedroom communities where most people live are all bedroom and no community."

"That's true. An amazing number of twentieth-century people don't even know their neighbors."

"Community doesn't come from our towns anymore. But the need for community is still in us. For most of us, the best chance of a community is at work."

Mr. Tompkins needed to pinch himself. He was sitting here next to a bag lady in a Morovian park talking about soul and community. Stranger things must have happened to someone, somewhere, but certainly not to him. Oh well. He pressed on, "So what you referred to earlier as 'building soul into the organization' is really an exercise in community building."

"Uh huh. It is. The soul you foster in the organization is like the sand in an oyster; it is the seed around which community begins to form."

He looked out over the harbor, letting his eyes go unfocused. Belinda went back to sorting cans and bottles.

"So, that's it then?" he said after a long pause. "Gut, heart, and soul. That's what management is all about."

"Mmm. Gut, heart, and soul . . . and nose."

"Nose?"

"Yeah. The great manager also needs a nose for bullshit."

Mr. T. stayed on for most of the afternoon, chatting with Belinda Binda. As the dusk was coming over them, he made his pitch.

"Belinda, I'd like to put your expert gut to work. Would you consider that? Would you come to work with me."

"You want to bring me on as a consultant?"

"Yes."

"It will cost you dearly, Webster."

"Name your price."

"A shopping cart."

"That's it? A shopping cart?"

"That's it. You can't imagine what a bummer it is to be a bag lady without a shopping cart. No place to put your stuff."

"A shopping cart. Okay, you got it then. It's a deal."

They shook hands soberly.

"You'll have to clean up a bit," he told her. He looked down pointedly at her bare feet and ankles, which were black with grime.

"You want me to wash, maybe put on some clean clothes?"

"Yes," he said firmly.

"You want me to imitate a normal person."

"Yes. At least in appearance. The rest of you, I don't want to change at all."

"She wants a shopping cart," he told Lahksa.

Lahksa rolled her eyes.

"How difficult can that be? We just go to the local super-market and requisition one."

"Webster, there are no supermarkets in Morovia."

"Oh."

"This is the third world, remember?"

"Well, we'll have to get one from abroad then. Go to London and steal one from Sainsburys. That should be right up your alley. That's what industrial spies are good at, aren't they? Stealing stuff?"

"I'm certainly up to that. Sainsburys will be no problem. It's British Air I'm thinking about. Can you imagine the belly-aching when I try to bring back a shopping cart as checked baggage? They'll have a kitten."

He left Lahksa to work it out. Back in his office, he opened his journal and took out a pen.

From Mr. Tompkins' Journal:

The Manager's Essential Body Parts

o   Management involves heart, gut, soul, and nose.

o   So . . .

lead with the heart,
trust your gut (trust your hunches),
build soul into the organization,
develop a nose for bullshit.

7

TAKING ON STAFF

ی

*B*elinda showed up at his office in a fresh sundress. She was sparkling clean. The only accommodation she was unwilling to make was footwear. She came with bare feet. "Shoes? Never again," she told him when he asked. He decided he could live with that. She towered over him by a good six inches anyway, even in her bare feet.

"Well," he said, "I guess we should get started." He pulled up a chair for her at his desk and gestured toward the pile of resumes. "There's what we've got to get through."

Belinda didn't sit. She picked up one of the resumes with a look of some distaste on her face. "How far away are these people?" she asked after a moment. "Hours away?"

"More like minutes away, I should think. They're all somewhere in the complex, I guess."

She brightened. "Oh, that's good." She pulled up a wastebasket and swept the whole pile of resumes into it. "Let's look at the people instead of looking at their resumes."

Mr. Tompkins stared at her in amazement, but she was already on her way to the door.

Waldo had a list for them of the people they'd need to interview and where on the campus they could be found. Within a few minutes, they found themselves in the office of the first candidate, a bright-looking young man, dressed impeccably in sports jacket and brown slacks.

"Tell us about your view of management," Belinda suggested. "What's it all about, this business of managing projects?"

The man got a glow in his eyes, obviously relishing what was to come. "Management . . ." he said. "When I think about management, I always remember the movie *Patton*. Did you see that movie? You remember, with George C. Scott as Patton?"

Both Belinda and Webster nodded.

"Well, I am like Patton. I mean, the project manager is like Patton. Has to be. Like Patton in that first battle scene in the movie where he directs the attack on Rommel. He is the one who gives shape to the whole battle. He calls all the shots."

The young man was on his feet now, waving his arms over an imaginary battlefield. "Bring in the air support! he says. And the air support comes in. Ack-Ack-Ack-Ack! Kaboom! Turn the flank! Here there, left squadron, attack! Attack! And now fall back. Quickly there, quickly! Now wait, wait, wait for my command. . . . NOW! Attack, attack, give them all you've got! Right wing, come to their support. Yes, that's it, that's it. Now more tactical air: bombs right up the middle. And now, the pièce de résistance, the Reserve: Come on, Reserve, down from the left side, hurry up. Yes, right there, exactly where the enemy is not suspecting it. Poweeee! Kaboom! Wipe them up. Yesss!!!"

Mr. Tompkins' jaw had dropped. He made an effort to close it. He looked over at Belinda. She seemed impassive, maybe a bit sleepy.

"I see," Tompkins said, after a moment. "So, that's your view of management."

"Absolutely. Just like commanding a tank battle. The manager is the brains and everybody else is just foot soldiers."

Afterward, out in the hall alone with Belinda, Mr. T. observed, "Seemed an earnest young man. You were not overly impressed, I gather."

She made a face. "You did see that film, Webster? *Patton?* Did you see it, and do you remember it?"

"I did and I do."

"The scene at the beginning where Patton 'commands' the battle, as our young friend would have it: Well, Patton doesn't give a single command in that scene. He just watches the whole thing through his binoculars. He picks up the front of the Panzer division as it comes through the pass into the valley, just as he had expected it would. And there, standing in the well of the first tank, is an officer with a riding crop under his arm. Patton focuses in on him and says, 'Rommel, you magnificent bastard. I read your book.' He's read the book so he knows exactly what Rommel would be likely to do. Now the battle begins. The attack, the flank maneuver, the feigned withdrawal, the re-attack, the air support, the arrival of the reserves. Patton just watches. He never gives a single instruction."

"So, the kid had it a bit turned around. I didn't remember the details exactly myself."

"He remembered what he wanted to remember. What he wanted to remember was that the General, the manager in his mind, was the only active intelligence in the battle, that everyone else was 'just foot soldiers.'"

"Ah."

"That wasn't Patton at all. He was not the active intelligence of the battle. That intelligence had been spread around to all his subordinates. By the time the battle began, Patton's job was already done. And he knew it."

The second interview was over before it began. They sat down in front of a second earnest-looking young man, also rather nicely dressed.

"Well, tell us a bit of your philosophy of management," Mr. T. suggested, taking his clue from Belinda's earlier opening.

"Um. . . ." the young man began.

Belinda turned to Webster. "Hire him," she said.

"What?!?"

"Hire him."

"Wait, I haven't even got his name written down yet."

"Kartak. Elem Kartak," the man told him. "Do I really have the job?"

"Well, I guess so. . . ." Tompkins said.

"Definitely," Belinda said.

Tompkins dutifully wrote the man's name down on his clipboard. Oh well, that was one. Only seventeen more to go.

Out in the corridor again, Tompkins turned to his colleague. "Belinda, what on earth was that all about?"

"Well, I talked to some of his people while you were in the men's room. When I asked them about Elem, the lights went on in their eyes. And did you notice how his office was set up?"

"Uh . . ."

"It wasn't an office at all. It was set up like a war room, a command center, with all the work artifacts pasted up on the walls."

"I did notice that the walls were totally papered with drawings."

"Designs, interface templates, schedules, milestone charts. It was beautiful. And no desk. Only a long table with lots of chairs. It's obvious they're all involved in running the war room."

"So, that's what we're looking for? Managers without desks? Managers who turn their offices into war rooms?"

"What we're looking for are managers who are awake enough to alter the world as they find it, to make it harmonize with what they and their people are trying to accomplish."

They completed nearly thirty interviews the first day. The interviews fell neatly into two types. In the first type, Belinda would smile politely, looking only a bit sleepy, and wait for the candidate to finish; then they'd make their exit. In the second type, she would cut the candidate off and tell Webster to hire him or her. It wasn't always clear to Tompkins what she was seeing, but they all felt pretty good to him. She obviously trusted her hunches. Occasionally, he would make the call, with Belinda nodding her agreement. Before leaving one of their new hires, Belinda would always ask for pointers about who that person thought were the best of the other managers in the organization.

By the last interview that day, they were both wearing down. They were shown into the office of a woman named Molly Makmora. Belinda asked her to describe the project she was currently running, an effort to produce some report generators for the Morovian Port Authority. Molly started off with reasonable enthusiasm, but was interrupted by a knock at the door.

"Um, excuse me," she said. "One of my people, I guess."

The man at the door was obviously distraught. "Molly," he said, "there's a guy out here who needs to go to confession. He needs to, bad."

"Oh, sure," she said. "Let me get my scarf." She walked back to a cupboard and leaned over it, keeping her back to the door. Webster and Belinda, unable to contain their curiosity, stepped out into the corridor, where they saw the back of the same man disappearing into an ornately carved wooden cabinet with two doors. He pulled the curtain closed behind him, and a moment later, the green light over his door turned red.

Molly came out behind them, placing a flowered silk scarf around her neck. "This won't take two minutes," she told them.

She stepped into a second door and closed it solidly. They heard the sound of a sliding panel opening between the two separate parts of the little enclosure, and then, after a moment, murmuring voices from inside.

There was a silence, then the sound of the same panel being closed again. The light turned from red to green and the man exited, moving quickly down the corridor and around the corner. Shortly thereafter, Molly emerged. She took off her scarf and led Belinda and Webster back into her office.

She shut the door. "You're wondering what that was all about."

"Actually, we were," Mr. T. confirmed.

"Well, he needed to tell me that his testing work was going to take longer than expected. In fact, he's going to miss the milestone date by at least two weeks, maybe as much as four." She walked to her white board and drew a red circle around one of the milestones. Then, she sketched in a band of possibilities some four weeks wide to show where the revised milestone was likely to occur.

She turned back to them, found them looking unenlightened. "Sometimes, it's hard just to look your boss in the face and say you're going to be late. Sometimes, it's easier just to be late. But then the problem is that the boss finds out weeks after you might have told her, often when there's not much she can do about it. Anyway, we worked out this idea for a semi-anonymous mechanism. Of course, I always know who it is that's confessing, but I pretend I don't. And they know that I know, but they pretend that they don't. The result is that bad news has an easier way to get to me."

Belinda was on her feet, looking at Mr. T. "Anything else you want to know about Molly Makmora?" she asked him.

"No, I think that will be fine. Welcome to the team, Molly. We'll be back to you with your specific assignment."

"One other thing," Belinda said, turning to Molly. "You called your confessional a 'semi-anonymous' mechanism. Would it be of any use to you to have a truly anonymous way to communicate? For example, suppose we set up an anonymous e-mail ID with a password known to all your people so that any of them could get a totally anonymous message to you."

Molly was nodding. "We tried to set that up. The powers that be, the network administrators, turned us down. They were horrified by the very idea. I suspect they were afraid it might be used for poison-pen messages, or something like that. Anyway, they said no, loud and clear."

"I'm going to reason with them," Belinda replied. "With a hammer, if necessary. You'll have it by this time tomorrow. Let's say the ID will be ANON and the password will be, well, how about 'MOLLY'? Count on it being in place tomorrow. You can tell your people."

"Won't it be used for poison-pen messages?" Webster asked her, on the way back to his office. "I mean, that *might* be a problem."

"Oh, I don't think so. There are plenty of other ways to send such messages, if people want to. What there isn't in most organizations is a clean way to send a truly anonymous message to your boss. So, bad news that everybody wants to tell and every good boss wants to know never gets through until it's too late. I bet the ANON ID is practically never used at all. But when it is, it will be invaluable."

Upon their return, Belinda asked Waldo to do a little research on the projects each of their selected managers had run in the past. What she was mostly interested in was knowing the largest group that each of them had managed before. Waldo had the list for them in no time.

"Well, here we see Molly, for example. In her management career, she has run four projects: three people, five people, five people, and six people."

They walked together over to the display wall where they had earlier pasted up the profile sheets for the first six projects (eighteen teams). Mr. T. picked up her train of thought: "She'll be perfect for PMill, the Web Page Designer project, then. We'll give her a staff of eight or ten developers."

"Mmm," Belinda said. "I'd rather see her on this one." She pointed to the profile sheet for QuickerStill, the Quicken look-alike project. It was the smallest of the six projects. In the box for maximum staff size, they had written '6.' She tapped on that number with one big, blunt finger."

"Six? But she's already done that. She'll want something more, something to stretch against, to help her grow."

"She will. She certainly will. But we'll ask her, as a favor, to do her growing on the next project. We'll ask her to do one time for us what she has successfully done before for others. We'll do that for each project, ask people to defer for a bit the chance to take on a real stretch goal, and repeat, just one time, what they already know they can do successfully. It's a trick, Webster, a trick that has never let me down."

Belinda left to head back to her spot in the harbor park for the night, and Mr. T. sat down in his office reading corner, in the chintz-covered, overstuffed chair that Lahksa had chosen for him. What a day! Thirty interviews and they had come up with no fewer than five managers that they both felt comfortable with. This was progress beyond his wildest hopes.

Looking back over his notes, he knew that he'd never felt better about any new hires than he did about the five managers they had just selected. If they could round out the management team now with others that inspired the same level of confidence, he knew they'd have a winning combination.

It was already dark outside by the time he stood up. He was ready for a bath and dinner. But before heading out, he dutifully sat for a few moments at his desk to write some observations from the day. Most of what he wanted to write had to do with the hiring process, but there was also Belinda's fascinating insight about Patton as a manager. . . .

From Mr. Tompkins' Journal:

Battle Command As a Metaphor for Management

    o   By the time the battle begins, the manager's real work is already done.

Interviews and Hiring

    o   Hiring involves all the managerial body parts: heart, soul, nose, and gut (but mostly gut).

    o   Don't try to do it alone—two guts are more than twice as good as one.

    o   Ask new hires to undertake one project at exactly the level of competence they have already proved, to defer real stretch goals till the next time.

    o   Ask for pointers: The person you are most inclined to hire may well know of other good possibilities.

    o   Listen more than you speak.

This last point was something he had picked up from Belinda during the day. He himself had a terrible tendency to gush on about the new organization he was building, the project, the nature of the challenges, or whatever. It was as if he could not bear to be quiet. If the candidate wasn't speaking, Mr. Tompkins felt compelled to fill the silence. Belinda didn't. When he did manage to contain himself and let Belinda direct the interview, she was prone to allowing long, uncomfortable silences. During this time, she would sit calmly, looking at the interview subject. At the end, the candidate would invariably break and begin to speak. What was said at such points was almost always the most useful part of the interview.

Now that he looked back at the list in his journal, he saw that it wasn't just the very last item that had come from Belinda, but virtually everything on the list. Hadn't he contributed anything at all to the process? Well, of course, he had. The night before Belinda's arrival, he had finally worked up the resolve to read through all the resumes. And then he had sorted the stack into a vague order, with the most likely candidates at the top of the stack. The list that Waldo later made up, showing all the candidates' names and locations, was made from the sorted resume pile; it was in the same order. So, he and Belinda had spent the day talking to the managers that his earlier scan had indicated were the best bets.

He bent down once again over his journal to add a final item to his points about interviews and hiring:

> o   All these things work better if you
>   stack the deck.

8

THE EMINENT
DR. RIZZOLI

&

*L*ahksa Hoolihan had a mischievous look in her eye. Since she behaved mischievously even when she didn't look that way, Mr. Tompkins suspected trouble.

"I need your approval for what I've just done, Webster. I've done something rather extraordinary."

"Oh, dear. I can't imagine why you need my approval, since you've already done it."

"I just do. Who knows why? I have these moments of needing approval. So approve, please."

He shook his head, expecting the worst. "Well, I'll bite. Tell me what you've done."

"Of course. But you must approve first, then I'll tell you."

"Lahksa! I can't do that. You're asking for a blank check."

She pouted. "A little blank check of approval. You would deny me that? C'mon, Webster."

He stared at her. What an exasperating woman. She waited patiently for him to approve before going on. Tompkins gave a long sigh. "Okay, I approve. Now, what have you done?"

She grinned. "Well. You know as well as I do that this business of setting up a Project Management Laboratory is something none of us really knows how to do. We're going to run multiple instances of a project, each one chartered to develop exactly the same piece of software. By altering some one or maybe a few factors, and then observing the results, we can hope to learn exactly how such factors affect project work."

"Right."

"Only, what are the factors? What should we vary? What are the controls? What do we conclude? If two people do a given piece of work faster than four, what does it prove? That two always do the work faster? Suppose one team goes faster but introduces more errors, what does that mean? How do we compare their performance?"

He nodded. "I've been wondering the same sort of thing. We have a ton of questions like that. Here we have the chance of a lifetime to set up some controlled experiments in project management. But it's not as easy as it looks."

"It isn't. So, we have an unusual and highly specified need here. We need to know how to do something that has almost never been done before. How do we do that?" She pretended to ponder the problem. Then, her face lit up with pretend revelation. "Sounds like a job for a consultant."

"I'll buy that. But who? Is there anyone who has ever set up a project laboratory before?"

"Well, there is. There is one man who has done just that: Dr. Hector Rizzoli."

"Oh, yes." Tompkins certainly knew that name, one of the most respected in the field. "Well, that's true enough. He has run some very cleverly controlled experiments to determine, for example, the usefulness of certain inspection techniques. I remember reading about that. He ran a kind of software engineering laboratory for some U.S. Government agency. Did a whole series of controlled experiments."

"The very man."

"You're a step ahead of me, Lahksa. I see what you mean. He could be a most useful consultant for us. As soon as we began talking about running a set of experiments, our Project Management Laboratory, I should have asked you to contact Dr. Rizzoli. I wonder when we could get him here?"

"Tomorrow afternoon."

"What?!?"

"Tomorrow afternoon. He'll be on the three o'clock flight from New Delhi. We'll meet him at the airport."

Mr. Tompkins was immediately suspicious. "Wait a minute. Wait a minute. How does it happen that's he's stopping in Morovia tomorrow afternoon? You haven't been up to your old tricks again, have you? Secobarbital and LSD? You haven't kidnapped the poor man?"

A hurt look. "Webster. Would I do a thing like that? Certainly not. No, he's coming of his own free will." Again the look of mischief in her eyes. "Sort of."

"Sort of? Explain, please."

"Well, he's coming of his own free will, only he doesn't know exactly where he's coming to. You see, he thinks he's arriving in Latvia. The Latvian government invited him months ago to a conference they're having in Riga, to give the keynote address. It worked out fine for him, since he's on his way back from India, so he accepted. And we have arranged for the flight to stop here. He'll be so jet-lagged, he'll have no idea where he is. One of our agents is serving as the stewardess of the flight. She'll wake him up and put him off here."

"This is outrageous."

"But the chance of a lifetime . . ."

The next afternoon, a very sleepy looking Hector Rizzoli stepped off a British Air flight at the Varsjop airport. Mr. Tompkins and Ms. Hoolihan were there to meet him. They waited for him under a huge banner that read "LATVIA WELCOMES THE EMINENT DR. RIZZOLI."

Mr. Tompkins approached him. "Dr. Rizzoli?"

"I guess."

"I'm Webster Tompkins. And this is my colleague, Ms. Hoolihan."

The man shook hands and looked around, somewhat befuddled. "Palm trees," he said. "I never knew there'd be palm trees in Latvia. Isn't Latvia in the north?"

"Not as far north as you might think," Lahksa told him.

"And then there is the effect of the Humboldt Current," Tompkins added helpfully.

"Oh, yes. Humboldt."

In spite of the slight deceit they were practicing, Mr. T. was excited to meet one of the icons of the field. "This is a great honor, Dr. Rizzoli. I have long been an admirer of your work."

Dr. Rizzoli blushed becomingly. There were crinkle lines around his eyes, implying a ready smile, which, sure enough, was soon in evidence. His beard was flecked with gray, but his thick head of hair was still quite black. There was about the man an air of solidity; he seemed like the kind of person you could tell almost anything to, and count on a thoughtful and caring response.

"We hope you're going to love your stay here in . . . Latvia," Tompkins enthused. "We have arranged a huge audience for you tomorrow afternoon, for your keynote. And then a little tour, lunches and dinners of course, and then I just wondered if you might be interested in learning about some experiments we'll be running."

"Experiments?" Dr. Rizzoli looked instantly awake. "What kind of experiments?"

They had the entire software engineering staff, nearly fifteen hundred in all, show up for Dr. Rizzoli's keynote address. The speech was a tour de force. At the end, the audience stood and applauded for what seemed like several minutes. By the time he was allowed to step down from the podium, Dr. Rizzoli was looking dazed and happy.

There was a reception that followed and then a tour of the town and of its ancient fortifications, then dinner, then another reception, then a chamber concert, then brandy out on the terrace with a small group, waiting to see the moon rise over the valley. There was not a moment during the day, only his second in Morovia (Latvia), for Dr. Rizzoli to look at the Project Management Laboratory experiments. But the third day he spent entirely with Mr. Tompkins and Belinda Binda. By late afternoon, they had sketched out a series of controlled experiments. Each and every product was to be constructed three times, by three teams working in parallel. For each project, they had a single, designated learning goal, a particular effect that the relative performance of the competing teams would help to prove or disprove.

Table 8-1.
Six Products: Eighteen Projects.

PRODUCT	COMPETES WITH*	A-TEAM		B-TEAM		C-TEAM	
		MGR	STAFF	MGR	STAFF	MGR	STAFF
NOTATE	NOTES	????	12	????	10	Taichi	4
PMILL	PAGEMILL	Gradish	9	????	8	Onyon	4
PAINT-IT	PAINTER	Alweez	13	????	11	Nefer	5
PSHOP	PHOTOSHOP	????	17	Isbek	16	Alterbek	7
QUIRK	QUARKXPRESS	????	13	Apfels	12	Kabach	5
QUICKERSTILL	QUICKEN	Grosz	7	Kartak	3	Makmora	6

During the evening after their long workday, there was a dinner buffet and wine-tasting party. "It seems we're tasting exclusively Morovian wines this evening," Dr. Rizzoli observed.

"Part of our 'Wines of the World' program," Lahksa told him smoothly. "Today Morovia, tomorrow Spain or Algeria or Luxembourg, who knows?"

"What a charming program," Dr. Rizzoli enthused, draining his glass of Zelenikë white. "I think I like Morovian wines, particularly the whites."

"Now you must try some of the darker ones from Bilak and Viziçë in the east." Mr. Tompkins was becoming something of an expert on Morovian wine. He poured a glass for his guest. "Look at the color, almost amber."

---

* Notes is a registered trademark of International Business Machines, Inc. PageMill is a registered trademark of Adobe Systems, Inc. Painter is a registered trademark of Fractal Design Corporation. Photoshop is a registered trademark of Adobe Systems, Inc. QuarkXPress is a registered trademark of Quark, Inc. Quicken is a registered trademark of Intuit, Inc.

Dr. Rizzoli tasted the clear, dark wine. "Mmm. Nutty and delicious. Now that is a wine. I think I might like to go to Morovia one day. Wonder what it would be like."

"Bit like this, I should think," Tompkins told him. "Pretty scenery, nice people, and, of course, lots of splendid wine."

The wine party was being held on the ground floor and garden of the Residence building where Mr. Tompkins had his private suite upstairs. Dr. Rizzoli, too, was staying at the Residence, so when the evening was wearing down they had only to climb the ornate staircase to find their way to their rooms. They each took a glass of Mogradec Tokay, an elegant pale orange dessert wine, for the trip up. As sometimes happens with two gentlemen in their cups, they stopped for a chat partway up the stairs. And an hour later, they were still there, seated side-by-side on the plush burgundy stair runner, talking shop.

"You know, Hector, we've talked so much about the controls and the learning goals for the projects, I almost think we've forgotten to tell you that the projects are not just experiments. I mean, they really do need to produce something in a timely way, software products of extremely high quality."

"Not a pure experiment, perhaps, but still a marvelous opportunity to learn important things about the dynamics of projects."

"Oh, yes. But there are also the dynamics of my job to think about. We could learn lots of things and not deliver anything, in which case my stewardship would have to be judged a failure. Or, we could learn nothing but deliver six stupendous software products, in which case, strictly from a job point of view, I would be judged a success."

"And you want to be a success in both of these respects."

"Exactly."

"Exactly. Just as I would."

"We want to learn from a few interim failures perhaps, but mostly from our ultimate successes."

Dr. Rizzoli nodded. "Well, just for starters, I suspect that the very fact of the experiments you're running can only help ultimate project results. How can you go wrong running three copies of a project in parallel and then selecting the one that finishes first and best as your product? It's a luxury that most organizations can't afford. The little competitive goad that will exist between the teams is a fair reminder of the competition that the products will face from the exterior; it can only help to keep the developers focused."

"Yes, I'm aware of that. But now here's the thing: I have sitting opposite me none other than the world-famous Dr. Hector Rizzoli, a man who has made his name as a master of most of the science of software building, a man who has published literally hundreds of scholarly papers, plus articles, books, tutorials. . . ."

"Mmm. I have been accused of being a man who has never had an unpublished thought."

"I'd like to meet the boor who would say such a thing!"

"Well, I suspect it was a compliment, actually."

"I should hope so. Anyway, here I find myself in a private moment with the eminent Dr. Rizzoli. I'd be crazy not to ask you for some advice. Tell me, Hector, What should I do to give the projects their very best chance of success? What would you do if you were in my place? What one thing?"

Hector let his eyes wander out over the wide stairwell. "One thing. That's a tough question."

"Should I focus on process improvement? You know the folks at our Software Engineering Institute are trying to convince me that a take-no-prisoners process improvement program to move the entire staff from CMM Level 2 to Level 3 is the best thing I can do to help the organization. Is that what you would do?"

"That's an easy one. No."

"Ah."

"Process improvement in the abstract is always a good thing. It means you get better and better at doing your job. But I am less enthusiastic about process improvement *programs* like the CMM. They sometimes become an end in themselves."

"But there must be something I can do, some short-term fix that will improve productivity, for example, . . ."

Hector shook his head energetically. "There is no such thing as a short-term fix in our business. There is never a way to improve productivity in the short term. When you're all done, the productivity you will achieve will be the direct result of the long-term investment made by those before you. And the only real impact *you* can have on productivity is to make a long-term investment now to benefit your successors."

Mr. Tompkins sighed. "I think I knew that. It's refreshing, nonetheless, to hear it stated so bluntly."

"The cold slap of reality on the subject of productivity improvement."

"Thanks, I needed that."

An observant waiter from downstairs arrived with two more glasses of the orange Tokay. Hector and Webster accepted the glasses and sipped thoughtfully.

"So, what would you do, Hector? What one thing?"

"Since there really isn't anything you can do to change productivity, at least not in the short term, I think you have to focus entirely on avoiding wasted time. If you assume a fixed production rate during effective work hours, then the only real variable you have to play with is the proportion of work hours that are effective. So, you concentrate on reducing the proportion of ineffective ones."

"I see that. So, I look for the sources of wasted time and rout them out of the workday."

"Yes, that couldn't hurt. But it won't help too much either, since people are always trying to perform such basic hygiene themselves, just to avoid their own frustration. The result is that you won't find huge opportunity for systemic improvement in the number of effective hours in the workday. Some, but not a lot."

"So, what nonsystemic waste do I look for?"

"Well, consider what happens when something goes wrong on a project. A risk materializes: Before it had just been a possibility, and now it's a reality, a problem."

Mr. Tompkins nodded. "Something like a piece of hardware that was on the critical path doesn't get delivered on time? Something like that?"

"Exactly. Or a key piece of critical path development finishes late, just because the time allocated for it was too little. So, people are inconvenienced, work gets pushed off, some people are idled because they can't go ahead on the next task until the critical path contingencies have been satisfied. What do you do now?"

"Well, I guess I would think of trimming functionality from the product. That might relax the critical path and it might also help us make up time in the work that remains."

"Okay. So you trim. That too suggests waste, since it's probably pretty late to be doing the trimming. After all, some work has already been applied to the very functions you are now trimming."

"I see."

"Waste, waste, waste. Waste and risk, I think, are always tied hand-in-hand. The real wasted effort of project work, the huge wastes that really set you back, are always a direct result of a risk materializing. So, the one thing I would do is to manage the risks. I would manage each project by managing the risks faced by that project. Software development is a risky business and managing that business is, most of all, an exercise in risk management."

"Most of my projects, of course, have the same risks: They might come home late or cost too much."

"Well, those are your ultimate risks, the ultimate undesirable outcomes, but those aren't the ones I'm talking about. The risks you have to manage are the causals, the things that might cause such ultimate failure. So, you don't just have a few big end-result risks, but lots of smaller, causal ones."

Mr. Tompkins chewed it over. "Manage a project as an exercise in managing the causal risks. I like that. Software development is a risky business and what are you managing if not the risks? I like that idea, . . . at least, I like it in the abstract. But I'm still not sure what it means in the specific. How do I know if I am really managing the causal risks?"

"Think about it backwards. How would someone prove that you *hadn't* managed risks? Imagine that you're being dragged into court and accused of not doing sensible risk management. What would they have to prove against you?"

"Well, I guess, that I didn't maintain a census of risks, that would be one thing."

"Or that you didn't assess each identified risk as to its probability of materializing and its likely cost if it did materialize."

"Or that I didn't set up a mechanism to detect materialization when it happened."

"That's a good one. There is always some earliest indication that a risk is actually in transition—becoming a problem—so you need to figure out what that earliest indicator will be and watch for it like a hawk."

"Maybe appoint some person to be the hawk, a kind of risk officer."

"Yes. Finally, I think it would be very damning in court if the prosecution could prove that you had not set up mechanisms for people to tell you when bad news was happening. Or worse, that you inhibited the flow of bad news by establishing a culture of fear, where people were afraid to tell you whatever you so plainly didn't want to hear."

"I wouldn't do that, of course," Mr. Tompkins assured him.

"No, not on purpose. No good manager would. But you may be so successful in instilling a Can-Do attitude in your people that they are inhibited from telling you an important piece of Can't-Do information."

"That isn't exactly a 'culture of fear,' but . . ."

"But it has a similar effect."

"I see that."

"So that is my 'one thing,' then. I would manage the projects by managing their risks."

Dr. Rizzoli was planning to be off on the first morning plane. He would leave none the wiser for where he had spent the last few days. (Someday, Mr. Tompkins was going to have to come clean about that with his new friend.) By tomorrow, all the stirring words exchanged on the stair might be lost in a post-alcoholic haze. Mr. T. had a hunch that he wasn't going to remember much of anything by morning. So, instead of going directly to bed, he now made himself sit down at his writing desk and commit Dr. Rizzoli's advice to black and white.

From Mr. Tompkins' Journal:

Productivity Improvement

o There is no such thing as a short-term productivity fix.

o Productivity improvement comes from long-term investment.

o Anything that promises immediate term results is likely to be snake oil.

Risk Management

o Manage projects by managing their risks.

o Create and maintain a census of risks for each project.

o Track the causal risks, not just the ultimate undesirable outcomes.

o Assess each risk for probability and likely cost.

o Predict, for each risk, the earliest symptom that might indicate materialization.

o Appoint a risk officer, one person who is not expected to maintain a Can-Do attitude.

o Establish easy (perhaps anonymous) channels for bad news to be communicated up the hierarchy.

9

EX-GENERAL MARKOV

è**

Since NNL was in town for the day, Belinda suggested that they press him into service. There were still dozens of interviews to be conducted. The man obviously had some experience in hiring software managers, Belinda observed, so why not let him take part? They would conduct interviews as a team of three. Even more important, they could break up and work singly, interviewing some of the lowest-level people to get their take on those who managed them. With three of them, that part of the work would go faster.

The man who fashioned himself as Morovia's 'tyrant' was not only willing to get involved in the interviews, he was positively enthusiastic. Mr. Tompkins had the sense that NNL was bored to tears with the tyrant business and itchy to do something more in line with his real skills. He turned up for the interviews wearing a disguise: a pair of dark-rimmed glasses with a false nose, bushy black eyebrows, and a mustache attached. He introduced himself at each interview as "Mr. Lider."

A young manager was telling them, "Management shman-agement. You wouldn't be hiring me as the manager, but the team that works for me. They are the best. They have worked under me for two years and with each other for two years before that. I acquired them as an integral team. Believe me, anybody could manage these people."

"Hire him," Mr. Lider said. Mr. T. looked down at his watch. The interview had only begun two minutes ago. He was beginning to suspect that he was the only one who ever agonized over a hiring decision. Certainly, NNL and Belinda Binda weren't inclined to. Oh, well, the candidate seemed like a winner to Tompkins, too. He got the fellow's name and copied it down on the clipboard.

"Respect for the team is always a good sign in a manager," NNL told them later, over coffee. "But you have to be a bit careful on this one, because it's politically correct in most organizations today to be pro-team. Some of the most flowery praise you hear on the subject of teams is only hypocrisy. Managers learn to talk a good game about teams even when they're secretly threatened by the whole concept."

"Who could admit to being anti-team or anti-team-work?" Belinda added.

NNL was nodding. "But some managers *are*. Deep down inside, they're threatened by a tight little workgroup that seems elitist, exclusionary, . . ."

"Sometimes, even excluding the manager herself," Belinda picked up. "I've managed teams that made it ever so clear that I wasn't a team member. That hurt at the time, but it was also realistic. Teams are made up of peers, and the manager is different—less tightly connected to the work details and more of an authority figure. Anyway, definitely not a peer."

Mr. T. was waiting for a chance to get a word in. "But our young friend in the last interview was not just mouthing politically correct things. He really meant it. The proof was that he had acquired an already formed team and kept it together. Someone who was secretly threatened by tight teams wouldn't have touched that . . ."

"Or would probably have broken it up," NNL added. "Breaking up teams is a sore spot with me. Some companies even have a formal policy about that. They break up teams as a matter of principle as soon as each project is done. What a dumb idea! To my mind, a well-knit team ought to be declared as one of the major project deliverables. So you're judged at the end, not just by the software you produce but also by being able to provide at least one good solid team that is willing and eager to do another project together."

"Well," Mr. Tompkins said after a moment. "We're obviously too much agreed on this subject to have a good argument. Who's our next interview?"

Belinda looked down at the list. "Fellow named Gabriel Markov."

"Oh, yes," NNL said. "That would be ex-General Markov."

"A general?" That seemed odd to Belinda.

"One of *the* generals. Before I came along, he was one of the ruling council of Morovia. So, he was one of the ones who was deposed by my coup. By the coup, that is, and a few million in stock and options."

Mr. T. objected: "But I thought you said all the Morovian generals had gone off to the Riviera to live it up on their new-found wealth."

"They did, all but ex-General Markov. He asked me if he could stay on and become a software manager. I can't imagine why he would want to work when he's got all that money."

"Look who's talking!" Belinda said pointedly. Conventional estimates were that NNL was worth a few billion.

"Oh. Well, my case is a bit different," NNL told them. "I'm building a new house. You can't imagine what plumbers and carpenters and electricians are charging these days. Everything costs a fortune!"

Belinda and Webster tried to look sympathetic.

"Anyway," NNL went on, "the ex-General had been in charge of software development in the Army, so he knew something about the subject. He has some pretty impressive credentials, but he is really more an administrator than a manager."

"Don't knock it," Belinda said. "We've got a ton of people on our hands. We could use a good administrator."

"Just what I thought," NNL agreed. "I've already put him in charge of everybody who is not assigned to one of our new lead projects. Ex-General Markov runs the rest of the organization. Everyone that we don't decide to put on one of the shrink-wrap software product efforts ends up working for him. He is, so to speak, our pool manager."

That worried Mr. Tompkins. "So each person and each team we do choose for one of the new projects is effectively removed from his domain. Isn't he going to be made uncomfortable by that?"

"I don't think so," NNL said. "He really has no idea what to do with the people he's got."

"What on earth are they doing?" Belinda asked. "They all seem to be working on something, building software, producing designs, testing modules, writing documentation. But you tell us they're also all available. I'd be fascinated to know just what the ex-General has got them all assigned to do."

As soon as they were assembled in Gabriel Markov's office, Belinda put her question to him: "What are they up to, all these people who work for you?"

"Most of them are building software for the Morovian Central Planning Office," the ex-General told them. He was a large, extremely fit man, who seemed still to be in uniform, even dressed as he was in a business suit. He had one gold tooth in front. Because he smiled almost constantly, the gold tooth was always in evidence. Now the smile was slightly sad. "I haven't the heart to tell them."

"Tell them what?" Tompkins asked.

"Tell them that the Morovian Central Planning Office has been abolished. It was a decision made by Himself." At this he winked and grinned broadly and pointed toward Mr. Lider in his false mustache.

"Why, that's awful," Tompkins said. "All those people are doing useless work."

"But only temporarily," the ex-General hastened to assure them. "We have already made contact with offshore agencies in the U.S. and Great Britain. I assure you, that by this time next year, we shall have them all busy doing contract work, at least all the ones you don't choose for the shrink-wrap software projects."

That came as a surprise to NNL. "I didn't know you were doing that, Gabriel, looking for offshore work."

"Well, I thought it made sense. And there is plenty of market out there. True, there was no great pressure to have them generate revenue, since their present salary level is still small by international standards. We could just keep them at busy work until we need them ourselves, manage them like a huge pool of available labor. Only it all seems so pointless. Even if there were still a Central Planning Office, the work would still be fairly pointless: endless automation of bloated, useless bureaucracy. To keep the morale up, I needed to find real, meaningful work for them."

Belinda changed the subject: "What is the largest group you have ever managed?"

"Thirteen thousand five hundred seventy-one people, the combined Morovian first and second Armies and the Air Force," the ex-General answered her promptly. "One hundred ninety-one million U.S. dollars in annual budget, eight hundred fifty-three million in capital investment, six hundred eighty-eight in officer-level staff including nine general officers, three hundred sixty-two in support staff, seventy-two thousand square meters of interior space, and a little more than eleven hundred square kilometers of bases and stations, five hundred nine in technical staff, including three hundred eighty-eight programmers, systems analysts, and designers."

"Oh," Belinda said.

"Well," Tompkins observed after a moment. "I think that is certainly a qualification for running our staff. Does that job appeal to you?"

The ex-General was smiling again. "It does. I am something of a novice at the technology, but I am also a great believer in it. I think the future is in information, in processing it to make knowledge and in moving it around via networks to get the knowledge to its market. That is the great revolution that is upon us. And I want to be part of it. It would be an honor to work for you and with you, the three of you, and to learn from and teach each other."

There was another silence after he spoke. The man's sincerity and warmth were palpable. Tompkins was marveling at how good it felt to hear what he had just heard.

Belinda, on the other hand, was still marveling at the numbers. "You know, Mr. ex-General, I have never managed even a tenth of the number of people you had. Give us the benefit of some of your insight. What did you learn from all your experience? Pick something and tell us about it."

Ex-General Markov looked thoughtful. His eyes became unfocused. After a moment he began, "The lesson you never stop learning is to cut your losses. When you're doing something valuable, there is always a lot of associated risk, always the chance that the effort will be a failure. This is particularly true of software work. Look at the number of projects that never deliver anything, or that are canceled, or that deliver a product that turns out to be useless. Maybe a quarter of all projects, at least of the big ones, are in that category.

"If you judge your performance based entirely on how well you run the projects that eventually do succeed, you get a false picture. You also have to watch how well you contain the failure rate, and how quickly you cut the failing efforts off. That is the biggest and hardest lesson I have ever learned."

The staff that was shaping up was impressive, but still full of unknowns. In his prior positions, Mr. Tompkins had always had at least a few known quantities to depend upon, people he'd worked with for five or ten or even fifteen years. The new faces on his Morovian management team all looked good, but he still had to wonder what his impression would be of them a few years from now. Still, it was hard to repress his optimism. The ex-General, in particular, was a welcome addition. He had the sense that this likable and intelligent man would always be able to supply a good complement to his own thinking. Most of all, it was a relief to know that the pool of some thirteen hundred and fifty of his people who would not be working on the six key products were in good hands under the ex-General.

Tompkins looked up at the new org chart that he and Belinda had put up on the white board in the late afternoon:

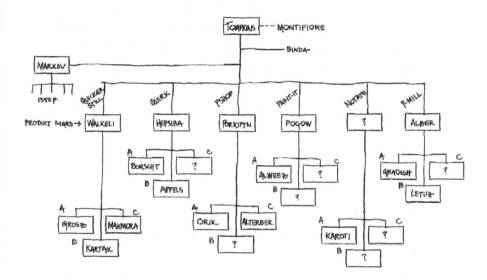

He had seven direct reports: Ex-General Markov and the six product managers who were responsible for delivering products to compete directly with Quicken, QuarkXpress, Photoshop, Painter, Lotus Notes, and PageMill, respectively. Under each product manager was an A-Team, a B-Team, and a C-Team, the three separate units competing to produce the best product fastest.

He was still looking for eight key people, including one of the direct reports. He would use the ex-General as a sounding board when he needed an experienced administrator's opinion, and other than that just treat him as manager of a human resource pool. The ex-General would be free to take on offshore contract work as he thought best, only promising to give first priority for people requisitioned by the six product areas.

Not perfect yet—he was still worrying about that key open slot right under him—but they certainly had come a long way in one short week. Eleven of the eighteen workgroups were staffed and started. Belinda said she felt positively high about their progress so far, and he was coming to depend on her gut for an overall indication of his ultimate prospects for success. He might have let his own expectations be as optimistic as hers but for the grim reminder of the countdown display on the board just beside the new org chart. He had instructed Waldo to put it up and to decrement it each day. The display now read:

ONLY $\boxed{705}$ DAYS TILL D-DAY!

Allowing for weekends and holidays, that left fewer than five hundred workdays left before the end of his contract. That was almost certainly not enough for a big product like PShop (and he still had no manager for the PShop B-Team!). So far, there were no deadlines set; he had been adamant that no schedules were to be handed down on him from above. But really, who was he kidding? Everyone expected the six products, or at least most of them, to be delivered before he was done. So, in spite of all his determination not to let it happen, here was another highly aggressive deadline staring him in the face. Seven hundred and five days left....

He picked up his bound leather book and his pen.

From Mr. Tompkins' Journal:

<u>Playing Defense</u>

o   Cut your losses.

o   You can improve overall performance more by containing your failures than by optimizing your successes.

o   Be aggressive about canceling failed efforts early.

o   Don't take chances on team jell if you don't have to: Seek out and use pre-formed teams.

o   Keep good teams together (when they're willing) to help your successors avoid problems of slow-jelling or non-jelling teams.

o   Think of a jelled team—ready and willing to take on a new effort—as one of the project deliverables.

o   A day lost at the beginning of a project hurts just as much as a day lost at the end.

That last one had come from Belinda, something she said at some point nearly every morning. He looked up one last time at Waldo's countdown sign. When he came in tomorrow, it would already be adjusted to 704. Had the seven hundred and fifth day been made to count as much as he might have hoped? Or would he eventually come to see it as just another dropped opportunity? Time would tell. He looked back down at the journal and added one final point on defensive management, something he had come to realize years ago and now was facing up to again:

> o There are infinitely many ways to lose a day . . . but not even one way to get one back.

10

ABDUL JAMID

❧

*M*r. Tompkins was in Rome for a bit of essential business
and perhaps a little R&R as well. With all the projects now
fully staffed and working effectively, he could afford to attend
to a matter that had been nagging him. At the front desk of
the Hassler Hotel, he slid his new corporate American Express
card across to the clerk.

The man puzzled over the inscription. "Morovianze Naczonal Byru av Data Schmertczung," he read. "That would be
the Morovian National Bureau of Data . . ."

"Schmertzing," Mr. Tompkins helped him out.

"Ah, data schmertzing. That's what it means in English.
Um . . . You wouldn't happen to know the Italian word for
'schmertzing,' would you?"

"Shmerziazione?" Tompkins offered.

"Ah. Well, welcome to Rome, Mr. Tompkins. Welcome
to the Hassler."

"Thank you."

A few moments later, he was being shown into a comfortable apartment with splendid views out over the Spanish

Steps. As soon as the porter was gone, Mr. T. set up his Power-book on the desk, plugged it into the hotel phone jack, and sent out a two-page fax to a number in New York.

He was awakened the next day around 7 A.M. by a call from the lawyer, Spofford.

"Webster! Rise and shine, Webster. It's me!"

"Hello, Jack."

"Hello, indeed. I got your fax. I've been on the phone all day, and I dropped by in the late afternoon at the main Fidelity office here on Wall Street. Had a chat with Ms. Lampool, just as you told me to. She was all ready for me. Most cooperative. Said that you had supplied all the proper notices and releases to enable me to act as your agent."

"Good."

"We checked out your account and compared it to the screen dump you included in your fax, the image you accessed on-line from Morovia."

"And . . . ?"

"And they checked out perfectly. You're definitely getting through to Fidelity and you're definitely accessing your own account. We saw no sign of tampering."

"I just worried that . . ."

" . . . that your KVJ friends might be up to pulling shenanigans. I know. Well, breathe a sigh of relief. They haven't."

Mr. Tompkins breathed a sigh of relief. "So, the money really is there. They really did deposit it as a lump sum."

"To the penny, just as promised. It even arrived a day ear-lier than they said."

"Good. Thank you for that, Jack. And you set up the new accounts and made the transfers?"

"As you specified. The old account is closed and the new ones are set up to hold the funds. The access passwords are the ones you asked for in your fax. But, of course, you're going to change those, aren't you?"

"Of course."

"And don't forget to keep the passwords in your head, not in your computer. Otherwise, those rascally Morovians might be able to get their money back just by grabbing your laptop. You had already thought of that, though, hadn't you."

"Of course." The truth was that it had never crossed his mind. He would have to remove all the passwords from the access programs and memorize them.

Jack was moving on. "Good. So, I think that's it. Your money is in and you're definitely secure on this end. Oh, one more thing."

"Yes, Jack?"

"Turn your mind back to last summer, to the party I attended at your house. Remember the elderly gentleman you introduced me to that day, Johnny . . . ?"

"Johnny Jay, my old boss. Yes, I certainly remember him. Too bad he retired. If he had stayed on, I'd still be there, still working for him, the best boss a person could ask for."

"He is a real gentleman."

"You know, Jack, I think about him almost every day. I sometimes believe my whole life as a manager is an attempt to discover and intellectualize the management wisdom that that man had in his bones. I think he was the best. It was a privilege to work with him."

"Well, the feeling is, apparently, mutual. I saw him here in New York last Saturday evening. . . ."

"No. Really?"

"Really. He and his wife were at the opera at Lincoln Center. He came up to us at the intermission and we chatted, mostly about you. He was already in the know about your Morovian escapade."

"The old son of a gun. How is he?"

"Fit as a fiddle. They both are. They were to set off sailing the next morning, headed for Martha's Vineyard and points beyond, maybe up to Maine. He asked me how he could have someone get in touch with you. He told me he had a young fellow that you really need to get to know. Asked me how you could be reached. I said I didn't have a number for you in Varsjop, but that you would be staying at the Hassler in Rome today and tomorrow."

"Anyone Johnny wants me to talk to is someone I'm more than willing to hear out. So, I'll be getting a call here?"

"No, I think the guy is coming in person to see you. Johnny said he was in Europe around the same time. His name is . . ."

"Wait, I'm getting a pen. Okay."

"His name is Abdul Jamid."

Mr. Tompkins tromped around ruins and fountains for most of the morning, enjoying the delicious, cool weather and a fine lunch near the Villa Borghese. By the time he got back to the hotel, it was almost three.

"Mr. Tompkins, I believe." A dark, astonishingly handsome man approached him. He looked like a young Omar Shariff.

"Yes, that's me," Mr. T. told him. "Or I. I'm him."

"I am Dr. Jamid. Your friend Mr. Jay . . ."

"Oh, yes. Dr. Jamid. This is an honor. The name of Johnny Jay is an instant key to my attention. Anyone he recommends . . . well, I'm delighted to meet you."

"You are too kind."

"Not at all. Mr. Jay wanted us to meet, and I'm quite looking forward to it. Any idea of what he wanted us to meet about?"

"My work. I have done a piece of work on management dynamics, and when I showed it to Johnny, he thought of you. He thought it might come in handy in your new position."

Mr. Tompkins nodded. "Johnny was always on the lookout to do someone a good turn, in this case, two someones, I suspect. I would be delighted to learn about your work, Dr. Jamid. I am here for two more days. Will that be enough?"

"For a beginning, yes."

"Well, on with the beginning, then." He offered his hand. "Webster."

"Abdul."

They shook hands solemnly. Webster showed him up the stairs and into the little parlor adjacent to his bedroom.

A few hours later, Mr. Tompkins pulled back from the display of Dr. Jamid's laptop Mac. His head was spinning.

"Time out. Time out. I'm on overload here. You keep talking about my hunch base. . . ."

"The set of all the hunches that you use to run your project."

"I understand, but you talk about hunches in a way I have never heard before. You talk about a hunch as though it were a little database and a program inside my gut. The program looks at the data and comes up with an answer. Is that really the way hunches work?"

"Well? Isn't it?"

"Well, more or less, I suppose. I mean, there is definitely data in there, that's the sum of my experience to date. And I suppose there are some algorithms as well that tell me what sense to make of the data."

"Precisely."

"But, you're telling me to make an explicit model of my hunches about how project work proceeds and then use that model to simulate the results."

"Right."

"But why would I want to do that? Why can't I keep my hunches in my head or my gut or wherever? Seems to me that's where hunches belong."

"Well, you could, but then you don't have a good mechanism to improve your hunches. If you believe that the best managers are the ones with the best hunch bases, the ones whose 'gut feel,' as you put it, is most often on target, then you must care about improving your ability to make your hunches be accurate predictions of reality."

"Of course, but how does the modeling help?"

"It gives you a nice clean way to make pictures of your theories about how the work is actually going to get done. And then you track the actual results back against the model to learn what you need to improve. If you have a colleague who has also got a good hunch base . . ."

"I certainly have that. Her name is Belinda."

"Then, you can work over these models together and learn from each other. Without the model, all you have is a vague sense in your stomach that, for example, a project is going to be inefficient due to adding staff too quickly. It's entirely interior. You feel it, and maybe I feel it or Belinda feels it, but we don't have a way to discuss it among ourselves. Maybe Belinda is, in some sense, twice as uneasy about it as you are, but we're not even likely to understand that, since we don't typically quantify the vague senses in our stomach. When we produce a hunch model, on the other hand, we have an eloquently expressed theory of how useful production is affected by the rate at which staff is added."

Mr. Tompkins laughed, uneasily. "Even if it's eloquent, it may still not be right."

"So true. It's just a theory. But now we have a mechanical way to test the theory out, by comparing it to what actually happens. And in the interim, we have an excellent vehicle for you and Belinda to use to address your differing senses of the thing and try to combine your gut-level wisdom."

"Well, let's say I buy that idea. I'm going to want to see some examples of it in use, but let's say I like your concept of modeling hunches, just to get them out in the light of day. I still don't see why I'd ever want to run the model through a simulator to see a precise calculation of its results. Isn't that overkill?"

"If you only had one hunch, you'd be right. But suppose you have half a dozen of them. How do you figure out what their aggregate effect is?"

Mr. Tompkins still wasn't convinced. "The simulator figures out the aggregate, that's what you're saying. Big deal. Since the input to the simulator would only be my hunches anyway, how can the simulation's prediction of the aggregate effect of them be any better than my hunch about the aggregate?"

Dr. Jamid nodded. "You think you're quite capable of figuring how the various effects combine? You're capable of doing that rather computational task in the entirely non-computational processor where your hunches reside. You've variously referred to that hunch processor as your head, your gut, and several times, your bones. Do you do accurate calculations in your bones, Webster?"

"Well . . ."

"Let's try you out. We'll try a little example from the literature of simulation modeling. Suppose you're running a project with one hundred people on board as of January first. They've been there for a couple of years and you have observed a consistent personnel quit rate of four people a month. Every time one quits, you hire a replacement immediately and train him or her for two months, after which the new person is integrated onto the project."

"Okay."

"Now you learn, or you suspect, that the quit rate is going to go up as a result of some new personnel policy that's being instituted on May first. Let's say you figure it will double."

"Okay. We're now expecting to lose eight a month."

"Right. What's your hunch about how many people you'll have fully integrated into the project as of August first?"

"Huh? Isn't it a hundred?"

"Is it?"

"I thought you said I had a steady state of one hundred people. And I hire one person immediately for each one that is lost. So, I've always got a hundred in total staff. I train the new hires. . . . Oh, wait a minute, I see what you mean. There are always some people in the training loop. And now I have more people in training on average." He thought for a moment. "Well, certainly, the very first month, I have some decrease in integrated staff due to the sudden bump in loss rate, so that month I am down from one hundred to ninety-two. But then, don't I get them back? I think I do, don't I?

As to whether I'm back up to a hundred by August, well . . . Okay, I don't know. The arithmetic processor in my gut is not up to this example."

"But it's a trivial example, Webster, utterly trivial. Far less complicated than the kind of simulation you are trying to do in your bones nearly every day. Here, let's see what the simulator has to say about this particular example." Dr. Jamid began drawing a model on the screen.* "I use a rectangular 'reservoir' to stand for your usable staff. The higher the level, the more people you've got. We'll set its initial value to one hundred.

Usable Staff

"That's already a model, but it's not very dynamic, since there are no flows of people leaving the project or new hires coming on board. If we ran the simulator, it would tell us that the staff level stays constant at one hundred over time.

"Next, we add a pipeline for the flow of people out of the project and a valve on the pipe whose value determines how rapidly they leave. We set the valve initially to a rate of four people per month.

---

* Dr. Jamid's example is borrowed from *Introduction to Systems Thinking and* **ithink** (Hanover, N.H.: High Performance Systems, Inc., 1994), pp. 17–18. Used with permission.

Usable Staff

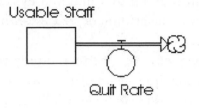

Quit Rate

"The little cloud icon indicates that when they leave, they pass out of the context of our model. Finally, we add a pipeline of new people coming onto the project through a Hiring Rate valve. Let's just connect the setting of the inflow valve directly to the outflow valve, so however many people we lose in a given month, we just hire exactly that number back. We place a two-month training delay between the hiring valve and the flow into the project. So, here we see our resultant model:

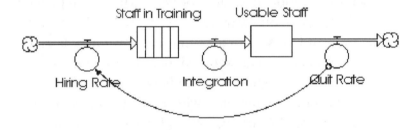

"To add our hunch about a sudden bump in Quit Rate starting in May, we set up an equation for the Quit Rate valve, keeping it at four people per month up till May, and then increasing it in a step function to eight people per month. Select RUN to see the simulation results."

Mr. Tompkins watched in fascination as the animated display showed the reservoir rate changing over time. When it had stabilized, Dr. Jamid stopped the run and, with a few mouse clicks, made the system display a graph of the reservoir level over time.

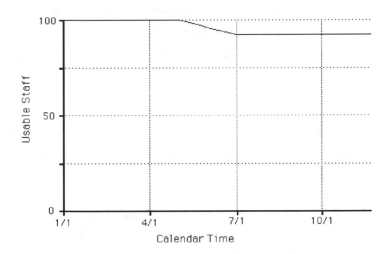

"Well, that's not exactly what I expected," Mr. T. admitted. "It declines steadily for a few months, steadies out in July, but then never comes back. Wonder why that is?"

Dr. Jamid pondered. "It's not immediately obvious to me either. Increasingly many people tied up in training, perhaps? My point is that even this trivial network of connected effects is pretty hard to dope out without some help. The simulation works out the connections for us, doing effortlessly the kind of arithmetic analysis that the problem really needs."

A laugh from Mr. Tompkins. "The kind that we don't do well in our bones. I do see what you mean."

Dr. Jamid kept his silence for a moment. Mr. Tompkins turned away from the screen and let his eyes, unfocused, seek out a region of the ceiling above the far corner of the room. What did all this have to do with him and his little Morovian world of projects to build six shrink-wrapped software products? What did it have to do with getting actual work done?

He wasn't entirely sure, but he was beginning to suspect that the models and simulation might be of use.

He turned back to his new friend. "Let's say I'm entirely persuaded by what you've described, Abdul. What would you have me do? How would I start to make use of what you have shared with me today?"

"Well, we pick some element of your hunch base. An easy way to ferret out a strong managerial hunch from your base is to challenge it a bit. So, I'm going to say some outrageous things and then interrogate you a bit as to why you find them outrageous."

"Okay, go for it."

"Suppose I'm your boss. You tell me that ten people working for a year can get a given piece of work done. But I'm impatient for the product, so I tell you to use twenty people and get it to me six months from now."

Mr. Tompkins could not keep his expression from clouding up. "I'd tell you to go jump in a lake."

"You have a hunch that twenty people for six months is not the same as ten for twelve months."

"It's more than a hunch," Mr. T. sputtered. "It's a conviction."

Dr. Jamid picked up a yellow pad and sketched quickly on it. When he was done, he shoved the pad over to Mr. Tompkins and pointed to it.

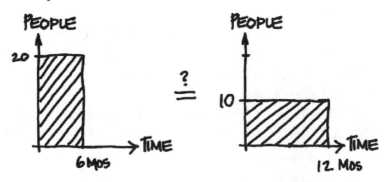

"So these two manpower loading schemes can't be expected to get the same amount of useful work done?"

"Absolutely not!"

"The total production capacity of the one is different from the other?"

"Quite different."

Dr. Jamid now looked slightly cagey. "Um . . . how different?"

"Excuse me?"

"How different are they? Let's assume ten people for a year can build a software product of size one thousand something-or-others, for example. Don't worry about my size units for the time being, just assume I've got some reasonable way to size software. If the ten can complete a thousand-unit product in a year, how big a product could we expect the twenty-person team—assuming equally capable people—to develop in six months?"

"Less than one thousand."

"How much less?"

"A lot less!"

"How much is a lot?"

"Tons. Those twenty people are falling all over themselves. They aren't going to be able to do nearly as much work as the smaller team over a longer period of time." Mr. Tompkins was becoming exasperated. "Can't you see that?"

"Oh, I can. Definitely. I'm not disagreeing with your hunch, Webster, only trying to get you to quantify it. How much less will the larger team accomplish in six months?"

Mr. Tompkins threw his hands up. "Half. Or even a quarter. I don't know."

"No kidding." Dr. Jamid was laughing gently.

"Well, I guess I *don't* know. I mean, not exactly."

"Even within a factor of two."

"Why is that so funny?"

"Because you *need* to know. The trade-off between people and time is something that concerns the manager nearly every day. You're always making such trade-offs. How do you do it?"

"Well, I guess I have a feel for it."

"That feel is your model. You see, you've already got a model, but just now, it's entirely internal. It's so deeply buried that even you can't just look at it when you want to. Let's bring it out into the open. Let's recreate in the form of a model your 'feel' for how adding people to a team affects the team production rate."

"Okay."

"Just talk to me about it, and I will reduce it to terms that the modeling and simulation package can understand. What happens when you add a person to a team?"

Tompkins thought it over. "The initial impact is always negative," he began. "The guy does nothing useful on his first day, and he uses up other people's time to learn. So, aggregate team production rate takes a hit."

Dr. Jamid was modeling on the laptop as he listened.

"Then, little by little, he becomes a full member of the team." Tompkins picked up the yellow pad and pen and sketched his concept quickly. "Something like this."

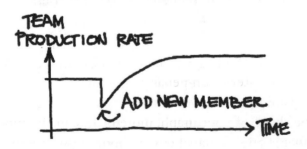

Dr. Jamid peered at the graph and integrated its concept into his emerging model with a few dozen keystrokes and mouse clicks.

Mr. Tompkins plowed on: "Only there's not as much advantage in adding him if he's the seventh person, for example, as there would be if he were the sixth. So, I guess, there's a kind of penalty that is a function of team size. The more people on the team, the more interactions, and therefore the more time lost."

"Commit yourself. Make me a graph of that, too."

"Well, let's see. If we look at the total production rate of the team as a function of team size," he sketched as he spoke, "then the forty-five degree line would represent the ideal. Staying on that line would mean that each added person contributed as much as the one before. Doubling the size of the team would double its capacity, no interaction penalty. The truth is a little less than the ideal. Something like this."

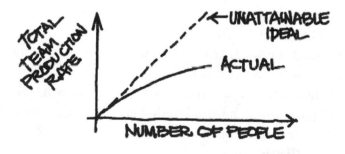

"The difference between the Actual and the Unattainable Ideal is your interaction penalty."

Dr. Jamid peered over at the drawing. "I see. I can replicate the shape of your graph, more or less, in the model." He put a finger on the Actual curve, about midway across the diagram. "Tell me, how big does the team have to be before the interaction penalty is up to a third?"

"Huh?"

"I've picked a point on your curve where the interaction penalty is about half the Actual value. So, that means about one third of Unattainable Ideal capacity is wasted at that point."

"I follow you that far."

"How big is the team at that point?"

"I don't know."

"Of course you don't *know*. We're not trying, just now, to find out what you know. We're trying to find out what you *feel*. Ask your gut. How big does the team have to be before a third of capacity is used in interaction penalty?"

"The best answer I can give you is very loosey-goosey."

"Commit yourself. How big?"

"Well, I'd say about four."

"So, the net capacity of four people working together is about a third less than four times the capacity of a single person who got to do the whole job alone?"

Mr. Tompkins shrugged. "Of course, I'm not sure, but that answer seems about right to me."

"Good." Dr. Jamid entered a bit more into his laptop. When he was done, he displayed the result and turned the screen for Mr. Tompkins to see. "Here is our model of your hunch about team size.

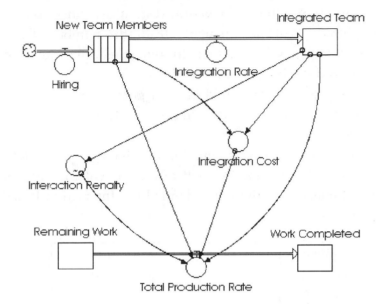

"The entire project is portrayed as an effort to move work from one reservoir to another. We start out with the Remaining Work reservoir full and the Work Completed reservoir empty. The units of work have to be expressed in some kind of synthetic metric of job size. . . ."

"Lines of code? Something like that?"

"Well, that would do if we failed to come up with something better. The capacity to get work done is modeled by one valve, called Total Production Rate. The higher its setting, the faster the work moves out of Remaining Work and into Work Completed. Obviously, the values of Total Production Rate have to be expressed in the same size units used in the reservoirs."

"I see," Mr. Tompkins said. He wasn't at all sure that he did.

"Finally, the thin arrows are dependencies. They tell us, for example, that Total Production Rate is dependent on four things: the size of the Integrated Team, the number of New Team Members still only partially integrated, the Interaction Penalty, and the Integration Cost."

"Integration Cost would be, I'm guessing here, the proportion of lost effort due to bringing the new members up to speed?"

"Yes. Now I write an equation or build a graphical definition for each valve and for each of these circular meters. So, for example, here is the way I defined the Interaction Penalty meter."

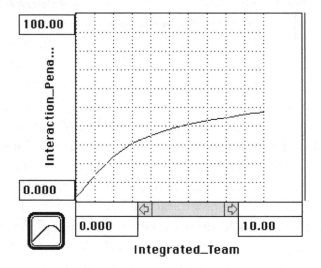

"As you can see, it starts off at zero and builds to approximately a third by the time you have four people on the team. I just guessed what you'd want the rest of the curve to look like."

Mr. Tompkins stared at the graph. Did that in fact represent his best hunch about how much penalty there was as team size increased?

Dr. Jamid seemed to be reading his mind. "As we play with this model, you may find you need to adjust either this curve or any of the others. Or you may need to change the model itself."

"To make it conform to what my hunch base really says."

"Exactly."

"Well, right now my hunch base is telling me a change is needed. It's not happy with the static value of Interaction Penalty. Maybe the penalty ought to be a dynamic function of time. After all, people do learn to work together."

Dr. Jamid nodded agreeably. "Talk to me about that."

Mr. Tompkins reflected for a moment. "Well, teams in my opinion have a potential of achieving almost a negative interaction penalty over time. Something happens and the team dynamic becomes so strong that it overcomes the interaction penalty. The whole can become greater than the sum of the parts. The team comes together and . . . I don't know, it unifies."

After a moment, Abdul turned the screen to him again. "Like this?"

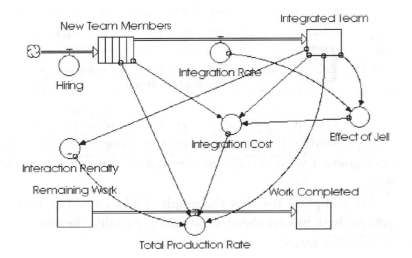

"Well, yes, something like that. There is definitely an effect of jell, as you call it. Now we have to go back and redefine Integration Cost."

"Of course."

Mr. Tompkins studied the screen for a long moment. "You know, I think that is my model. It looks pretty much like what's going on inside me when I try to figure out how well the team will perform. Of course, it may be quite wrong, not at all the way real teams perform, . . ."

"Of course. But now at least you have a way to test it out. You simulate to see what your combined hunches predict, and then you let the real project run for a while to collect tuning information to perfect the model."

"I see."

"Little by little, you integrate this tuning information until . . ."

". . . the hunch on the screen is better than the hunch in the gut."

"Precisely."

In the cab out to the airport, Mr. Tompkins asked, "What's the name of the modeling and simulation package you use? I'm going to want to order a copy as soon as I get back to my office."

"The one I use is called *ithink*," Dr. Jamid told him,* "but you don't have to order a copy, Webster. I've already bought one for you." He reached into his briefcase and pulled out a boxed software package, still sealed in its shrink-wrapping.

"Oh, Abdul. You didn't have to do that. I could have . . ."

---

* *ithink*® is a registered trademark of High Performance Systems, Inc., Hanover, N.H.

Dr. Jamid held up his hand. "Please, Webster. This was meant to complement all that we have been talking about, to make it a complete and accessible delivery of my scheme. Besides, it didn't cost so very much. You bought us a lovely lunch in Rome this afternoon. And I bought you this software product from a mail-order house in California. I assure you it cost me less than our lunch cost you." He passed over the box. Then he reached into his case again and pulled out a diskette. "And here is the set of models we developed together yesterday and today. It will be a starting point . . ."

Mr. Tompkins finished for him, ". . . a starting point for a modeling effort that won't stop till we've got all our hunches captured. I promise you that, Abdul. I promise you that."

From Mr. Tompkins' Journal:

<u>Modeling and Simulation of the Development Process</u>

o   Model your hunches about the processes that get work done.

o   Use the models in peer interaction to communicate and refine thinking about how the process works.

o   Use the models to simulate results.

o   Tune the models against actual results.

11

THE SINISTER
MINISTER BELOK

ঽ৯

A crisp Morovian spring morning. Mr. Tompkins was on
his way before seven, taking his usual constitutional walk on
the way to work. When the morning was so lovely as this one,
he liked to dawdle on the way, breathing in the freshness of a
new day. From the Residence in Varsjop to his office building
on the Aidrivoli Campus was a one mile walk, all of it on a
breathtakingly pretty pathway cut through the vineyards and
along the side of a little brook. Why is it, he wondered (as he
did almost every day), that the developed world has so much
material advantage, but can't seem to provide a pleasant
walking path from A to B? No matter what your A and B
were in Morovia, there was a fine walking path between them.

As he was early, he continued on along the brook well past
the turnoff for the office campus. Half a mile farther on was a
little pond, and beside it a wooden bench where he liked to sit
on nice mornings and reflect. He stepped quietly for the last
hundred yards of his approach to the pond; there were sometimes deer there, or the occasional baby rabbit with its mother,
and he didn't want to disturb them.

He settled down onto the bench and sighed deeply, pervaded by a sense of well-being. He'd been in Morovia now for a little more than three months and he could not remember a happier time in his life. Being fired had turned out to be the best thing that could have happened to him. Well, that wasn't quite right. Lots of people got fired and didn't land on their feet as well as he had. It wasn't being fired that had been his lucky break, but being kidnapped by Lahksa Hoolihan.

He looked up at the sound of a splash at the edge of the pond. There was a rapid flapping after the splash and, just a moment later, a cheerful call from up in the tree just at the water's edge. Moving very slowly, he reached down into his bag for a bird book and a pair of binoculars he carried for just this purpose. He focused the binoculars on a chunky little bird with a huge head of green feathers. Without too much trouble, he found the same bird pictured in his book. He turned to the note pages at the back and wrote down "April 4: Belted Kingfisher." Then, he put the book and pen and binoculars on the bench beside him until something else should show up.

That he was feeling so content just now did not imply that there weren't a few problems. Of course there were problems. You didn't run a group of talented developers without problems here and there. Morovia was no different in this respect than any other place he had ever worked. People who are good tend to know it and to make sure you know they know it. Sometimes, they could be a pain in the butt, and he certainly had his share of prima donnas. But he'd learned long ago to appreciate, or at least *try* to appreciate, even the most obnoxious of them.

And, of course, there were schedule problems. If he looked at his contract end date (a year from next November) as a deadline, then most of the projects under him would be challenged to make it. He was optimistic that some of the smaller ones might be complete by that time; however, a project like PShop would be lucky to come in even a year later. So, what he was faced with, in that project at least, was to figure out some way to gain a full year.

Oh, well, don't worry about that on such a pretty morning. He knew he'd be sitting down later in the day with ex-General Markov and Belinda Binda for a brainstorming session on that very problem. For now, he could relax and feel good about all the things that were going right: lots of sharp people on his staff who were happy to be doing good work; excellent managers at two levels underneath him; truly superior facilities; and most of all, two of the best peers he had ever had to work with. In Belinda and Gabriel, he knew he had assembled the ultimate management "dream team." He had come to rely on them both for savvy counsel and continued insight.

In retrospect, this was the first time in his professional life that he had been turned loose to do the best work he could without there being some idiot somewhere above him in the chain of command to ruin everything by trimming reasonable schedules or overriding his best decisions. NNL seemed like a pretty sensible fellow once Tompkins had taken a firm stand and laid down the law to him. Since their first meeting in Korsach, Morovia's tyrant had been almost putty in his hands. He seemed comfortable to let Tompkins run his shop the way it ought to be run. What could be better than that? A supportive manager above and competent people and challenging work below.

Mr. Tompkins repacked his bag and headed off toward the office. He walked with a bounce in his stride. By the time he arrived, he had gone beyond being merely content and was feeling positively ebullient.

Waldo met him at the door to his office and pulled him aside. He whispered, "Boss, there's something you need to know."

"What's that?"

"NNL has gone back to the States for a while, to look out for his other interests. Evidently he's going to be gone for quite a while."

"And . . . ?"

"And, in his absence, he's placed a certain Mr. Belok in charge."

"Oh oh."

"Oh oh, indeed." Waldo gestured back toward the office door. "Mr. Belok is waiting for you in your office."

Tompkins nodded and stepped through the door. There, seated behind his own desk was a short, very smug-looking man. Their eyes met briefly. Then Tompkins looked up at the wall behind his desk where Waldo kept the countdown display of days remaining till Delivery Day. Just the afternoon before, it had shown 607 days left, so now it should show 606. But it didn't. What it showed instead was

ONLY $\boxed{420}$ DAYS TILL D-DAY!

"Oh, shit!" Mr. Tompkins said.

The card that the little man offered Mr. Tompkins read "Allair Belok, Minister of Internal Affairs and Deputy Tyrant."

"I think that should make things clear," the man said.

"It doesn't make anything clear at all. I work for NNL, directly."

"Not all that directly, as it turns out." Minister Belok looked particularly pleased with himself at this. He passed one hand through a greasy head of hair, then wiped it absently on his jacket. "Not so directly as you might have thought."

"I'll wait for NNL himself to confirm that."

The little man glanced down elaborately at his fingernails. Seeing something black under one, he lifted it delicately to his mouth and cleaned it against a lower tooth. He studied the nail again at arm's length. Without eye contact: "Oh, I wouldn't wait if I were you. NNL is planning on being away for the foreseeable future."

"Where is he?"

"Away. Mr. Tompkins—Webster . . ." Belok spread his hands out, palms up, the gesture of appeal to reason, "I see no reason why we shouldn't get along. We should. I expect we're going to get along swimmingly. You'll find that I am a most reasonable man." He smiled nastily.

"Right."

"Most reasonable, really. And I go back quite a long way with Himself."

"Big deal."

"And I'm here and he isn't. Do you get my drift?"

Mr. Tompkins shook his head. "I'm not sure I want to get your drift. But go ahead. Drift on."

"'Drift on,'" the Minister repeated the words distastefully. He looked heavenward, his saintly patience tried. Then, looking back at Tompkins with a sneer: "I am, quite simply, the *only* indispensable person in this Morovian venture. In the past, I have been responsible for financial matters, *all* financial matters in NNL's various interests. The dear boy is—how shall I put this?—not too swift about the financial side of things."

"He is a billionaire," Tompkins said pointedly.

"My point exactly. He is not swift about finance, and yet he has become one of the richest men in the world. Now, how do you suppose that happened?"

120

"You, no doubt."

Belok smiled again. "Modesty forbids that I take *all* the credit. I mean, Himself does have a certain flair for things technical. However, suffice it to say that without my little contribution he would probably be running a two-bit operation today."

"I see."

"He has his talents and I have mine. It's as simple as that."

"Uh huh."

"One of the things he is not too talented at is imparting—how shall I say this?—a sense of urgency to those who work under him."

"You, on the other hand, are rather good at applying the old pressure. Am I getting this right?"

"Quite right. It is a kind of genius of mine. I hope I'm not being *too* immodest."

"Heavens, no. Just realistic, I suspect."

"You see? We are getting along. This is going to be even easier than I thought."

"I doubt it. But go ahead."

"Well, as I said, my particular focus is the financial. Now we'll just ignore the financial aspects of you and your rather over-rewarded staff and the outrageous costs of all those computers and networks and hubs and satellite dishes and high-speed modems and all that other rather irresponsible spending. . . ."

"We're going to ignore all that. Good. I think that's wise."

A tight little smile. "Fine. You see how reasonable I am. We'll ignore all that. What we're not going to ignore however is the cost of lateness."

"Ah."

"Lateness costs money. That shouldn't surprise you. The six products you have been charged with producing have all got projected revenue streams. The PShop product, just to take one example, is eventually going to produce something on the order of . . ." he looked down at a notebook lying open on the desk in front of him, ". . . a revenue stream of some thirty-eight million dollars a year. These are, of course, U.S. dollars."

Tompkins knew where this was going. He stared at the man glumly.

"The Quicken replacement product will generate some twenty-three million dollars; eleven million for Paint-It, et cetera, et cetera, et cetera. All together, the six products should generate about one hundred sixty-four million dollars per year. Discounting that for materials and sales and promotion, the net income would be just a little over ninety million dollars. You see where I'm going?"

"Of course." He'd been there many times before.

"Ninety million a year works out to . . ." he punched some numbers into a calculator, "$246,575.34 a day. Just to use round numbers, that's a quarter of a million dollars a day *of profit.*" He leaned heavily on the last two words. Again, the slimy smile.

"Yawn."

The smile faded away. "Every day you *dick around,* Tompkins, costs *me* a quarter of a million dollars. Could I be more clear?"

"Oh, no. You couldn't be more clear. I understood you exactly, even before you started."

"Splendid. We are beginning to understand each other. Now I've decided to give you just the littlest nudge on these projects, something to help galvanize you and your people. What I've decided is to make a tiny change in the deadline. . . ."

"There is no deadline."

"Oh, I quite understand. NNL himself told me that. Said you were quite persuasive on the subject. No deadline. But the fact is that you did set a deadline yourself for the November after next. It wasn't made public and you certainly didn't allow anyone else to impose it on you, but you did set that as a tentative deadline. I know that from the amusing little display you keep up here on the wall."

Tompkins conceded a point. "We've barely finished the detailed estimates, but it is true that I was hopeful of getting most of the products done by that November."

"There you are. So, there really was a deadline. And now there is a new one: the first of June of next year."

Tompkins saw red. "That's absurd!" he sputtered.

"Not absurd. It is ambitious, perhaps. Maybe even aggressive. But not absurd."

"It is utterly absurd. We have sized these products precisely. We have very reasonable measures of past productivity. And even allowing for a substantial improvement over the past, we can barely hope to finish even the smallest projects by the November after next. A project like PShop goes way beyond that November. June is simply out of the question."

Again the gesture of reason. "Not at all, not at all. I'm sure you can do it. In fact, I'm going to be giving you an important bit of help, just to make sure you succeed."

"I hardly dare ask what."

Belok stood up and walked over to the org chart on the white board. He drew a circle around the three PShop projects. "What an amusing little experiment we find here. Three projects vying to produce the same product. And here, . . ." he draw another circle around the three Quirk projects, "three projects to produce one product. And here, . . ." He continued down the board circling the sets of competing projects. "It's what you're calling the 'Project Management Laboratory,' I believe. Charming. Perfectly charming . . . BUT NOT WHEN IT'S COSTING ME A QUARTER OF A MILLION DOLLARS A DAY!!!"

Belok walked back to the desk and sat down. He made a visible effort to compose himself. "Excuse me. I think I may have raised my voice. Calm yourself, Allair, calm, calm. There, that's better. All calm again. You see, it's just that the thought of lost profit can be so very disturbing, particularly to someone of my very refined sensibilities."

Mr. Tompkins groaned inwardly.

"So, there we have it. I think we've come to an agreement, haven't we? You will combine the three Quirk teams into one Quirk super-team. With those extra people, you will achieve, of course, an earlier delivery. Note that I am allowing you to triple the team, but all I ask is that you reduce the project by a mere six months, not even a twenty-five percent reduction in calendar time. Now I call that reasonable: Triple the team to reduce delivery time by six months. That's what I mean when I say I am a most reasonable man. Triple the size of the QuickerStill team, triple the Paint-It team, triple the PShop team. . . ." He was at the board again, merging all the teams into super-teams.

Mr. Tompkins took a deep breath. It probably wasn't worth it, but he had to make an effort. "Minister Belok . . ."

"Allair, please call me Allair."

"Um, yes." He swallowed his pride. "Allair. Look, we've been giving a lot of thought to some of these very questions over the past few weeks, my assistants and I. We knew we were up against it with the PShop project, for example, so we were looking for ways to cut the delivery time. As luck would have it, we have just stumbled on a new technology that allows us to simulate the effect of various management decisions, to see how they will work out. One of the things the simulation tells us is that projects can't always save time by adding staff. The problem is that there is an absorption rate effect that says teams can only build up so fast. If you try to push them faster than that, you do more harm than good. Further, there is an interaction penalty that causes the nth person added to a team to be worth less than the ones before."

Mr. Tompkins opened a file drawer and pulled out some of the simulations they'd been running over the past few days, using Dr. Jamid's model. "Now, here, if I can just find the right sheet . . . yes, here. Look at this." He spread the results of one run on the desk in front of Belok. "Look at this. We're currently projecting 524 workdays for our PShop-A project with twelve people on board. Now, if we were to bump up staff to twenty-four people, our simulation shows that it would take them *longer* to do the same work. Instead of 524 workdays, they will require almost six hundred!"

Belok suppressed a yawn. "Right. So what?"

"So what?!? So instead of finishing earlier, we'll finish later, that's what."

"Look, Tompkins. I don't care about any of this. Combine the teams and publish the new delivery date. Do as you're told. Make sure that everybody knows that every day the work is late beyond June first will cost us a quarter of a million dollars of lost profit."

"But that won't help. It's going to hurt. You're going to lose more profit by overstaffing these teams. You're just going to make us later. We could deliver the product to you in 524 workdays, but because of this decision it will take us six hundred."

"The deadline is June first. That's the last word. I will not hear talk of delivering any later than that."

"Even though this will result in being later still than we would have been?"

Belok smiled without humor. "Tompkins, let me make this even clearer for you. I want the deadline changed, I want the pressure put on, and I want the teams combined. If that makes the delivery later than it might have been otherwise, so be it."

"All those quarter-millions of dollars lost."

A shrug. "So we lose some money. When your team eventually delivers PShop, say in six hundred days as you predict, we'll begin coining money. And when it comes time to hand out the credit for that, NNL will be looking square at the fact that, but for my intervention to triple the people on the PShop team, the project would probably have dribbled on for as much as eighteen hundred days."

A long silence as Mr. Tompkins digested that. Finally he said, "You've been very clear. Let me be clear as well. Stuff it in your ear."

Belok chuckled. "A man of principle. I like that. Our Mr. Tompkins is willing to put his job on the line."

"I am. Every day, if need be. If you're not willing to put your job on the line, your job is not worth having."

The Minister put his pen down on the blotter and spun it idly, looking smug. "He's willing to put his job on the line . . . but is he willing to put his *life* on the line?"

Tompkins stared at him, stunned. "What the hell does that mean?"

"A little joke."

"Are you suggesting . . . ?"

"Just some light humor."

"I don't think it was very funny. If you're thinking of any such thing, I want you to know that I have some resources in that area myself."

"Ah, the lovely Miss Hoolihan. Yes, she would be a formidable ally, if it came to that. She would. Unfortunately, she has accompanied our Noble Leader on his swing through the States. That was my rather inspired idea. I don't expect to see her back here for the next few months. . . ."

ஃ

The management "dream team" of Tompkins, Binda, and Markov sat around the glass coffee table in Mr. T.'s office. The afternoon light was failing but no one moved toward the switch. They had been there a long time.

Ex-General Markov broke the silence. "He is a dangerous man, this Belok. There is no question of that. And, this being Morovia, there are probably plenty of people who would carry out his dirty work for him. We have a long tradition of dirty work. I had hoped that would all come to an end." He had said all of that several times already.

"What I feel stupidest about," Mr. Tompkins said, "is my own willingness to believe that here at last I had found myself a job with no politics. I guess there is no such thing as a job without politics."

"There is no such thing as a job with no politics," the ex-General agreed. "Politics is the bane of every manager's life."

Belinda objected. "Come on, Gabriel, this isn't politics, this is criminal mischief."

"But there is always politics," the ex-General told her. "There is politics in every job. And it's often just another form of criminal mischief."

"I don't agree with that at all," Belinda said. "Politics is a noble science. It's one of the five noble sciences that Aristotle named, the five branches of philosophy. There was Meta-physics, Logic, Ethics, Aesthetics, and Politics. The noble sci-ence of Politics is what we've been practicing, the three of us, over the past three months. We've been building a community that could act together ethically and harmoniously to achieve a common purpose. That's what politics is all about. Don't dignify Belok and all he stands for with a good Aristotelian word like that."

"But you know what he means, Belinda," Mr. Tompkins offered. "He means politics in the sleazy sense, the way we often use the word to mean, I guess, a kind of pathological politics."

Belinda nodded. "Yes, I understood that, Webster. But let's use our words precisely. The three of us are trying to practice Politics in the Aristotelian sense. Belok is just trying to be an amateur greaseball."

Ex-General Markov nodded. "Still, an amateur greaseball can cause a lot of damage."

"So, what do I do?" Mr. Tompkins asked them.

They both looked to Belinda for an answer, an answer that took its time coming. "You don't accomplish anything by standing in front of a train," she told him gently.

"No," Mr. Tompkins agreed.

"No," the ex-General agreed.

After another long silence, ex-General Markov cleared his throat. "Why are we here?" he asked.

"Hmm?"

"What is it that we're trying to accomplish? Forget about this greaseball for a moment. What are we really trying to do?"

"Well, good work for one thing," Mr. T. said. "We're here to do good work, and to enable other people to do good work."

"There's that," Belinda agreed, "but we're also here to learn something. What has made this so wonderful, at least up until this morning, was the Project Management Laboratory experiment. We were hell-bent toward learning some truly fundamental things about the dynamics of projects, about how management decisions really affect a project. That was part of why I was here, and I think the same for you, Webster."

"Right. All the things we've been simulating this week and last were effects that our experiments would have validated. We could have come away with an extraordinary result, a completely tuned model of project dynamics, one that could guide us and the rest of the world from that point on."

The ex-General leaned forward to reach out to each of them, placing one of his big hands on Webster's shoulder and one on Belinda's. "Well, let's not give any of that up. That's what we're here for. To do good work and to learn. Let's stick to our guns."

"But how do we do that without putting Webster in danger?" Belinda objected.

"We don't put Webster in danger because we have Webster do exactly as he has been told."

"You mean, I do combine the eighteen teams into six super-teams, all of them horribly overstaffed?"

"Yes, because you have to. And, you publish the June first date. And you make an announcement that the price of lateness is a million dollars a moment. You do all that. Just hold your nose and do it."

"But Gabriel, how do we still manage to do good work?"

"And how do we ever learn anything from six stupidly overstaffed and overpressured projects?" Belinda added.

"We've been looking at it as a false dichotomy," the ex-General told them. "We've been thinking all day that either we do the projects the way we always planned to do them and preserve our Project Management Laboratory, or we give in to the greaseball. That has been our error. It doesn't have to be a matter of OR. It could also be a matter of AND."

"Explain that."

"Yes, please do."

"We combine the projects. We combine three Quicker-Still teams into one. That gives us one overstaffed team and two free managers. . . ." He left a long silence.

"Ah," Webster said. "I see what you mean. We have a pool of available workers to draw on, so we just set up two new teams under those two free managers. We do the same thing for all the other products. And, again, we've got three teams doing each project."

"Exactly."

"Only the new teams are a few months behind, . . . so what's a few months?" Belinda was looking more cheerful. "We've learned a lot, we have our simulations to guide us, and we can make some of the early project deliverables that were generated by the old B- and C-Teams available to the new teams that take their places. I think it would work, Gabriel. What do you think, Webster?"

Mr. Tompkins was thoughtful for a moment. "Of course it can be made to work. We have to be a little careful here, though. We'll have to keep the new B- and C-Teams a secret; otherwise, they'll be a threat to Belok."

The ex-General smiled. "Leave that to me, my friends. I am an expert in concealing things. This was an important skill in the old Morovia."

"And in the new one," Webster added. "As we all now know."

"So, we move all Webster's B- and C-Team managers over to Gabriel's building, restaff their projects, and keep them there under wraps."

"Right. Only one problem that I see, though."

"What's that Webster?"

"One of the B- or C-Teams is likely to finish long before its corresponding A-Team does. We know that from the simulations. When that happens, Belok is shown up for exactly the meddler he is; his overstaffed and overpressured projects are going to be trounced by our leaner teams. He is not going to take that lying down."

"So, we don't tell him," Belinda suggested. "We'll publish the product and tell the world that it was Minister Belok's reformulated super-team that got the work done so quickly. Without his intervention, it would have taken three times as long."

"But that's terrible," Mr. Tompkins wailed. "All the credit will go to the wrong people."

"But we'll all know, and our people will all know, so who cares, as long as Belok doesn't know."

"She's right, Webster," ex-General Markov told him. "Remember why we are here: to do good work and to learn. That we don't also thwart the greaseball is a small matter. He will get what's coming to him one day."

"Hmm." Mr. T. was beginning to feel better, too. He wasn't sure it would work, but at least they'd be doing something more than just caving in. "Of course you're right. We'll do it," he said at last. "And so the Project Management Laboratory is saved, for the moment at least. I have a hunch we're going to be learning something we really hadn't counted on: We're going to come away with a very precise understanding of how over-staffing hurts projects, how much, and in what ways. Well, folks, let's get the lights on here. We've got work to do."

Many hours later, Mr. Tompkins stumbled back to the Residence and up to his suite. He got into his pajamas. He would have liked to turn in directly—it was already after 2 A.M.—but instead, he sat down at the little writing desk beside his bed and took up his pen.

From Mr. Tompkins' Journal:

Pathological Politics

   o   You have to be willing to put your job on the line any day . . .

o   . . . but that doesn't guarantee that pathological politics won't affect you.

o   Pathological politics can crop up any-where, even in the healthiest organiza-tion.

o   The defining characteristic of patho-logical politics is that goals of per-sonal power and influence come to override the natural goals of an organi-zation.

o   This can happen even when the patho-logical goal is directly opposed to the organizational goal.

o   Among the bad side effects of pathology: It becomes unsafe to have a leanly staffed project.

He looked back over what he had written. The last item was the most depressing of all. The more they worked with the Jamid simulations, the more they were coming to realize that there were substantial productivity advantages to running very small teams. Sometimes, a small team could do wonders in a short time, while large teams could barely get going in the same period. But small teams were impossible in a sufficiently political climate. You wouldn't dare try to pull off a miracle with only four or five people on board. If you tried and failed, there would always be someone willing to suggest that you could have succeeded if only you'd added another dozen or two dozen people. In such an environment, managers have to take the only safe option and overstaff their projects, even though they know in their hearts that it's exactly the wrong thing to do.

12

THE NUMBERS MAN

છે.

*T*hey had spent most of each day since Minister Belok's bombshell interviewing new teams. This work had gone somewhat faster than expected because they'd had the assistance of the six product managers and the twelve newly redundant B- and C-Team managers. They'd divided themselves up into groups of three and blitzed through ex-General Markov's staff, looking for the best people. Sadly, the most talented people were the ones they'd chosen before, during the earlier set of interviews in January and February. After all, they had set out then to take the cream of the crop, and they undoubtedly had. Now all those good developers had been combined into the six A-Teams:

PRODUCT	A-TEAM	
	MANAGER	STAFF
NOTATE	Karoti	35
PMILL	Gradish	33
PAINT-IT	Alweez	48
PSHOP	Orik	60
QUIRK	Borscht	42
QUICKERSTILL	Grosz	26

All the A–Teams were, in all of their judgment, too heavily
staffed for their own good. They were hell-bent for failure.
That didn't mean Mr. T. could ignore them, however. He still
had to manage their managers. That alone used up a big piece
of his time. The official org chart showed him sitting directly
on top of the six A–Team managers. This was something of a
fiction, generated to keep Minister Belok off their backs. The
real organization was similar to what had existed before the
shake-up. It had six product managers plus ex-General
Markov reporting directly to Tompkins.

The six product managers each ran three project teams, as
before: the reformulated A–Teams and the newly formed B-
and C–Teams. By the time they were finished staffing, they
had eighteen totally independent projects:

PRODUCT	PRODUCT MANAGER	A-TEAM		B-TEAM		C-TEAM	
		MGR	STAFF	MGR	STAFF	MGR	STAFF
NOTATE	Churchi	Karoti	35	Kungfu	10	Taichi	4
PMILL	Alber	Gradish	33	Letuz	8	Onyon	4
PAINT-IT	Pogo	Alweez	48	Somtyms	11	Nefer	5
PSHOP	Porkipyn	Orik	60	Isbek	16	Alterbek	7
QUIRK	Hepsiba	Borscht	42	Apfels	12	Kabach	5
QUICKERSTILL	Walkeli	Grosz	26	Kartak	3	Makmora	6

Tompkins and the A–Teams were housed in the prestigious
and very visible Aidrivoli-1 building. The six product managers and the B- and C–Teams were all hidden away in space
that the ex-General had found for them in Aidrivoli-7.

Just three week after Lahska's sudden disappearance, Mr.
Tompkins found a breezy postcard from her in his morning

mail. The picture side showed students clustered around street musicians in what was almost certainly Harvard Square. On the back she had written in her fine script,

> *My dear Webster,*
>   *I have come across a charming small company here in Massachusetts. They measure things, all kinds of things, but software in particular. They have a special way to determine the size of a software product entirely from the outside. The result is expressed in units they call "function points." Of course, I thought immediately of you. I have contracted with their consultant, a Mr. T. Johns Caporous, to pay you a visit.*
>   *All the best,*
>   *Lahksa*

A few days later, Mr. Tompkins received a fax from a Cambridge company instructing him to meet T. Johns Caporous at the Varsjop airport the next morning. When the flight touched down, the first person to step off the plane was a genial-looking man with sparkling eyes who seemed to be running at an internal clock speed at least twice that of a normal human. He also spoke about twice as fast as anyone Tompkins had ever met before.

His words came like bullets out of a machine gun. "How many programmers do you suppose there are in Morovia?" he asked Mr. Tompkins, as soon as they were in the car.

"Well, I couldn't say exactly, but ..."

"Two thousand eight hundred sixty-one, as of first of the year. How many computers would you guess?"

"Um ..."

"Just over three thousand workstations, thirty-six percent Macs, fifty-five percent Windows, eight percent Unix boxes, and the rest mixed. Twelve Internet servers. One hundred sixty hand-held organizers, a few old-fashioned mainframes, mostly used by the military."

"Oh."

He smiled easily at Tompkins. "I've never been to Morovia. It's nice here, isn't it?"

"It is."

"Average ambient daytime temperature, 78 degrees Fahrenheit; that would be, let's see, 25.6 degrees centigrade; average annual rainfall, 66.8 inches a year, . . . say, I'll bet they could make some fine wine here."

"Delicious, actually."

"And they certainly make a lot of it, almost fifty-eight million liters a year. That's as much wine as is imported by the New England states plus New York and, say, Pennsylvania combined. Not that the northeastern states drink so much wine . . . only about 4.2 liters per person per year. All of which is not imported of course. Only thirty-eight percent."

Mr. Tompkins nodded dazedly.

Four and a half hours later, T. Johns Caporous was gone again, delivered back to the airport by Waldo. He had flown in on his way from Ankara and had to be in Helsinki that very evening. Then, the next day he would be off to Dublin, and from there to South America for a five-country lecture tour.

Mr. Tompkins' office looked like a tornado had come through. There were manuals and reports open on every surface. There were pads of paper littered with calculations, and the white board was full. Mr. Tompkins was trying to collect together and annotate what seemed like a mile of calculator tapes from the furious morning of work. In one corner, ex-General Markov was sprawled on a folding chair, still looking stunned.

Tompkins as well was still slightly in shock. It was as concentrated a morning as he had spent in years. He certainly didn't want to go through another one like that, not without a good rest in between. But as hectic as it had been, it had produced one very interesting result: a compact table of numbers written in T. Johns Caporous's distinctive scrawl. The matrix occupied only a single flip-chart sheet, now displayed on the easel by the desk. It showed the sizes of the six software products:

PRODUCT	SIZE
NOTATE	3,000 Function Points
PMILL	2,200 Function Points
PAINT-IT	3,800 Function Points
PSHOP	6,500 Function Points
QUIRK	3,200 Function Points
QUICKERSTILL	1,500 Function Points

"Hi, guys." It was Belinda Binda. She had missed the morning meeting. "Hey, looks like you've had a fun day. What hit this place?"

"A certain T. Johns Caporous," Mr. Tompkins told her.

"Ooooh. I've heard of him. I've heard he is a kind of unstoppable force."

Mr. Tompkins and the ex-General nodded in agreement.

Belinda turned to stare at the flip chart. "What's a function point? Wait a minute, don't answer that. I think I don't even have to know." After a moment she turned back to them. Her eyes were alight. "Why, this is beautiful. Gabriel, Webster, do you realize what we've got here?"

The ex-General was shaking his head. "It feels like it's going to be useful. I do suspect it's good for something. But as to exactly what, . . ."

Belinda was practically dancing with excitement. "This is beautiful, this is beautiful! Think how it ties in with the simulation models we've been drawing. We've been drawing flow models," she walked over to one of the models pinned up on the wall, "reservoirs emptying into pipes, flowing through valves. But what exactly is it that is flowing? What is it that moves through our models? What is it that's in the reservoirs?"

"I don't know," Tompkins told her. "Done-ness?"

"Or goodness," the ex-General suggested. "Some kind of an abstract quantification of work."

"No, you sillies. It's function points that flow through the models. Look!" She flipped the flip chart to get to a blank sheet and took up a pen. "Look at it this way." She was sketching quickly.

"We can look at each project in exactly the same way. At the coarsest level, the project is just a valve." She tapped her pen on the valve in the middle of her diagram. "On the left side, we have a reservoir of product to be developed. On the right side is a reservoir of product completed. We start off with the right side completely empty, since we haven't done anything yet. The left side starts off filled with function points. How many? Well, . . ." She flipped back to the Caporous data. "Here we have it: three thousand function points for the Notes project, for example." She wrote the number in at the level of the left-side reservoir.

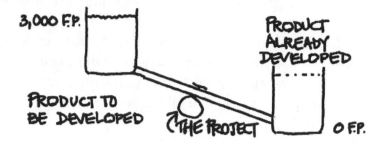

"Now the guts of our model is the next-level decomposition of that valve called The Project. We model it in terms of the teams and the partitionings and the effects of pressure and deadline and staff level and critical-path delays and . . . whatever. All of those we simulate using lower-level pipelines and valves and reservoirs. Now, when we run the project, the left-side reservoir empties through the complex valve or network of such valves that is The Project into the right-side reservoir. When all the function points have gotten through, the project is done!"

For the rest of the afternoon, they closeted themselves in Mr. T.'s office, reconstructing the sizing algorithms that Caporous had shown them. They were also trying to make sense of the mountain of information that he had thrown at them during the morning. While he was calculating, T. Johns Caporous had the habit of spitting out rapid-fire facts like "Average American software cost is $1,050 per function point as of 1994," or "Software maintenance on average requires one maintainer per five hundred function points of product," or "Undebugged code has a defect potential of 5.6 per function point." Mr. Tompkins had struggled to keep up, writing fact after fact on index cards, almost, but not quite as fast as Caporous spewed them out. Now they were sorting through the cards, looking for gems.

"What we don't know," the ex-General said, with some discouragement, "is what the productivity of our organization is. Look at the variation in the figures Caporous gave us: from two function points per month all the way up to ninety. But where are we?"

"I have no idea," Tompkins told him.

"Not impossible to figure out, though," Belinda Binda said.

"Sure, given a little time," Mr. T. agreed. "By the time our first project is done, we'll have one data point. And shortly after that, a bunch more. A few years from now, I think we'll be able to answer Gabriel's question. We'll know the mean production rate of this organization and the variation around the mean. We'll be able to sort the data by project size, staff size, anything you can think of. If we only had that data now. . . ." He drifted off, considering that metric ideal.

"C'mon, guys. We don't have to wait two years." Belinda was looking at them like they were school kids. "We can have the data next week."

"Well, I'd sure like to know how we're going to pull that off!" Tompkins sputtered.

"Yes, Belinda, please clue us in."

"Look, there have been projects here before, scores of projects."

Ex-General Markov was shaking his head. "But we don't have the data, Belinda. No data. Almost none."

"I'm sure there's salary data."

"Well, of course there is that. We had to pay people, and that creates records."

"So we know about months of effort expended. And we know what projects they were working on. If we don't remember, we can ask them."

Gabriel conceded her a point. "I suppose we could establish person-months expended for each project. We wouldn't know what kind of work they were doing, but we could, I suppose, reconstruct the aggregate cost, how many people-months on each project."

"That'll do it. The aggregate is all we need. And then we correlate it to the size in function points of the products that those projects built."

Mr. Tompkins still didn't see. "Where on earth do we get that?"

Belinda looked at him pointedly, leaving a moment for him to figure out the answer for himself. He was so worn down by the exertions of this very intense day that he could barely keep himself awake. Just as he was facing up to how tired he was, Waldo, the ultimate office assistant, opened the door and wheeled in a tray of Morovian coffee. "Ah, coffee," Tompkins said, thankful for the interruption. Ah, reprieve.

"We'll calculate function points delivered for all those old projects by looking at the products they built. We'll apply the Caporous formulas to the products." Belinda helped herself to a cup of coffee. "It's a mountain of work, but not beyond us."

"Where are we going to find the time for all that work?" Mr. Tompkins moaned. "We're up to our armpits already in things to do."

Belinda was grinning. "Hey, we're captains of industry here. No need to do the work ourselves. We'll form a measurement team, teach them how to calculate function points and how to dredge up the salary data, and send them on their way."

He still wasn't convinced. "Where are we ever going to get someone to take on that task? We need a specialist in data recovery. . . ."

"Archaeology," Belinda corrected him. "This work is pure archaeology. It's just tromping around the bones of dead projects to form a picture of the past."

"Archaeology, then. Where are we ever going to find a software archaeologist? The guy has not only got to be able to digest the data, but he's got to have connections throughout the organization to know whom to go after to get it. Where do we have to go to find such a person?"

The ex-General was grinning. "'What seeketh ye abroad that cannot be found at home?'" he quoted.

"What does that mean, Gabriel?"

"It means, look under your nose, Webster."

Immediately under his nose, on the desk in front of him, was a jumble of index cards and tables of numbers. Waldo was busy straightening them into neat piles. "What? What's under my nose?"

"Waldo."

Waldo looked up. "Me? What about me?"

"He is perfect," the ex-General said. "You're perfect for the job, Waldo. How would you like a new job?"

"What job?"

"Manager of the metrics group."

"Me, a manager?"

"Well, I don't know about that . . . ," Mr. Tompkins began, slightly panicked at the thought of losing Waldo. "For all his good qualities, . . ."

Belinda strode across the room. "Of course," she said, taking Waldo's hand and shaking it. "Of course you can do it. Congratulations, Waldo. Poof, you're a manager. That's all it really takes. A little magic wanding by one of us, and there you are."

"But . . ."

"Don't you see how perfect he is, Webster? He's been here forever. He knows absolutely everyone. I doubt there's a person in any of the seven buildings who hasn't had some interaction with Waldo by this time. And a good interaction, too. When he makes a contact, he makes a friend. You do see it, don't you? He is perfect for the job."

Mr. Tompkins did indeed see it. He smiled a resigned smile. "Of course. I'm just sorry to lose him, that's all."

"We're not losing him, we're just putting him to work at something that can make use of all his talents. That's what we do as managers. Apply people where their skills and talents can really shine. That's what management is all about."

"Um, what's going on here?" Waldo wanted to know.

"I've got a good statistics person to help him," ex-General Markov contributed, "someone who mixes up statistics like Julia Child mixes food. We'll throw in a programmer analyst, just to give the team its full complement of the necessary skills."

"Um, what's going on?"

Tompkins told him. "I think you just got promoted, Waldo. Congratulations, you are now manager of the metrics group."

Belinda stayed on for another two hours, helping him bring Waldo up to speed. By the time they were done, he had pretty much mastered the function point counting rules and had a game plan for how to conduct the software archaeology study. He told them confidently that he would be back to them with data from the first past project within no more than a week.

Belinda and Webster had dinner downtown, and afterwards he walked her back to the little park up over the harbor where she slept. He took real satisfaction from the fact that Belinda seemed to be recovering from burnout. There remained, however, a few odd quirks in her ways: She still wouldn't wear shoes or sleep indoors. On a night like this, of course, it wasn't hard to understand the appeal of bedding down outdoors. The park was peaceful and quiet, the stars bright and large in the absence of much artificial light.

"What a difference a day makes," he told her. "It was a lucky day for us that T. Johns Caporous showed up here. I can't think when we've made so much progress. Today, we really got a grip on things."

"It's true. He has been a catalyst for our thinking. But I've been kicking myself all afternoon."

"Why on earth?"

"Why did we wait for him, Webster? Shame on us for not having done that work months ago."

"Well, we needed his concept of function points. That was an important discovery for us."

"Without knocking its importance, I point out that we could have plowed on without it, if only we'd given ourselves a good swift kick to get started."

"I can't see how."

"Think about it. Without the concept of an objective sizing formula, we could have at least done some intelligent approximations. We could, for example, have worked out a relative sizing scheme."

"Such as?"

"Well, sizing the various products in terms of each other. If we hypothesized, for example, that QuickerStill was one hundred 'Galoobles' of software, then couldn't we have figured out how big Quirk was in Galoobles? Couldn't we have figured out how many QuickerStills in a Quirk? It would involve some seat of the skirt estimating, but if we'd put our heads together, I think we could have come up with a pretty good assessment."

"If QuickerStill is one hundred, I guess Quirk would be, maybe, two hundred fifty Galoobles."

"More or less. And PShop would be five hundred or six hundred."

"But those are just numbers pulled out of the air, just gut-feel numbers."

"Yes, but once we'd pulled them out of the air and written them down, they could only get better. We would be obliged to refine our concept of a Galooble, to invent some function metric of our own."

"I hardly think we were going to invent a fundamental concept like function points all on our own. Caporous and his people have been working on this for years."

"Well, he was trying to solve a much harder problem than we needed to solve. He was trying to come up with some size metric that would work for all software, everywhere. He had to worry about hundreds of variables that do vary over the global population, but never vary here. Our problem was much more contained. All we needed was some size metric that was useful, just for Aidrivoli."

"I don't know how we would even have begun," Tompkins said.

"Function points are a *synthetic* metric, like tax bracket in the IRS code. You can't measure it directly; you need to measure other things, and then apply them in a formula to derive the synthetic. The 'other things,' in the case of function points, are the countable characteristics of software. Viewed from the outside, those would be input and output streams, database segments, data elements. Those are the primitive metrics on which any synthetic has to depend."

"Yes. . . ." He didn't see where this line of thinking was headed.

"All we had to do was speculate that there was some synthetic that could be formed from these primitive metrics. Then, we could perform a software archaeology study to collect the primitives along with effort data for a dozen past projects. . . ."

"Ah." He got it at last. "Then we just run multiple regressions, correlating combinations of the primitives against the effort numbers."

"Right. Some specific combination would emerge as best, the one that gives the least noisy relationship to effort. That would be our unit, the Galooble, or the Morovian Standard Unit of Work, or the Aidrivoli, or whatever we wanted to call it."

"I see. You're right, we could have done that on our own."

"By the time Caporous got here, we would have had all the primitive data collected, and been working with our own, local synthetic size metric. Then he would have shown us, I don't doubt it, a better way to form the synthetic. So, we might have switched from Galoobles to function points to take advantage of the emerging standard, and because it's probably a better metric. But in that case, the improvement would only have been marginal. We would have had the advantage for months of working with pretty reasonable metrics."

"You're right. We should have done that. It's as plain as the nose on your face once a T. Johns Caporous has demonstrated it for you. But we couldn't see it before."

"Shame on us."

"No. Good on him. The people who point out things that should have been obvious but weren't are the ones who do the most real good. They see the simple fundamental truths that the rest of us miss, and they help us to see them as well."

A long, comfortable pause: They sat quietly side-by-side absorbing the spectacle of the night sky.

"You can see shooting stars over this way," Belinda said, after a while, pointing out over the Ionian Sea. "Keep your eyes just over the green navigation light, and up about twenty degrees."

She turned him to face the sea. Webster looked above the green navigation light, as instructed. He let his breath out slowly, let his shoulders relax. The night was almost perfectly still now, the only sound was Belinda's soft rustling just behind his back. Suddenly, a long, slow arc of light trailed across the sky. "Ooooh."

"Did you see one?"

"I did."

"They're there every night. Sometimes, I count a dozen of them before I fall asleep." She put her ground cover down beside him, and sat on it, dressed now in a flannel nightgown. He hadn't considered what Belinda might sleep in, but somehow he wouldn't have expected it to be a flannel nightgown.

She lay back, fully reclining on the ground cover, arranged a light blanket over her, put her hands behind her neck, and stared off straight up into the heavens. A long time passed with no need for either of them to say anything. Finally, Belinda told him what was on her mind: "What's it all about, Webster? What are we up to here? Here I am, forty-something, and I still don't know what to do with myself. What's enough for a life? Is it enough that we're helping a little third-world country come out of the woods and develop a world-class software industry? It's amusing, I know, but is it amusing enough? Is it important enough?"

"I think so. But I know what you mean. I wonder, too, sometimes."

"We're helping nice, young people build decent careers for themselves and live with a bit of dignity. . . ."

"And we're not doing any harm, not adding to pollution or building weapons."

"Right. And still I wonder. Is this what I am here for on this earth?"

"I don't know. Maybe we'll never figure it out, what matters, I mean."

"Sometimes, I think that what matters is doing something so spectacular it will astound the world. And then, other times, I just want to help the world. And still other times, I want to sneak up behind the world and give it one humongous goose."

"To astound, help, or goose. That is the question."

"Or what combination of the three—that is the question. Maybe each of us has to find his or her own perfect combination. Do you suppose that our career choices are as simple as that, Webster? To find our own particular point in Astound-Help-Goose space?"

"I like that. We're each of us a point in that space, defined by our positions along those three axes, defined by our values of the dimensions A, H, and G."

"How many parts Michelangelo, how many parts Mother Teresa, and how many parts . . . ?"

"Milton Berle."

"Milton Berle."

He was watching the sky again, looking toward the green navigation light for more shooting stars. All he had to do was keep his eyes fixed there, and sure enough, they continued to appear. By the time he had seen three more traces, Belinda's breathing had become regular and deep. He tiptoed away so as not to disturb her, and made his way slowly back to the Residence through the splendid summer night.

From Mr. Tompkins' Journal:

<u>Metrics</u>

o   Size every single product.

o   Don't sweat the units—while you're waiting to achieve objective metrification, use subjective units.

o   Form synthetic metrics from all the primitives (countable characteristics of the software) available to you.

o   Collect archaeological data to derive productivity trends from now-ended projects.

o   Tinker with the formulation for your synthetic metric until its values give the best correlation to Effort for the set projects in your archaeological database.

o Draw a trend line through your database, showing expected Effort as a
   function of values of the synthetic
   metric.

o Now, for each new project to be esti-
   mated, compute value of the synthetic
   metric and use it to pick off expected
   Effort from the trend line.

o Use the noise level around the productivity trend as an indicator of what
   tolerance to apply to the projections.

13

QuickerStill

ಶ

From the beginning, NNL had decreed that the Quicken look-alike product would be called QuickerStill. The name caught on with the teams. Of course, the direct result was that the performance requirement for the product had to be bumped up in order to justify the name. Mr. T. let that happen. He rather liked the name. He liked the suggestion that the projects might be done "quicker still" than he had hoped, maybe even quicker still than the dumb deadline imposed by Minister Belok. Sitting in his office, Webster stared up over his shoulder at the countdown sign, which now read:

ONLY 345 DAYS TILL D-DAY!

Now just a little less than a year remained till next June 1. As a deadline for all six products, Belok's date was truly ludicrous. They now knew what the average production rate was for products built over the past five years at Aidrivoli: a little less than five function points per person-month. And that was for one-off products that didn't have to meet the rigors of the shrink-wrap software market. In developing the six products, Mr. T. knew, they'd be lucky to achieve anything more than three function points per person-month. That meant that a product like PShop would take at least three years to put out the door. Three years from their start date back in the winter would work out to more than six hundred days from today. There was no chance of even one of the PShop teams finishing even close to Belok's deadline.

While Tompkins knew that the larger projects—PShop and Paint-It and Quirk—hadn't a prayer of being done by the deadline, he still harbored some hope that one of the QuickerStill projects might be able to finish by then. That was the challenge he had set for himself. If they achieved that, he would call his whole Morovian venture a success.

He savored that idea for a long, pleasant moment. He might pull off some measure of success in spite of Belok. What a feat that would be! The more he thought about it, the better he felt. Now that they had come face to face with the awful reality of Minister Belok's schedule, at least the worst was past. After all, what else could possibly go wrong on that scale?

Mrs. Beerzig, the grandmotherly assistant who had taken over for Waldo, bustled into his office in some distress. "Oh, Boss. Something here you need to take a look at. There's a delegation outside from the Morovian Software Engineering Institute. They say they're here to perform an audit of the project groups."

"We're acting on the specific instructions of Minister Belok," the Audit Group manager told Tompkins. "He has laid down the law on this one. All these projects must be put under the gun to demonstrate improved process. They're currently rated at Capability Maturity Model Level 2. And Minister Belok wants them at Level 3 before the end of the year. He has set that as an absolute requirement." The man shook his head uneasily. "I don't know if it can be done, but he says it must."

"Whether it can be done or not is *not* what's foremost in my mind," Tompkins told him. "What I'm thinking of is, What's it going to cost me in lost time to put this group through a process improvement program? We're up against a deadline, you know."

The Audit Group manager replied confidently, "Well, I wouldn't worry too much about that. Process improvement results in productivity improvement. We know that from the Americans. Bumping up a single CMM level should push your productivity up by twenty-four percent."

"I doubt it. But even if it is true, that doesn't guarantee that the twenty-four percent increased capacity will be available before my deadline." He was thinking back to Hector Rizzoli's observation that there is no such thing as a short-term fix. "We know that process improvement programs take time, a lot of time. So, in the short run, we lose capacity."

The man shrugged. "But in the long run . . ."

"Yes, I know. Starting someday, maybe a year from the end of the program, some of the good things you'll have taught my people may start to pay off. How long does the program take?"

"Ten months, maybe. We'll tie up your people for a day, or perhaps only half a day, per week."

Tompkins groaned. He didn't have to run the simulation to know what this would do to the schedule. "What's your charter? Are you process-improving just these six projects, or the whole organization?"

"Well, the whole organization. That's what Minister Belok wants."

"I see."

"Sorry, Mr. Tompkins. I can see this is not such welcome news. But do try to take the long view of it. I'm sure that . . . "

Tompkins was shaking his head in disgust.

"Well, you might take heart from this then, Mr. Tompkins: The truth is that we're not ready at all to begin the process improvement program. It will take us, maybe, six weeks before we can even start."

"So, what is all this today, all these people?"

"We're just the Audit Group. The one thing we can do right away is to determine that your organization hasn't slipped from CMM Level 2. So, we need to go around and assure that everyone is indeed using the process steps that they were certified for a year ago."

"I see."

"Even as many as we are, it will take us most of the day to do just Aidrivoli-1. Then, we'll audit the people in the other buildings during the rest of this week and next."

By the end of the day, the Audit Group manager and a few of his lieutenants were assembled in Mr. Tompkins' office. They'd brought along with them a rather sheepish-looking Bigsby Grosz, the QuickerStill A-Team manager. Ex-General Markov sat in.

The Audit Group manager made his report: "Look, here's what we found, Mr. Tompkins. Not too bad really, but there was one rather upsetting deviation from process; that's Mr. Grosz here and his group."

"I'm sure he had a good reason. . . ." Mr. Tompkins began.

"Well, you know, there are always good reasons for deviating from standard procedure. When the MSEI certified your group last year as CMM Level 2, it was specifically confirming that the process, the set of disciplined steps the people undertake on each project, had become Repeatable. That's what Level 2 is. It's called Repeatable, meaning that whether your approach is good or bad, ideal or imperfect, at least you're doing it the same way each time. Now, most of your people in Aidrivoli-1 were doing just that. We looked into six projects, all of them in the Requirements stage, and of these, five were going about requirements capture and documentation using the same standard procedures they have always used on past projects. This was true of all the projects except Quicker-Still. Mr. Grosz here seems to have abandoned the Repeatable process entirely. His group has left off the requirements stage without even finishing the document, and gone right straight into design!" He said this as though it were a crime against nature.

"I'm sure he had his reasons," Mr. Tompkins repeated.

"I did," Grosz said. "I had very good reasons. Look, this is not at all like other projects we have done. This is a project to build a look-alike to a well-understood, well-documented, commercial product, Quicken. We had all the documentation from that product. There was no need to build a requirements spec at all. . . ."

"No need to build a requirements spec!" the Audit Group manager sputtered. "I have never, ever seen a project that had no need to build a requirements spec. Never. Every project has to build a good, thorough requirements document. Every MSEI-certified CMM Level 2 project has to build the requirements document using the same methods and notations it was certified as using. That's what it means to have a Repeatable process."

"But this project is different!" Grosz wailed.

"All projects are different," the Audit Group manager shot back. "They're different, each and every one of them. But we use the same process nonetheless."

Tompkins ventured in. "But suppose there is something special about a given project that makes the certified process not worth following?"

"We follow it anyway," the MSEI man said. "It has to be followed. If we let people make exceptions due to the exceptional nature of their projects, we'd never have any consistency."

"So, they have to proceed exactly the same way on each project?"

"Exactly the same way," he confirmed. "And if they don't, then they're not worthy to be certified as Level 2. That is not just my opinion. That is the opinion of the MSEI."

"Not worthy to be certified as Level 2," Mr. Tompkins considered. "Well, maybe that's our answer. Maybe you could just *de*-certify the QuickerStill project."

"I hardly think that's the right answer, Mr. Tompkins. The MSEI is not about to preside over any backsliding. I mean, once that sort of thing gets started . . ."

"Well, we could keep it all very private, just among ourselves."

"I don't think so," the man said firmly. "And I don't think Minister Belok would be pleased at all by this. He wants the whole group up to Level 3 by year-end, and here is one of his very important projects going in exactly the opposite direction, right back to Level 1. No sir, I am going to be issuing a written Cure Notice to Mr. Grosz and the QuickerStill project today. We're going to put them on notice that they have seven days to get themselves back onto the straight and narrow, producing requirements documents in the standard form. . . ."

"Copying requirements over from one form into the other," Grosz said bitterly.

" . . . in the standard form, as I said, using the standard Level-2 process. If they don't demonstrate that within seven days, then they will be officially and publicly decertified. Do I make myself clear?" There was a note of menace in his voice.

"Perfectly," Mr. Tompkins told him. "Perfectly clear. Of course, this project is only a small part of my full organization. I understand you'll be auditing the other buildings beginning tomorrow."

"Yes, about one building a day, if today is any indicator."

"Well, then, would you accommodate me by starting on Aidrivoli-2 tomorrow? And then, from there, on to Aidrivoli-3 the next day, and so on. You might as well do the buildings in numerical order, ending up at Aidrivoli-7 on the last day." That at least would give him a few days to decide how to pro ceed. "Would you do them in that order for me?"

"Well, sure, Mr. T. We're here to help. So, it's Aidrivoli-2 tomorrow. I take it you've got some pretty important things going on in Aidrivoli-2 that you want us to take it next."

"Er, yes, that's it precisely. And Aidrivoli-3 and -4, as well. All very important work. We are intensely interested in your audits of Aidrivoli-2 and -3 and -4, and to a lesser extent, Aidrivoli-5 and -6. Those are key ones, so I'd like you to do those first."

"You got it, Mr. T. The MSEI won't let you down."

"I'm sure of that."

Gabriel stayed behind after the others had left. "Looks like we're even further behind than we thought," he observed.

"Well, certainly further behind by whatever time was spent on process improvement."

"No, still worse than that."

"Why?"

"It is such a natural management decision to shortcut the requirements documentation on these look-alike projects where you have excellent user documentation from the commercial vendors. But Grosz was the only one who saw the opportunity and took it. The others all knuckled down and applied themselves to writing requirements documents just the same way they always had on other projects, not realizing that this one was different and required a different approach."

Mr. Tompkins stood up. "I see what you mean. I think we need to wander over to Aidrivoli-7 and perform a little audit of our own to see whether the B- and C-Teams are willing to take sensible shortcuts or not."

"The user document *is* the requirements spec," Molly Makmora told them. "Of course, we didn't copy it over into the standard form. That would have been a total waste of time."

"A total waste," Elem Kartak agreed. All the other B- and C-Team managers were nodding their heads in agreement.

Avril Alterbek, the PShop C-Team manager held up her hand. "The Photoshop manuals we got from Adobe are as thorough and comprehensible a statement of requirements as I have ever seen. I never looked at a user manual before to evaluate it as a spec, but this project has forced me to do just that. And I came away thinking that a user manual makes one very fine specification document. I'm wondering why we don't, in general, push up the work of writing the user manual, or at least the guts of it, to the front of the project, and make it do double service: act as user manual and functional specification. I know the others are mostly of the same opinion, since we've been comparing notes on the subject." She looked around at her peer managers and they all showed signs of agreement.

"But just because the manuals made a good functional specification," she went on, "didn't mean that we had *no* requirements work to be done. There are also the nonfunctional requirements to worry about: things like response time and file capacities and number ranges and precision of variables and expansion characteristics. . . ."

"We each of us wrote up a set of nonfunctional specifications," Kartak picked up. "Those together with the manuals made up a complete requirements document. Its form was unorthodox, but its content was excellent. It contained all the requirements, both functional and non-, and it was readable, unambiguous, and full of examples. I think our projects have got some of the best requirements specs ever seen."

Mr. Tompkins was considerably relieved. The very nonstandard requirements process they all seem to have adopted was a huge and meaningful shortcut. And the result of that shortcut was that all of the B- and C-Teams had put requirements stage work to bed and were now fully involved in design. Of course, it also meant that every single one of them would be decertified when the Audit Group finally arrived at Aidrivoli-7. That was his problem, not the project managers'.

Maybe this was the moment to give them a well-deserved pat on the back, Tompkins thought. "I'm delighted to see that you have been willing to approach this project in a nonstandard way. When there are intelligent shortcuts to take, we have to take them. And you have. That shows you're thinking on your feet, and that's what I want to see. But what I'm wondering is, Why didn't my A-Team managers all take the same shortcut?"

A moment passed while they considered his question. "I think I know," Avril suggested.

"Tell me, please."

"Well, put yourself in the position of my colleague Tomas Orik, who runs the PShop A-Team. He's got sixty people on his team. And there's talk that the Minister of Internal Affairs has got an eye on that project, because it's the one that is most stressed to deliver on time."

"So . . . ?"

"So, Tomas is obliged to keep all his people working. He's supposed to crack the whip and even make them work overtime. Otherwise, he stands out like a sore thumb as the wrong man to manage that effort. But what are they to do?"

Mr. Tompkins considered the implications of Avril's dreadful question. He'd have to sound out Tomas on the subject, but he had a hunch she was onto something. Translating requirements from one form to another wasn't exactly useful work, but there was a lot of it, enough to keep all the overstaffed teams busy, and, more important, looking busy. It was just possible they were working in an admittedly inefficient way just to have enough work for everyone to take part.

It was still early, but he decided not to go back to his office; he was too discouraged. His way home led him through the perennial gardens in front of the MSEI building, but he couldn't even enjoy them. The only bright spot of the day was that he had postponed audit of the people in

Aidrivoli–7 for another week. That gave him some time to do something. But what?

From Mr. Tompkins' Journal:

<u>Process and Process Improvement</u>

- o Good process and continually improving process are admirable goals.

- o They are also very natural goals: Good technical workers will focus on them whether you tell them to or not.

- o Formal process improvement programs cost time and money; a given process improvement effort may well set project work back. Even if productivity gains materialize, they are unlikely to offset the time spent on process improvement for those projects that host the program.

- o A project can hope to gain enough from a <u>single</u> well-chosen method improvement to repay the time and money invested in the change.

- o Projects cannot realistically hope to accommodate more than one method improvement over their duration. Multi-skill improvement programs (for instance, increasing by an entire CMM level) are most likely to make projects finish later than they would have without the program.

o   The danger of standard process is
that people will miss chances to take
important shortcuts.

o   Particularly on overstaffed projects,
standard process will be observed rigorously as long as it generates sufficient work (useful or not) to keep
everyone busy.

14

MOROVIA'S
FIRST PROGRAMMER

❧

"*I*'m going to tell him to stay away from my projects." Mr. Tompkins was sitting in Gabriel Markov's office. He punched his hand down on the desk, hoping to imply more determination than he really felt.

The ex-General raised his eyebrows. "You're going to tell that to the Director of the Morovian SEI?"

"I am. I'm going over there this afternoon to beard the lion in his den. Or her den."

"His."

"His. Thank you. I'm going to lay down the law to him." He stood and began to pace as he talked. "Yes, we want to invest in training and process improvement, but not for projects on deadline. No way. That's final."

"And you think he's going to agree to that?"

"I'm not going to give him any choice."

"He's likely to mention this to Minister Belok. He'll have to because it is Belok who has told him to start the process improvement program. Are you ready to take Belok on?"

Mr. Tompkins shook his head emphatically no. "I'm going to tell the Director to stay away from my projects and not mention it to Belok. I'm going to tell him this with so much conviction and persuasiveness that he will just have to agree. I think it's going to work."

"I don't think so."

"Neither do I. . . . But I have to try."

"Webster, my good friend, this is going to be a very tough sell. The Director's motivations are almost precisely the opposite of yours. He doesn't care much about the projects—he will tell you that your focus on the projects alone is too short-term—what he cares about is the long term and the skills and aptitudes of our people. And, he honestly believes that his various process improvement programs will help. I have the occasional doubt about some of this myself, but he believes in what he is doing. He is a very sincere man."

"So, help me. How do I say what I need to say?"

"I will help you practice a bit. Try it out on me. I am the Director. Pretend I am the Director. Give me your spiel."

"Now see here . . . um, what is his name?"

"Menotti. Prospero Menotti."

"Now see here, Mr. Menotti . . ."

"It's Dr. Menotti. Everybody is a doctor here. Even me, I am Dr. ex-General Markov."

"Okay. Doctor. How about this: You many think, Dr. Menotti—and I don't doubt your sincerity in thinking this thing that I'm about to utterly demolish because it is the dumbest thing that any thinking person has ever thought to think of—that process improvement—I mean, Just who do you think you are, coming in and disrupting my projects, probably costing us weeks or months off our schedule, weeks or months that we certainly can't afford, and I know this

because we have these simulations that prove conclusively that
the kind of woolly-headed fuzzy-thinking ..."

The good Dr. ex-General was shaking his head. "You are
too angry, Webster. Now, just indulge me for a moment. Tell
me what you feel about Dr. Menotti, not what you think, but
what you feel."

"I feel he is a woolly-headed, fuzzy-thinker, thinking up
woolly-headed fuzzy ideas and then imposing them, institu-
tionalizing his dumb notions willy-nilly on innocent people
for some kind of misguided, totally bureaucratic concept of ...
Why are you looking at me that way?"

"Webster, you never even met the guy. A minute ago, you
didn't even know his name, and you hate him."

"Meddling so-and-so."

"How are you going to convince somebody when you
don't like him?"

Mr. Tompkins paused for a moment to consider that one.
Of course, Gabriel was right. "Oh. I guess you're saying that
if I let my dislike show, then he probably won't do what I
want him to do."

"That is certainly true."

"And I was letting my dislike show?"

"I'll say."

"Well, that's a good point. I will have to be careful to
keep my feelings for the man under wraps. I'm certainly
capable of that. I'll do it. Thank you for that advice, Gabriel."

"That was not my advice at all. And you are probably not
capable of keeping your feelings under wraps anyway. Webster, think about this as a management problem. You are our
boss here and a damn good one. We are all falling over each
other to do the things you want us to do. Do you think that's
because you have authority over us?"

"Isn't it?"

"No. Wake up, dummy. Your power comes from something else entirely."

"You're saying, people do what I want because they like me? Maybe that's true, but how can I get Dr. Menotti to . . ."

"It's not because *they* like *you*. It's because *you* like *them*."

"Huh?"

"You like and respect the people who work for you. You care about them. Their problems are your problems; their concerns are yours. You have a heart as big as a train and it shows. You give trust before a person has really demonstrated trustworthiness. You make us all feel like you've adopted us into your family. That's why we follow you."

"Well." Mr. Tompkins wasn't quite sure what to say next.

"That's your power, Webster. If you use it on Dr. Menotti, you might just come away with what you need. I don't guarantee it, because it is going to be a bitter pill for him to swallow. But at least you'll have a chance."

"I have to like him?"

"You do. You can't convince anyone whom you don't like. Some people can, but you can't. Don't fight it."

"How can I like him? I mean, I can't just make myself like someone, just because it might help."

"I don't know, Webster. But I think it's your only hope."

The building housing the Institute was at the very center of the Aidrivoli complex. It was a handsome stone edifice, four stories tall. The sign in front read "Morovian Software Engineering Institute," but the letters cut in stone over the main entrance gave the building a different name. They read:

ARISTOTLE'S INSTITUTE

Mr. Tompkins looked back and forth between the two names, wondering about the difference.

Just inside the entrance, he found a large portrait that gave at least part of the answer. The man shown in the portrait was tall, with a pleasant angular face and a shock of white hair. There was something faintly bemused about his expression, especially in the eyes and one corner of the mouth. It was as if he were aware of something terribly funny and was just about to grin. Under the portrait, there was a plaque that read, "Aristotle Kenoros—Morovia's First Programmer."

Dr. Menotti's office was on the third floor. When he was shown in, Mr. Tompkins found himself shaking hands with a surprisingly young man of medium build and a cheerful expression.

"Mr. Tompkins. So, we meet at last. What a pleasure. I have heard so many good things . . ."

"Dr. Menotti." Tompkins withdrew his hand and stood stiffly, his stomach in a knot.

"So many good things. This dynamic model you have been running—well, it's quite the talk all around the campus. I do hope you'll be willing to show me through it one day. A brand-new approach for me, I'd never heard of such a thing. I am just delighted at the innovation. And, we've all heard about your splendid accomplishment in getting Belinda Binda engaged in doing good work again. What a waste it was to have her idle, a human tragedy and a great loss to our industry, but now she's turned quite around, thanks to you. And all the projects now staffed and on their way . . . Well, you've had yourself a busy few months."

"I, too, have been hearing some nice things about you, Dr. Menotti. Ex-General Markov has told me. . ."

"Isn't that man a treasure? His people love him, you know. They really do. He is a real people-person. Well, please

167

do sit down. I have asked one of my coworkers to send out for some cakes and a pot of tea."

"I'm afraid I've come on a rather distressing errand."

"Oh, I know. I know. I've heard about the audit."

"Frankly, it's not just that."

The Director shook his head sympathetically. "I can imagine. You know, you're not the first who's had some misgivings about what we do."

"No, but in this case . . ."

"Well, let's just put it on hold for a while, till we've had our tea. Oh, here's the tea." An elderly man in a blue smock was wheeling a tea tray toward them. "Yes, put it down right there on the corner table, Mario. Yes, that's fine. Now, Mr. Tompkins, just put yourself in that comfortable chair, that one right there, and tell me something about yourself. How are you settling? And how are you finding our little country?"

It was nearly an hour before Mr. Tompkins made his pitch. By that time, he both liked and respected the Director, so he thought he might just have a chance.

"Prospero, I'm sure you know this already, a process improvement effort may have a positive effect in the long run, but in the short run, it has costs."

"So true," the Director agreed amiably.

"Over the lifetime of a project, you may very well end up behind, since you pay for the improvement effort in time and effort lost. . . ."

"Let's say 'invested.'"

"The time you've invested in process improvement is time that was not available to do project work. So, you have paid the cost but the benefit hasn't started to kick in yet. Just for the purposes of that one project, you come out behind."

The Director nodded. "That can certainly happen."

"And, as you know, we have six projects that are under immense pressure. I was just thinking . . ."

"Well, of course. I *knew* what you were thinking when the receptionist announced you."

"So, you'll do it then, exempt the project work from the improvement program?"

Dr. Menotti smiled, somewhat sadly. "Webster, the deadline that these projects are toiling under is impossible anyway. Everybody in Aidrivoli knows that—every manager and every programmer and every secretary. The projects are going to come in very late because the schedule is very wrong. So, what difference does an extra few months make? The little bit of your people's time we take to make real improvements in their methods may cause the projects to be twenty months late rather than eighteen. Does it really matter? The skills we'll be working on will be quantification skills, the very ones that will make future projects less likely to begin with such unreasonable schedules. You can see, from my point of view . . ."

"Yes, I do understand your perspective, Prospero. And it's a good one. But, you see, there is one thing that you've said that is only very slightly wrong. You said that *everybody* knows that the projects will be late. The truth is that everybody knows that but me."

"Ah."

"And I know that most of the projects won't make Minister Belok's ludicrous deadline, but I do have hopes that one project might just be able to sneak in under the wire."

"And you have a lot of self-esteem riding on that."

"I do. I'm not sure how I let that happen, but I have."

"I see." The Director looked away for a moment out the window. With his eyes still averted, he said, "Perhaps we could agree to overlook that one project. After all, with such a big improvement program under way, it is only reasonable that one little project might slip through the cracks, only to be picked up later." He turned back to face his visitor. Again, the sad look.

Mr. Tompkins sat back in his chair. He had been offered a fair and reasonable compromise. It hadn't been easy; the man's expression showed that it was a painful concession he was offering. Simple fairness now required that he accept the Director's offer, but he couldn't. He needed to protect the other projects as well, all of them, most particularly the secret ones in Aidrivoli-7. He knew most of them weren't going to be able to finish on Belok's schedule, but he still had all of his pride on the line to meet his original November date. He had to ask for more.

"Thank you for making that offer, Prospero. I see that it didn't come easy, and I do appreciate it. But I need more. I have to ask for all six of the projects to be excepted, and the entire division now housed in Aidrivoli-7. I ask you to limit the process improvement program to the other five buildings, where, of course, we shall cooperate to the utmost."

"My friend, I don't really see how . . ."

"And further, I need to ask you to make these exceptions and somehow not feel the need to mention them to Minister Belok. That's what I need."

"You want me to neglect a third of the staff, and not even mention it?"

"Yes."

"I can't do that, Webster. I just couldn't." A sorry shaking of the head. "You know, the MSEI does not impose these programs. We are only a service group. We do what our client organizations ask of us. I'm afraid you need to take this up directly with Minister Belok."

A long silence. This had been, as Gabriel had pointed out, a bit of a long shot. But taking things up with Minister Belok was not even a long shot; it was futile. Oh, well, he had only one more card to play, so he played it. "I know this sounds terrible, but is there any way to go around you? I mean, is there anyone above the Director here?"

Dr. Menotti looked slightly startled. "What made you think that there might be?"

Mr. Tompkins pointed up toward the ceiling. "There's a fourth floor. Usually the controlling officer has his office on the top floor."

An extended moment to ponder. Finally, the Director said, "Mr. Tompkins. Suppose I do give you access to my superior. And suppose further that that superior should accede to your request. Would you be prepared to make a concession to me in return? I refer to something that has nothing to do with what we have been discussing."

"Name your terms."

"Montifiore. We have followed with fascination your new archaeological data collection experiment and your inspired choice of Waldo Montifiore to lead it. We have nothing like that at the Institute. We want him. If I give you the access you wish, will you transfer Waldo Montifiore and his entire group over to me?"

Tompkins laughed in relief. "Willingly. I would be delighted to do that."

The Director looked at him oddly. "You would be 'delighted' to lose such a good man?"

"No, it's not losing him that I'd be delighted about. His loss would be a real inconvenience to us, but think of it from Waldo's point of view. For him, it is a triumph—the beginning of a wonderful new career."

171

Dr. Menotti nodded appreciatively. "Yes. I think you're right. I am pleased that you look at the transfer in this way, pleased and rather charmed. Of course, we will make sure that Waldo carries on doing the work that you've already chartered him to do."

A significant pause. "There *is* someone above you then, Prospero? Someone upstairs?"

"Oh, yes. The president of the Institute. He maintains a very low profile. In fact, he almost never even shows up. The position is largely honorific. When he does come here, it's often just to take an afternoon nap. He's up there now."

"I'll wake him. His name is . . . ?"

"Aristotle Kenoros."

Dr. Menotti instructed him to make his way up to the top floor by himself. There was no need for anyone to phone ahead, he said. In fact, Kenoros had no phone. Mr. Tompkins headed up the stairs.

What he found on the fourth floor was one enormous dark room, an office with no lights. The windowed wall to his right was entirely closed off by drapes. There was a soft hum in the room, the sound of a humidifier, he thought, but aside from that—nothing, only silence. The air was fresh and cool, and had a faint odor of moist earth. After pausing a moment for his eyes to adjust, he could see that the room was full of plantings; there were potted plants and trays of cuttings and seedlings and glassed-in plant beds on nearly every surface. In the far corner of the room he could now make out a narrow daybed. There was a prone figure on the bed, under a blanket. He could see a shock of white hair, a bit of movement.

"Mr. Kenoros?" Tompkins ventured. "Mr. Kenoros, I am Webster Tompkins."

"At last. I thought you'd never get here"

"I . . ."

The figure in the dark sat up and stretched. "Hey, why have we got all the curtains closed? We have work to do." He jumped to his feet and threw back the curtains. "So, Mr. Tompkins is the manager of the whole shebang here. And he needs a little help. So, he comes to Kenoros. Of course. Who else to go to, really? But where was he last week and last month? He couldn't use a little help then, too? I am up here dying of boredom, wishing he would come for something. So, at last, now he is here. Tell me, Mr. Tompkins, how can I help?"

"Um, well, let me just give you a little bit of background."

"No background. Tell me what you want me to do."

Tompkins took a deep breath. "Write a letter to Minister Belok saying that you are personally taking on the process improvement of the people in Aidrivoli-1 and -7. Say that they are already at Level-3 and will soon be at -4. All you need is to be left alone to do this work your own way."

Kenoros considered. "This will cost you dearly," he said.

"Anything."

"A job."

"A job?"

"A job. I can program, debug, design, review, analyze, specify, plan, estimate, and document. I have been doing these things since 1954. I am very, very good at what I do. I am so good that they made me president of this Institute. But I am bored to tears up here. So, give me work."

"Give me the letter and I'll give you the job."

"It's a deal."

"Mr. Kenoros, I think this is going to be the beginning of a beautiful friendship."

"So you see, we have eighteen project teams, working on six different products. For each product, there are three competing teams, each trying to build the product better and faster than the others. What I want you to do, Aristotle, is to rove around those eighteen projects being my technical eyes and ears. I want you to look for whatever should be done to give those projects, each one of them, the best chance of success. I speculate that there is at least one thing you could do for each of them, probably a different thing on each project, that would help it most. I want you to go into that project and teach them how to do that one thing that they need to do."

"A piece of cake."

"Oh?"

"Easy."

"Well, I don't know about that."

"I'm going to go to eighteen different project teams, but I'm going to teach them all the same one thing."

"You know that already?"

"Oh, yes."

"How could you possibly know that?"

"Think about what we are up against here, Webster. All the projects have got impossible or nearly impossible deadlines, as you have told me."

"That's for sure."

"That means we have to save time. But—most people miss this—you can't save time by adding things to do."

"I beg your pardon?"

"The so-called process improvement that occupies Prospero and all his nice people downstairs is mostly additive.

174

They see a less-than-ideal process and they think, 'Add this skill or that procedure and the result will be improved.' That is process improvement as practiced on the first, second, and third floors. Of course, it is useful stuff they add; I don't mean to knock it. But process improvement as practiced here on the fourth floor is different. My theory is that you have to think not about adding but about subtracting."

"I'm fascinated."

"Let's think about one of your projects, Webster. Let's say we're going to start with the Quirk B-Team. We speculate there is one thing that needs to be improved. Okay? Right now, they are not doing that one thing. They're not doing it. Not at all." A pause for effect. "So, what are they doing instead?"

"I don't know. Some other thing."

"They are not loafing."

"Certainly not!"

"So, we have to look at what they are doing and figure out a way to subtract some of it. So, really, what are they doing?"

"I don't know."

"Imagine you got to look every day at all of the people on the project just for a minute at, say, three o'clock. Then you categorize all your findings for all of the people over the whole life of the project. What are most of the people doing most of the time?"

"Debugging, I guess. That seems to be the biggest category of work."

"That's our challenge then. We have to subtract some of that debugging time."

"We have to learn how to do debugging more efficiently?"

"No," Kenoros corrected him. "We have to learn how to do design more efficiently."

෨

175

What Kenoros proposed to teach the eighteen teams was a technique he called Last Minute Implementation, and it scared the hell out of Tompkins. The scheme involved deferring coding as long as possible, spending the middle forty percent or more of the project doing an elaborate, exaggeratedly detailed low-level design, one that would have perfect one-to-one mappings to the eventual code. It was this time spent on design that was supposed to result in a much reduced need for debugging.

In a project that was destined to last a year, for example, no coding would be allowed until the last two months. No testing would be done until well after that. That meant that when testing did begin, virtually every test had to pass. There was almost no time allocated for debugging.

"How can we run a project with no time for debugging?" Tompkins asked incredulously.

"The amount of time spent on debugging is a function of the number of bugs," Kenoros replied, as though he were talking to an idiot.

"Yes, but no time spent on debugging implies that we need to have . . ."

"No bugs. You got it. You're all right; you catch on quick."

"No bugs!"

"That's what you just said."

"How can we have no bugs?!?"

"Look, think about a bug you have just found in a module. Where's the bug?"

"In the module."

"No. It's on the edge of the module. On the very edge. Oh, sure, there are some easy bugs in the middle, totally local to that one module, but those are the ones that get picked up easily in inspections. The real bugs, the ones that take up your time, are the ones that have something to do with the interface between that module and the rest of its world."

"Right. Everybody knows that. So what?"

"So, when you find that bug, during debugging, you are looking at the wrong thing."

"What am I looking at?"Tompkins asked in some exasperation.

"You are looking at the module, at its inside. You are looking into the code."

"What should I be looking at?"

"At the design. The design is where you have all the information about interfaces arrayed in front of you."

"But we *try* to get the defects out when we review the designs. We already do that. Then, an enormous amount of debugging work is required to pull out the defects that slip though anyway."

"Wrong."

"Wrong? Wrong that bugs slip through design review?"

"No, wrong that you really try to get them out during design."

"How can you possibly say that?"

"I know that because I know from these years I have been knocking about that almost nobody ever does a design that gets close enough to the actual code to allow sensible review."

"Well, of course we do design. Everybody does."

"Of course. But they don't do it at design time. At design time, the team puts together a document. There is a bit of hand-waving about 'philosophy' and maybe a file layout or two, and then a proforma review. What they're doing is whatever it takes to get management off their backs so they can get on with the coding. Finally, the manager says okay. You can get on to the next part. The team rejoices and puts the so-called design on a shelf where it is never consulted again. It's pure shelf-ware.

"Then, while they are coding, they do the real design. While they are coding! That is when they decide what the actual modules will be and the actual interfaces. And those are the decisions that escape review."

Mr. Tompkins let out a long breath of air. He hated where this was leading. "Of course, it is true that most low-level design gets done pretty much as you say."

"Of course."

"But that's low-level design."

"What you call high-level design is just hand-waving."

"I don't know. My gut-feel tells me that you're at least mostly right about this, but . . ."

"Sure I'm right. Low-level design is the only thing that is real. The other, the so-called conceptual design, is just for show."

"I think you're right, but suppose you're not? I have to worry about that, don't I? Suppose I do what you're suggesting and you're not right."

Aristotle Kenoros looked at him cheerfully. "Then you're screwed."

"That's what I'm worried about." What a case of managerial nerves he was going to have if he actually did this. He would delay coding, delay and delay and delay, leaving all the closure till the very end. Then, if it didn't come together, if there were a ton of bugs anyway . . .

"Tell me, Aristotle. Who on earth dreamed up this crazy scheme?"

"A guy."

"You?"

"No, not me. Some other guy. I don't know his name. I've been doing this for years, but it was this other guy who dreamed it up."

"We don't even know his name?!?"

"No. He's on the Internet. We exchange messages all the time. He is some kind of oracle, but he doesn't give his name. I can give you his ID, though. Ask him yourself." He scrawled a line on a piece of paper and handed it to Tompkins.

Tompkins shoved the little piece of paper into his pocket and headed home.

From Mr. Tompkins' Journal:

Changing the Way Work Gets Done

    o   There is no way to get projects to perform substantially beyond the norm without making large reductions in the total amount of debugging time.

    o   High-performing projects spend proportionately far less of their time in debugging.

    o   High-performing projects spend proportionately far more of their time in design.

Mr. Tompkins put down his pen. All of that was certainly true enough. Since debugging could take up as much as fifty percent of total project resources, projects that managed to achieve wonders could only do that by "subtracting" most of the need for debugging. That would leave them with a relatively higher proportion of design time. There was no arguing with that.

But it didn't really prove that the converse was true, that increasing design time would necessarily result in fewer bugs. The point that he wanted to write down next in his journal was, "Spending more time on design allows still greater amounts of time to be saved during debugging." But he really didn't know if that were true. That was where a leap of faith was needed. He was going to have to trust Aristotle Kenoros on that one, or go it alone. He still didn't know which it was going to be.

If he did decide to go along with Aristotle's prescription, he was going to have near mutiny in the ranks. Programmers are addicted to debugging. They weren't going to take easily to this radical new scheme. He would have to spend most of his time from now on hearing out their doubts, reassuring them, and asking for their indulgence and trust. That at least was something he suspected he could handle. There was reason to believe he might even have a bit of talent along those lines.

He thought back to Gabriel's startling compliment earlier in the day. Even now, the memory of the ex-General's warm sentiments made him feel good. He could still hear the words, "That's why we follow you, Webster. That's your power." Mr. Tompkins picked up his pen to make one more journal entry:

> o   You can't get people to do anything dif-
>   ferent without caring for them and
>   about them. To get them to change,
>   you have to understand (appreciate)
>   where they're coming from and why.

He closed the journal book and picked up Kenoros's letter. It said precisely what he had asked for. At least he would have Minister Belok off his back for a while. He'd send the letter off to Korsach by courier first thing in the morning.

15

THINK FAST!

ᨏ

$\mathcal{G}$etting Belok off his back was not something to be done once and then forgotten. Kenoros's letter had bought him a few weeks of respite, but then at the end of August, Mr. Tompkins was summoned again. He had a 1 P.M. appointment in Korsach.

On the way up to Belok's office, Mr. T. wandered past the office suite occupied by NNL, hoping that Himself might be back in town. He figured he had a few markers to call in with NNL, maybe enough to have Belok refocused onto some other poor soul somewhere. But the suite was closed up. A hand-lettered note on the door said, "NNL stateside seeing to completion of new house. Back by June 1." June first had been nearly three months ago. Oh, well, nice to see at least that it wasn't just software people who missed their scheduled delivery dates. He looked at his watch and hurried on.

Belok's receptionist led Mr. T. back though several ornate rooms to the minister's secretary. The secretary led him through several more ornate rooms to the minister's aide. And the aide led him back to the minister's office. There, Belok looked up at Tompkins' entry and then, without saying anything, looked back down again at some papers on his desk. He read them thoroughly, frowning as he did. At last he looked up.

"Tompkins, you and your goddamned people are costing me $31.5 million a year. And what the hell am I getting for it?"

"Progress."

"Progress, indeed. Pfeeuuu. What the hell can I do with progress? Can I sell it?"

"Eventually. When the products are delivered, as you said yourself, you're going to be taking in a mint. $31.5 million for a few years doesn't strike me as an unreasonable investment for . . ."

Belok silenced him with a wave of the hand. "You'd better be on schedule with those products. You don't want to be here in front of me if you are not. It would be one damn sorry day for you if you had to stand here and tell me that you weren't going to make the June first delivery for all six products. One very, very sorry day, indeed. I am not kidding about this. Now, are you on schedule?"

"Sure," he said, his voice flat.

"I don't believe you for a second. If I did, I would move up the date. No, you're late, I don't doubt it. But you're going to make up the time, Mr. Tompkins, I assure you, you are. You are going to begin putting the screws on."

"Well, people are already working pretty hard."

Minister Belok's expression turned from unpleasant to poisonous. "You call this working hard? Look at this." He shoved a sheet of paper under Mr. Tompkins' nose.

"Um, what is this? Overtime hours? You're keeping track of how many hours of unpaid overtime my people put in?"

"I certainly am. These are the figures from July. Look at this pitiful portrait of six projects, piddling their time away. Notate: 144 overtime hours; Quirk: 192; PShop: 601. . . . Pitiful! Six hundred measly hours of overtime from our most aggressively scheduled project. That works out to barely ten hours of overtime per person on that project for a whole month! And, across your whole organization, Tompkins, do you know what the average per-person overtime was in July? Do you know what it was?"

"I haven't a clue."

"Less than TWO GODDAMNED HOURS."

"I'm amazed it's that high. Most of the people in Markov's division, for example, don't even have any real work to do."

"Well, give them work, Tompkins. Wake up here. Put them on the PShop project."

"All thirteen hundred and fifty of them?"

"I don't care how many of them there are. Get them working. And I don't mean regular forty-four hour weeks either. I want to see people working sixty hours, seventy hours, eighty hours a week. That's what I want and I am used to getting what I want. Do I make myself clear?"

"Oh, yes. I've never had any trouble understanding you."

"Thank god for small favors. Now, I see that you are pro-ceeding satisfactorily with the process improvement program. I want that kept up. I'm changing the target to Level 4 by the end of the year, and then next year, I am going to . . ."

"Excuse me, Allair, do you know what Level 4 entails? I mean, are you up to speed on the specific skills that people will have to acquire?"

"Details. Don't bother me with details. Your organization will increase by one or two levels a year through the year 2000 or my name is not Belok. Again, do I make myself clear?"

"Quite."

"There is no place for complacency in my operations, Tompkins. I want every man who works for me to . . ."

"Excuse me: 'man and woman.'"

"What?!?"

"There are women, too. Both men and women working here. You remember women . . ."

"Of course, there are women! What the hell are you muttering about? Why are you going on about women? We've got work to do. Products to put out. People to keep in line. What was I saying?"

"You want every man who works for you . . ." Mr. Tompkins prodded him.

"Oh, yes. I want every man who works for me to be reminded *on a daily basis* of his inadequacy. That is what keeps the work going. That is the essence of running a tight ship. Rub their noses in it. I want to see a specific nose-rubbing plan from you, in writing, by the close of business hours today."

"I guess that means by midnight?" Tompkins asked bitterly.

"Right." Minister Belok dismissed that matter with a wave of the hand. "Now, as to your responsibilities in regard to the Summer Games . . ."

"Excuse me?"

"The Summer Games, the year 2000 Olympics. They're to be held here in Korsach."

"What? What are you talking about?"

"The Olympic Games. NNL stopped in at Olympic headquarters in between his other projects and made the deal.

He can be quite persuasive, what with all the resources he can bring to bear. We'll be hosting the Olympics for the year 2000. That is your personal year 2000 problem."

"My problem?"

"You bet it's your problem. I am delegating a major responsibility to you, and it's going to have to be ready in time for the Games." He stood up and began gathering his papers together. The interview was evidently done.

"Now, wait a minute. I only signed up for . . ."

Belok gave him a look of barely contained fury. "Don't you tell me what you signed up for. *I* will tell you what you signed up for."

"He wants us to build an entirely new Air Traffic Control system in time for mid-summer, 2000."

Belinda rolled her eyes.

"He says we're going to have 2.4 million people coming through the Korsach airport during a six-week period. That works out to something like three hundred takeoffs and three hundred landings a day."

"Erghh. How many takeoffs and landings do we have now at Korsach?"

"Six a week. I checked. We don't even have a tower. They bring the planes in with flags."

"So, we need to design and build a tower, acquire and train controllers, build support systems, integrate the whole ball of wax. I don't know if we can possibly do all that. Did you make him understand about the risks?"

"C'mon. My life is too short to spend precious minutes on such a hopeless task. This is Minister Belok, remember? Besides, I've been thinking: Where does *our* interest lie in all this? We have people available in Gabriel's shop—why not put them to work? It's going to spread you and me and Gabriel a bit thin over the next few months while we set the project in motion, but if we do nothing more than start a meaningful Air Traffic Control system project and keep our people working on it for a few years, there will still be benefits. Think of the people working on the project. Think of the experience they'll be getting."

She shrugged agreeably. "I'm game if you are."

"Oh, by the way, Minister Belok also wants us to begin 'turning the screws,' his term. He wants us to get people to work overtime."

"I've been meaning to talk to you about just that. I've been looking at the figures for August. Overtime hours are way up, at least for our eighteen key projects."

"Whatever they are, I doubt they'll be enough to suit Belok."

"No, probably not. Frankly, I'm not too happy with the figures either."

"You think our people should be putting in more overtime?"

"Less."

"Belinda!"

"I know, I know. Good projects always have a certain amount of overtime. But the trend here is not what I consider healthy. Overtime is rising too early, so it can never be sustained. I worry that we're going to peak before the projects are ready for maximum effort and then dribble off as people burn out and leave. That's what my gut tells me."

Mr. Tompkins delivered his usual response to such observations. "We need to capture what your gut is telling you, Belinda, and put it into the form of a model. Let's work on that this afternoon. We'll model as best we can what the effects of overtime and pressure are on production rate, how much people produce as a function of how hard they're pushed."

"I'm game for that, too," Belinda said. "While we're at it, let's put Waldo to work on the same thing."

"Waldo? What's he going to do?"

"Look back over his archaeological data and extract projects conducted under high and low pressure and look at how their production rates were affected. We can use his data to refine and tune our own model."

A few hours later, Belinda had come up with an effects-of-pressure model, but it was so tentative in her mind that she wasn't even willing to key it in to the simulator. Instead, she sketched it on Webster's white board. She drew her own model next to what she proposed was the mental model inside Belok's head:

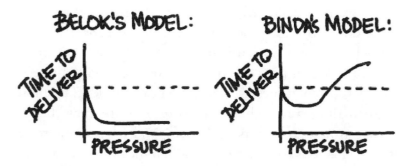

"Let's hypothesize some metric of pressure," she began. "It might include an indication of how the eventual delivery date compares to the date first imposed on the project. And, it might also have some component of overtime built into it. It is a synthetic indicator of Pressure. Call it P.

"Now, my model says that increasing P initially gives you a pretty big hit of productivity. People in our business like pressure and they respond to it, at least to a bit of it. They knuckle down and really tear into the work. My model says that moderate amounts of pressure might give you a twenty-five percent improvement in productivity and even a twenty-five percent decrease in total time to deliver. But that's only true if you apply the pressure moderately. A little more pressure, and the curve flattens out—that pressure does no good at all. And then a little more, and you start to lose ground. People tire out, they burn out, they lose heart. More still and you begin to lose them; if you really turn the screws, people leave in droves and the project goes down the toilet."

She turned her attention next to what she presumed was Belok's model. "Here we see an alternative view. This is the view of someone who is a 'management is just kicking ass' kind of manager, a real fascist. He believes that pressure gives you a *huge* improvement in work accomplished, maybe halving the time to get the project done, or reducing it by even more than half. More pressure than that, the model asserts, does no good—people just have no capacity to go faster—but it does no harm either. Since you can't know where the knee of the curve is, you should err on the side of applying too much pressure, rather than too little. The more you turn the screws, the more sure you are that they're working as hard as they possibly can. You apply pressure by setting a ludicrous date, and even though they miss the date by a year or more, you have kept them working at the maximum possible productive rate."

"You and Minister Belok seem to agree only on the first two percent of the curve."

"Nobody can be one hundred percent wrong, not even Belok."

Webster stared at Belok's curve uncomfortably. No wonder the man behaved the way he did, if that was really what he believed. "He seems to think that developers only work hard under punishing pressure; the earlier you want the product, the more punishment you need to apply."

"Punishment . . ." Belinda stumbled backward, away from the board. She sat down abruptly, her face slightly pale. She stared up at the graph for a long moment, and finally said, "Ugh."

"What?"

"Punishment. That is the graph of a child abuser, Webster. That is an abusive parent. Instead of pressure, let P stand for punishment. . . ." She went back to the Belok graph and relabeled the axes. "And on the vertical, instead of Time to Deliver, we'll show Misbehavior.

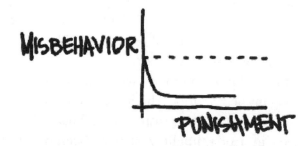

"That's the view of the world that drives an abusive don't-spare-the-rod parent," Belinda continued. "Don't you see? The more and harder the kid is spanked, the less and less he misbehaves. Until finally, extra punishment doesn't help anymore; the kid is maxed out. But the extra punishment, no matter how much, doesn't do any real harm either. So the parent reasons: 'Might as well lay it on hard.' Ugh."

Mr. T. went over to the board and erased the tail of the curve. Then he redrew it rising up sharply. He could feel the tension beginning to drain out of Belinda as he did. "Over-punished kids don't behave better," he told her gently. "They behave worse, even much worse."

"Of course. They just learn to hide it better."

"Of course."

"Erase the damn thing, Webster. It's too depressing."

He erased the Belok graph.

Belinda looked a bit drawn still. He crossed over and took the chair by her side. Time to lighten things up a bit. "Speaking of hiding bad behavior, Seafood, my old pussycat, does that. He knows he is not allowed to sharpen his claws on the Oriental rug. But he does. Only, when he does it, because he knows it's naughty, he lays his ears back. And he keeps an eye on me in case I might yell at him or throw the paper."

She remained serious. "That's exactly how an overpunished kid will act. He knows what's bad, but has no compunction about doing it. No moral sense at all. His only concern is how to get away with it."

The cat story had not led exactly where he'd wanted. "Of course, I never punished Seafood," he hastened to explain.

Belinda smiled a bit. "No. I suspect not. That behavior in a child, or even in a dog, might well have been a clue that someone had overpunished him in the past. But cats are different. Cats are natural cynics."

Once Waldo had gone through his archaeological data on project pressure and put his findings on OHP acetates, he set up a projector in the office and waited until Webster and Belinda had made themselves comfortable. Then he began to deliver his findings.

"We took fourteen projects out of our database," he told them. "Remember, these are all projects completed by our staff here at Aidrivoli over the last three or four years. We had already sized the products they built and expressed the result in function points. Then, we plotted the actual delivery time for each project, and derived a trend line showing the normal calendar time it takes to deliver products of any given size. The result looked like this," Waldo said.

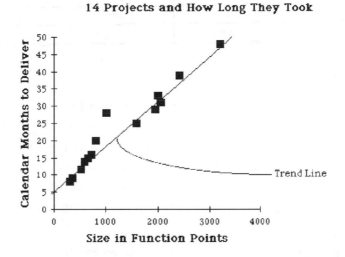

"Next," Waldo continued, "we used the trend line to determine the normal expected delivery time for each of the fourteen projects. We have now studied more than thirty projects, so you might wonder why we chose these particular fourteen to show you. Well, they were the ones that had left a good audit trail behind them. We could reconstruct, for example, the entire scheduling history for each of them, including initial published delivery date and each subsequent update. We used this to compute what the average expected delivery time was over the life of the project. We did that for each of the fourteen. Here are a few of the results." He showed them the next slide.

PROJECT NUMBER	COMPUTED NOMINAL DELIVERY TIME	AVG. EXPECTED DELIVERY TIME (PUBLISHED)	RATIO (Nominal/Expected)
9401	18 months	14 months	1.28
9404	9 months	10 months	1.11
9405	7 months	7 months	1.00
9408	34 months	22 months	1.54
9501	29 months	12 months	2.41

"You can probably see exactly where I'm going now. We reasoned the Nominal/Expected made a good metric of Pressure. You asked us to investigate the effects of pressure, so we looked at the actual performance of the fourteen projects as a function of their respective values of Nominal/Expected." He went on to the next slide. "This is what we came up with."

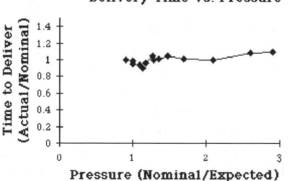

192

"Wait a minute, it's practically flat," Mr. Tompkins exclaimed.

"Right. More or less, there is no effect of pressure."

"This is crazy," Belinda said. She walked to the projector and turned it ninety degrees so that it cast its image on the white board rather than on the blank wall. Then, she lined it up so Waldo's graph was almost precisely overlaid on her own:

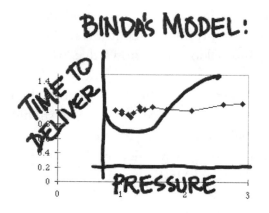

"Two questions here," she went on. "On the left-hand part of the graph, why don't we get more of a productivity hit from reasonable increases in pressure? And, over here on the right side, why don't people continue to leave as the pressure is built up more and more?"

A light knock at the door and Mrs. Beerzig showed in Gabriel Markov and Aristotle Kenoros.

Belinda addressed Kenoros directly: "What do you think, Aristotle? Why don't people leave when pressure is really punishing and unrealistic? Oh, some people obviously do, but then it looks like there is a core that stays on, no matter how bad it gets. Why?"

"Cynical," he said. "Programmers are naturally cynical."

"Like cats," Mr. Tompkins threw in.

"Sure, like cats. Look, you've been there yourself, Belinda. Somebody gives you an unrealistic date, what's your response? 'Oh, well. Such is life.' Then they make it still more unrealistic: 'Ho hum. So what else is new?' Am I right?"

She shrugged agreeably, "Maybe so. Programmers and cats," and then she pointed to Waldo's graph. "But what sense do you make of Zone 1? I would have thought we'd get at least some effect from turning on a moderate amount of pressure. Maybe twenty-five percent, or at the very least fifteen percent. But Waldo's data shows that we're getting next to nothing."

"Six percent at the best," Waldo told them. "There is some noise in the data, of course. So, you should think of it as six percent plus or minus maybe three."

"Almost nothing. I wonder why."

"I wonder why," Mr. T. repeated.

A long silence.

"So, ask the Oracle," Kenoros said.

As soon as the Internet message had been sent, Mr. T. composed a filter command to sound a beep at his workstation as soon as any reply came in with the word "oracle" in its From line. He looked at his watch. "I don't imagine we'll have an answer before tomorrow. Too bad. I'm fascinated to know what he might suggest." He hit Return to put the filter in place. There was an immediate beep.

"Hello, what's this? Hey, he has already answered."

"Not just your run-of-the-mill Oracle," Kenoros observed.

They gathered around the screen. The message was mostly header. In fact, the guts of the Oracle's reply was only a single line:

```
Date: 1 September 07:55:42 -0400
From: The Oracle <oracle@lister.com>
MIME-Version: 1.0
To: webster@morovia.com
Subject: Re: Pressure and Productivity

On 1 September you wrote:
> Why does the effect of pressure on programmers
> max out after only 6% productivity gain?

My answer:

    PEOPLE UNDER PRESSURE DON'T THINK FASTER.

Best regards,

    The Oracle
```

They went back over to the sitting area near the windows and plunked themselves down—Belinda, Webster, Aristotle, Gabriel, and Waldo. There was a long silence. Finally, Aristotle said again, "Not your run-of-the-mill Oracle." Then another long pause.

Webster broke the silence: "What do you call a guy who tells you something you should have known a hundred years ago, but didn't."

"A genius," Belinda offered. The others nodded.

"Our whole theory of pressure is kaput," Gabriel said. "Everybody's whole theory of pressure . . ."

"Which is," Belinda interrupted, "the standard prevailing theory of productivity improvement. We all talk a good game about the things that might increase productivity. But then, when we need it, what do we really do? We apply pressure. That is the one-trick pony used by almost all managers."

"Management's one-trick pony." Gabriel was smiling his wide, gold-toothed smile. "No wonder we managers are so well paid."

Mr. T. was still struggling to digest the meaning of the Oracle's message. "Look, if people don't think any faster under pressure—and who could deny it?—then the only effect that's left is that people work longer hours. No wonder we don't see larger productivity gains. Even fifteen percent would imply a continuing overtime rate of six or seven hours a week, week in and week out, across the whole team. That's an enormous amount of overtime. Probably too much to be practical. And even that doesn't give us a huge hit. Waldo, why are you shaking your head?"

"Because we looked at the effects of overtime. We thought we should factor overtime into our pressure metric, but when we looked for the impact of overtime hours, we couldn't find it at all."

"What?"

"We did a very simple analysis. We just compared all the projects in our database where there was overtime, paid or unpaid, against those where there wasn't. We calculated production rates in function points per person-month. The projects with no overtime had a slightly higher production rate. Not much, only a few percentage points."

Gabriel stopped him. "Wait a minute, Waldo. Surely you mean the *hourly* production rates were the same, not the monthly production rates. And since the overtime workers were putting in more of those hours, all at the same value, their total production over the month would be increased by the added number of hours. No?"

"No. The people who worked 190 hours in a month did slightly more total work than those who worked 200, and more still than those who did 210 or 220. I'm sorry, I know these data are not what you were expecting. But we checked and rechecked."

"C'mon people," Aristotle told them. "This is not news. You all knew it in your guts. Extended overtime is a productivity-reduction technique."

They all thought about that. "I can believe it," Belinda said at last. "We all know that overtime has its negatives: burnout, lost energy, increased error rate . . ."

"Wasted time during the normal workday," Aristotle added.

"Why that?"

"Because people convince themselves it's okay to have lots of meetings and to permit interruptions because they expect to make it up in the evening hours."

"I suppose. If you told them that no overtime hours were permitted, they'd have to clean up their act."

"Sure."

"So, add that to the list of negatives. What Waldo's numbers are telling us is that the negatives more than offset the extra work people do during overtime hours. As Aristotle said, this is something we've all considered at one time or another."

"So, what is a manager supposed to do?" Mr. Tompkins asked them, a slight tremor in his voice.

"The other stuff," Belinda replied. "The hard stuff: hiring, motivation, team dynamics, keeping good people on board, working inefficiencies out of the methods, meeting reduction, lightened overhead, trimming down excess documentation."

Mr. Tompkins was still aghast. "If overtime is really counterproductive, you're telling me we ought to be sending people home at night?"

"We should. In fact, I do."

"Belinda? You? You actually turn them out?"

"I do. I never used to, but since my own episode of burnout, I am reformed. I see people staying too late and I toss them out. I tell them I'm turning off the lights in ten minutes. And I do it, too. No kidding. I've begun to think that if someone had had the good sense to send me home occasionally when I was putting in so many extra hours, I might still be a working woman today."

"In case you haven't noticed, Belinda," Gabriel told her, "you *are* a working woman again. You have been in at eight each day this week and stayed all day."

"Aha," Mr. T. exclaimed. "And it is now . . . five thirty! You are working overtime, young lady. And I, caring manager that I am, am giving you the homeward shove. Off you go." He jerked his finger toward the door.

"Thank you, Webster. That's sweet. But I'm having too much fun to go now."

"Out," he said firmly. "Too much fun is no excuse. That's what they're all telling themselves, the ones that you boot out at night."

She laughed easily. "So true," she said, standing and gathering her notes. "Oh well, so long everybody."

"Back to your shopping cart," Webster added, maliciously.

She stuck out her tongue at him. "No, I've rather had it with my shopping cart. Think I'll go back to the Residence and soak in a nice long bath."

"The rest of you out, as well," Mr. T. told them. "Home. Everybody goes home. Me, too. In fact, I think I will pick up my trunks and go down to the shore for a swim. Lights off in ten minutes."

He would, too. He would be gone in ten minutes. As soon as the others had left, he picked up his pen and journal to make a few quick notes.

From Mr. Tompkins' Journal:

The Effects of Pressure

o   People under pressure don't think any faster.

o   Extended overtime is a productivity-reduction tactic.

o   Short bursts of pressure and even overtime may be a useful tactic as they focus people and increase the sense that the work is important, but extended pressure is always a mistake.

o   Perhaps managers make so much use of pressure because they don't know what else to do, or are daunted by how difficult the alternatives are.

o   Terrible suspicion: The real reason for use of pressure and overtime may be to make everyone look better when the project fails.

16

Planning for the
Summer Games

༄

*A*fter his breakfast, Seafood liked to go out onto the terrace and from there along the narrow catwalk around to the far side of the building where Lahksa always left her own terrace doors open for him when she was in town. Now, of course, her suite was closed up tight, as it had been since early April when Belok first arrived on the scene. Within a few moments, Seafood was back. He looked up accusingly at Mr. Tompkins and gave a long complaining meow.

"I know, I know. I miss her, too. And I don't know when she'll be back."

There was some news of Lahksa that day, though very indirect. When Mr. Tompkins arrived at the office, he found a huge pile of documentation in black, loose-leaf notebooks waiting for him. There was an accompanying note on the engraved stationery of the Ministry of Internal Affairs. The handwriting was angular and almost, but not quite, illegible. The note said: "I had Hoolihan steal this from the States.

With a head start like this, there will be no excuse for missing the summer year 2000 deadline." And it was signed with a flourish, "Belok."

Also waiting for him was Aristotle Kenoros. He had one of the black notebooks open on his lap. He looked up. "Specifications from the FAA NASPlan contracts," he told him.

Tompkins groaned. "Not the American NASPlan specs. All those projects ended up in litigation."

"Right. These are court-impounded documents. They've got court seals all over them."

"If Belok really wanted to help us, he might have stolen the specs from the French system, or even the Spanish system. At least those projects produced results. But these . . ."

"The good news: We've got a full set. I checked. There is a spec here for each and every component. I suppose there is a possibility that projects that went on to be a complete debacle still managed to produce decent specifications along the way. There is a possibility of that."

"I guess."

"About one in a million, but it's still a possibility."

"Oh, well, I suppose even grossly imperfect specifications might be better than nothing. I should think that even a competent list of components would be of some use. I'm counting on you to lend us a hand on this Air Traffic Control project as well, Aristotle. I mean, later, when they get into the design activity. By that time, you should be off the hook with the others."

"Oh, sure. Glad to help. Very amusing work, juggling airplanes in the air. A nice project for no deadline."

"But of course there is a deadline. A fixed deadline and a very aggressive one."

"Of course. I just thought that there might be, someplace on earth, a project where the goal is quality rather than time. I guess not, though. Guess I was wrong. You can see why I was thinking that, though. I mean, an Air Traffic Control system, you might think that would be a natural. You might think people would be saying, 'Hey, take your time, folks, no hurry. Really, just get it right. Take whatever time is needed.'"

"Fat chance."

"I guess I am a hopeless idealist."

"We have got an excellent team for you to work with, however. I said the magic words 'Air Traffic Control' to Gabriel, and he came up with seven people who had worked on the Spanish system. I took it as an omen and hired them on. And they're really good."

"More good news. And now the bad news. I have some bad news for you. Not from the ATC project, but from one of the others. You've got trouble."

"What else is new?"

"This is new trouble. PMill-A. You've got an angry manager."

"I have?"

"Abusive. Loud and abusive. Angry and abusive. People are starting to be afraid of him."

PMill-A was run by Osmun Gradish, a pleasant, soft-spoken, young manager. It was hard to imagine him being abusive. "I'll stop by and talk to him in the afternoon," Mr. Tompkins said. "In the meantime, give me a hand with these books, please, Aristotle. We'll drop them off downstairs where the ATC team lives. I'm determined to be entirely optimistic about these specs. Think positively; we have to. If these specs don't give us some advantage, then the summer of 2000 is going to be a major fiasco."

Between the two of them, they were just barely able to carry all the black notebooks. Mr. Tompkins began scooping them up and loading them into Aristotle's outstretched arms, and then into his own until there was only one notebook left. Mr. T. bent down and managed to slip the last one under his arm. "Why are we doing this?" he wondered out loud to Kenoros. "Why are we taking on all this extra work for the ATC system? We were overloaded before Belok ever mentioned this new wrinkle."

Kenoros's voice came out muffled from behind the pile of black notebooks. "We take on too much," the voice said, "because we are terrified of too little."

Osmun Gradish was still pleasant-seeming and still soft-spoken. But there were some strain lines around the man's mouth. At first, that was all that was evident. Tompkins invited himself to sit in on the weekly staff meeting for the PMill-A project. Also present was the PMill product manager, Melissa Alber, Gradish's boss. After the meeting, Mr. T. took a coffee with Ms. Alber out on the patio in front of Aidrivoli-1.

"So, what's up with PMill A?"

"Oh, Webster. Bad stuff. Osmun is not responding well to the stress."

Mr. T. shook his head. "I don't blame him. Our response to having the A-Teams overstaffed and overpressured was to set up B- and C-Teams. Now, when I'm feeling down at all, I just stop by Notate-C or PShop-C or QuickerStill-B or almost any of the others."

"Me, too."

"The A-Team managers don't have that luxury. We're treating them like sacrificial pawns, and it's kind of hard on the pawns."

"It is."

"How bad is it? Tell me."

"He can be extremely cutting," Melissa said. "Sometimes he yells. His face turns red. He calls people down in front of the others."

"Is there something else bothering him, do you think? Something besides the pressure?"

"He won't talk, but I don't think so, Webster. You know what he told me? He told me that Quirk-A is going to finish on time. He thinks he might be the only one late. I think that's what's getting to him."

"Should I talk to him?"

"Maybe later. Let me work with him a bit more."

"As you like."

"Oh, there are some transfer requests starting to come in. People are asking to be switched off PMill-A. I don't know exactly how to . . ."

"Let me think about it a bit."

"You know, Webster, you say that the A projects are sacrificial pawns. But we shouldn't think of them that way. We should think of them as training opportunities. Even if the work is frustrating and the deadlines hopeless, the team is learning to work together. A healthy and well-jelled PMill A-Team would be a real asset when the next big assignment comes along."

"I know. I'm thinking of the Air Traffic Control project. When that moves into implementation, we're going to need functioning work groups to apply to it. Osmun's team is not ideal—at least, their experience isn't the most germane—but there will be plenty of work they can do. They could be a real asset, as you say."

"They will if they ever do jell as a team. I don't need to tell you that groups of developers, when they don't feel appreciated, don't tend to form into a particularly strong team. Right now, I wouldn't hold out great hopes for PMill-A. . . ."

Belinda had been working for the past few days with the Air Traffic Control project group. Now she had them all focused on one of the recently pinched FAA specifications, the one covering the Radio Governance System. They were still a long way from sure about how elaborate the Morovian ATC system would be, but it would clearly have to tie into radio contact with the planes, so the RGS component, at the very least, was a requirement. Webster had taken just three hours to read through the RGS spec before joining the group at day's end.

"Hi, Boss." Belinda was looking particularly cheerful. He noticed that the rest of the group was subdued. Even the team leader, Gulliver Menendez, was not wearing his usual enthusiastic expression. In fact, he seemed a bit sheepish.

"Well, here's the question of the day, Webster: What do you think of the spec?" Belinda was grinning.

Mr. T. found himself slightly on the defensive. The truth was, he hadn't understood a word of what he'd read. "Well, I really only had a couple of hours to . . ."

"That's okay. Tell us your take after the first couple of hours of reading."

"Well, that is to say, of course, that basically, this spec is basically, how shall I say it?"

"How indeed?"

"Of course, there is just no question that the system being specified here is pretty complex. But having said that, you

know, the spec does seem to come to grips with the complexity, and I just think that, I'd have to say, that though I may
need a few more hours . . ."

"In other words, you didn't understand squat. Am I right?"

"Uh, more or less. You see, I think this is the kind of specification that one has to read pretty hard, and if you haven't
done that, well, of course, then you still haven't gotten to see
its thread or its inner logic. Is that pretty much what you guys
have all concluded?"

Gulliver nodded glumly. "That was more or less what we
had concluded, the nine of us. Belinda, on the other hand,
had an entirely different take on it."

"Ah. And what is Belinda's take on it, if I may ask?"

She was looking vastly amused. "It's gibberish, Webster.
Front-to-back gibberish. All of every page is pure gibberish."

"Well, I don't know that I would say that. After all, this
spec was written by some pretty high-powered people."

"Oh, yes. It was."

"And reviewed and accepted by the FAA."

"Yup. The spec writers wrote gibberish, the reviewers
read gibberish, and the FAA accepted gibberish."

He was annoyed by her smugness. "I don't see how you
can possibly say that. I mean, after all, this spec kicked off a
project that went on to spend a hundred million dollars or
more in development."

"One hundred sixty million dollars. I looked it up."

"Well, there you are. Nobody's going to spend that much
implementing a spec that nobody understands."

"No? Well, let me ask a test question. You read the spec,
for, let's say, two hours."

"Three, actually."

"So, you must have gotten through it at least once."

"At a *very* cursory level, yes. And, then I went back, still at a cursory level, and breezed through it again."

"Okay. Tell me, is there a keyboard connected to the system?"

"Um." Mr. T. had that panicky feeling you get in a college exam when you realize you haven't read a key chapter of the text and all the questions are on that chapter. "Um, I didn't exactly notice that. Perhaps it was in one of the parts that I read in a particularly cursory way."

She turned to the others. "You guys have been working on this all day, right? Tell me, did anybody notice if there is a keyboard connected to the system?"

They all shrugged.

"Good question," Gulliver answered.

"So, we don't know that," Mr. Tompkins conceded. "That is an outstanding question. There are always questions about system specifications. You haven't proved the spec is totally incoherent, only that it is imperfect. We could hardly expect perfection."

"Webster, think about what it is that I asked you. We're looking at a multiprocessor hardware/software system that has hundreds of configuration variables in its database. . . ."

"There, now. You see, we all got that out of the spec. There is both hardware and software, and there is a database— and it's full of configuration data of some sort. So, we definitely got something from the spec. It's not total gibberish."

"But where do they come from, those configuration variables?"

"Excuse me?"

"How do they get there?"

"Well, I suppose they get there from operator input; in which case, we would have to suppose there is an input device at the console. Or, maybe they are loaded at initialization time along with the software. Or, maybe they come from one of the upstream systems. Or, maybe the software actually constructs the configuration database on the fly by probing the hardware to see how it's connected."

"Right. Those are four possibilities. The system could be one of four totally different systems, depending on which one of the four is selected. But none of the four is selected. The spec simply doesn't commit itself as to where the data comes from. Or, for that matter, as to what configuration data specifically has to be included in the database. While we're at it, it doesn't ever say explicitly what the rules are for reconfiguration or whether the system can reconfigure on the fly or how the radio frequencies are loaded or reassigned or how messages are switched or whether there are multi-destination connections or . . ."

"Or anything," Gulliver nodded. "She's right, Webster. The spec doesn't specify anything. It's three-hundred pages of vague implications."

He knew he wanted to write something about the spec of "implications" in his journal, but what? Now that he'd spent another hour on the document, he could see that Belinda was quite right. As a specification, it was quite useless; the document simply refused to commit itself on any subject. But why had it been written that way? Was it such rocket science to write a system specification? And why had no one seen through its emptiness, none of his people except Belinda, and no one on the American FAA development project that had tried to implement RGS? Even he had been infinitely willing to give it the benefit of the doubt. Why was that? He'd seen other hopelessly vague specifications in his day, each one of them a milestone on a project that subsequently failed. Why did they get written that way, and why did they get accepted, and why did no one ever see through them? It made a kind of mystery story: The Puzzle of the Vague Specification.

On these still-warm autumn evenings, he knew that Belinda often swam laps at the Residence pool before supper. He took a chance on finding her there. Sure enough, there she was, moving smoothly through the water. Mr. Tompkins sat himself down on one of the recliners and watched for a moment, admiring her skillful somersault turns at each wall and all that boundless energy. As soon as she came out, he would seek her counsel on the vague specification matter. While waiting, he opened his journal to the first blank page and began to write some comments about Osmun and the curious way he had begun to emulate exactly the behavior that Belok had used to terrify him.

From Mr. Tompkins' Journal:

The Angry Manager

o   Anger and contempt in management are contagious. When upper management is abusive, lower management mimics the same behavior (much like abused children who go on to become abusive parents).

o   Managerial contempt is supposed to act as a goad to get people to invest more in their performance. It is the most frequent "stick" of carrot-and-stick management. But where is the

evidence that contempt has ever
caused anyone to perform better?

o   A manager's use of contempt to goad
workers is more a sign of the manager's inadequacy than of the workers'.

What he still didn't know was why angry managers were
angry. Why did they choose to display that particular emotion? Belok, for example, seemed monotonously furious, but
why? Another puzzle. Mr. Tompkins had set out to write a
journal of conclusions about how management works and
doesn't work, but now he was wondering if he shouldn't
instead have written a book of puzzles. There were certainly
more of them.

Soon Belinda was out of the pool and beside him, tow-
eling off. "Hi, Boss. What's up?"

"You're dripping on my leg."

"Sorry."

"I'm puzzling over puzzles, since you ask. Want to puzzle
with me for a while?"

"Sure." Belinda spread out her towel on the recliner
beside his and draped herself over it. "What's the puzzle of
the day?"

He laughed, somewhat bitterly. "Would that there were
only one. Let's take on the matter of the vague specification,
just for starters. I have two questions: Why was the spec
written that way? and, Why didn't anyone notice? Anyone but
you, that is? Why were the rest of us determined to believe
that it did specify a system, and that if we didn't understand it,
it was our problem, not its?"

"That's a tough one. Let me peel off a slightly easier piece
of it, though, one that I think I can answer: Why didn't any of

our highly competent team blow the whistle and say, 'This spec sucks'? If the spec had been a little less awful, we'd say they were just determined to make up for its inadequacies by trying harder. That would be a good, professional attitude. But the RGS specification is an abomination. In a course on specification writing, it would get an immediate F. Why didn't they tell us that?"

"Okay, why?"

"If any one of them were teaching the specification course, he or she would know enough to assign the F. But they didn't feel themselves to be in a judging position. Rather, they were in a competing position."

"Competing with the spec?"

"Competing with each other. I have a theory, Webster, that all of us have a few secret inner doubts about our mental capacities. I speculate that we are an entire race of creatures that have this strange characteristic: Each of us secretly believes he or she is of below-average intelligence compared to the others, and has to make up for it by trying harder. As we read through a horrible morass of complexity like the RGS spec, our secret doubt makes us believe that all the others who are reading it are understanding what they read. Now, the boss comes along and asks, 'How goes the spec reading? Are you getting along okay?' Panic. What do you say? You cover. You say, 'Oh, fine, Boss. I mean, sure, it's complicated, of course, but given a bit of time . . .' And all the others are doing the same thing."

"So, nobody blows the whistle."

"I learned this a long time ago, Webster. Nobody will ever tell you that the spec is lousy. People may grumble that the writing isn't as clear as it could be, but they won't tell you what you really need to know: That it isn't a specification at all; it simply doesn't do any of the things that a specification needs to do. It doesn't specify."

"So, how did you see through it? Don't you have inner doubts?"

"You're asking this of a woman who lives under a palm tree? Get serious. Sure I have inner doubts, as much as anyone else. But I've been burned on this one before. I know some specifications are utter rot, and I have schooled myself to see through them. I have a few mechanical rules, for example."

"Please share. I'd love to know your rules."

"Well, I'll give you one of them—in the form of a definition: A specification is a statement of how a system—a set of planned responses—will react to events in the world immediately outside its borders. There are two parts to every spec: first, a set of policies showing how the system's responses depend on events; and second, a set of inputs and outputs by which the events and responses are moved across the system boundary. No matter how complex the system is, the second of these parts is pretty simple: All of the inputs and outputs are listable data and control flows. They can each be named or numbered. They can be sized—by the number of data elements in a flow, for example. And they can be counted."

"You're saying that if the system is really complicated, all the complexity is in the policy."

"It is. The policy governing how inputs get transformed into outputs can be arbitrarily complex. But inputs and outputs are just that: inputs and outputs. You may never understand the transformations, but if a spec is worth anything at all, it has to tell you exactly what the boundary characteristic is. If it doesn't have at least a count of inputs and outputs, the spec gets an F. It isn't a spec at all."

"So, every spec has to have, at the very least, a complete census of inputs and outputs, maybe give each one a name and show what its composition is."

"At least. The spec may still not get an A, but at least it's not a nonstarter like the RGS spec was."

He pondered that. "Well, maybe that explains what happened on the RGS project. There was a really extraordinarily complicated transformation policy, and the specification writers got so bogged down trying to describe it that they just forgot to do the relatively easy part. In that case, we could conclude that the system was so complex that maybe it just couldn't be specified. And that's the reason the spec was a failure."

"I don't think so. There was something else going on. I'll give you my theory on that as well. But first, I point out that no matter how complex the policy is, you can specify most of the system with nothing more than the census of inputs and outputs. I want you to imagine an alternate RGS specification. Imagine one of merely twenty pages. It has a complete and elaborate census of inputs and outputs, each one named and defined down to the data-element level. Where the inputs and outputs have control significance, there may be a description of the signals, maybe even including voltage levels, pulse durations, whatever it takes. That's all part of your census. Let's say the census lists twenty kinds of input and thirty kinds of output. Now, for the transformation section, we have a simple one-sentence statement. It says, 'The twenty inputs and thirty outputs are related in the sorts of ways that you might expect these kinds of inputs and outputs to be related.' How's that for a spec?"

"Belinda, that's a horrible spec! That's about as ambiguous as it could be."

"It is in its description of the policy for transformation. But it's clear and complete in its description of inputs and outputs. In other words, the easy part is done to perfection, and only the hard part is lousy."

"So, what's your point?"

"My point is that such a spec, for all its imperfection, would have allowed the RGS project to proceed. It might have kept it out of litigation. The developers would have seen where the holes were. They would have written down all their assumptions about what they assumed the transformation policy would have to be. And they would have taken these back to the controllers and the administrators and gotten verification or correction. The twenty-page spec I've just described to you would have been a truly awful spec, but it would have been infinitely better than the spec the FAA produced."

He didn't doubt that. But now that she'd said that, it opened more new questions than it answered. "Why do you suppose they wrote the spec that way? Why did they make it so ambiguous?"

She laughed. "I finally know the answer to that. It wasn't easy to understand at first, but once I caught on to the general rule, the specific instances of it have always been easy to spot."

"The 'general rule' is . . . ?"

"Ambiguity implies unresolved conflict."

"Conflict?"

"Conflict. Systems are negotiated between interested parties: owners, users, stakeholders, builders, operators, administrators. On a complex system like RGS, there may be dozens of different kinds of interested parties. Sometimes, the parties don't agree. They're in conflict. Example: Imagine one party to the RGS negotiation that wants initialization variables to be controlled directly by the system operator, while another party wants them to be controlled centrally."

"Ah. They're in conflict. And if the conflict is unresolvable . . . ?"

"The spec has to be ambiguous. It can't commit itself on whether there is a keyboard to facilitate direct entry by the operator, for example. It can't state exactly what the configuration variables are. Each unambiguous statement on the subject would be a red flag to one or more of the parties, because it can only be unambiguous by choosing among their conflicting needs to own the data."

"The spec writers *could* write an unambiguous spec, but . . ."

"They would have to commit themselves, to come down on one side or the other of the conflict, and then they would have been eaten alive by the other side."

"How depressing. Instead of resolving the conflict, they paper it over with ambiguity."

"It happens all the time. Now when I come across anything unclear in a specification, I go nosing around for conflict. I always find it. I've become convinced that it's pretty trivial to make an unambiguous statement of anything. When we fail to do it, it's not our expression skills that need to be fixed, but our conflict-resolution skills."

Mr. T. stared off toward the hills and the sky just above them where a few dim stars were starting to appear. He let his thoughts take him where they would.

After a while Belinda asked, "How about some dinner, Boss?"

"You go on in, Belinda. Get changed. I'll meet you in the dining room."

She gathered her things and headed into the Residence. Mr. Tompkins picked up his journal and began to write again.

Ambiguous Specification

o   Ambiguity in a specification is a sign of unresolved conflict among the various system stakeholders.

o   A specification that doesn't contain a complete census of inputs and outputs is a nonstarter; it simply doesn't begin to specify.

o   Nobody will tell you if a specification is lousy. People are inclined to blame themselves rather than it.

17

THE GURU OF CONFLICT RESOLUTION

৵

"$\mathcal{W}$e don't know jack about conflict resolution," Mr. Tompkins was telling the assembled management dream team. "And here, I'm not just talking about the people in this room, but about our whole industry. We have skills of system design, system implementation, documentation, testing, quality assurance, and all that. But we have no conflict-resolution skills."

"It must be because there is no conflict in our business," Aristotle Kenoros offered, dryly.

"Sure," Belinda laughed. "None at all. It's only everywhere you look. Between us and Belok, between us and the Institute, between us and at least some of the teams, between the teams, within the teams. And that's just here at Aidrivoli, on this one small campus. Webster and I have been speculating that the FAA projects, the ones our Air Traffic Control specifications were taken from, were rife with conflict at all levels."

"Conflict is everywhere in our business," Mr. Tompkins went on. "You can't install a system of any magnitude at all without encountering some serious conflict. There are always many parties to the work, and thus many conflicted interests. Conflict is everywhere in our business, but our command of the subject of conflict is virtually nil."

"I, of course, know something about *armed* conflict," Gabriel observed.

"Well, that's a bit different, Gabriel. Besides, you only know about that from your past life, not from being a software development manager."

"True enough," the ex-General agreed amiably.

Mr. Tompkins made his pitch, "What I want to suggest is that we set out to become experts on conflict resolution. At the very least, we need to find a good book on the subject, or a seminar, or a consultant to guide us. Who is the international expert on conflict resolution in our field?"

A long pause followed as they considered the question. Finally, Gabriel spoke up. "Webster, my friend. I don't know who the international expert is, but how about a very local expert? How about a man who is a conflict magician? I know such a man. He is a former kindergarten teacher."

"Now, that is where some serious conflict resolution skills might come from," Belinda observed.

Gabriel was nodding enthusiastically. "In Morovia, those heroic souls who teach in kindergarten are called 'Maestro.' The man I would propose to you is Maestro Diyeniar. He is a programmer on my staff. When you add him to a team, problems tend to go away. He has never been very highly esteemed by his management, except myself, since nobody understands what he does. He may not understand it himself. His role seems to be catalytic. It took me a long time to understand what a great asset the man is."

"Can he teach us conflict resolution, Gabriel?"

The ex-General looked a bit dubious. "I don't think so, Belinda. I know he can *do* conflict resolution, but I doubt he can tell us exactly what he does. Like most people with a natural skill, what he does is not very apparent, even to him. But still, he can be invaluable. Would you have use of such a person, Webster? What would you do with him?"

"A catalytic personality," Mr. Tompkins mused. "If you can spare him, Gabriel, I will plunk him down in the PMill-A project and keep my fingers crossed. Maybe he can make some of that very unhappy team's problems go away."

"Done. I will arrange it later this morning."

Mr. Tompkins made a note on his desk pad. "We still need someone to guide us, though. Think, people, who is the expert? Who is the Guru of Conflict Resolution in our field?" He looked around the room to Aristotle, Belinda, and Gabriel.

After a long moment, Aristotle spoke up. "There is a guy."

"Not the Oracle again?"

"No, another guy. I forget his name. But he is the expert on conflict resolution for systems projects. He also does some metrics. He is the inventor of the 'Everybody Wins' circular methodology."

"Of course!" Belinda exclaimed. "He's our man."

"And who would that be?" Mr. Tompkins prodded her.

"Dr. Larry Boheme."

That very evening, Mr. Tompkins flew to London to catch the last day of Larry Boheme's two-day tutorial on the "Everybody Wins" circular methodology. A tall, soft-spoken, and somewhat shy man, Dr. Boheme seemed genuinely pleased when Mr. T. invited him out after the seminar for a beer in a nearby pub. They found themselves a table away from the worst of the crowd, but still had to lean their heads close together to hear and be heard over the din.

"Now, as I understand what you've said, Dr. Boheme . . ."

"Larry. Please."

"Larry—thank you—now, as I understand what you've been saying, we need to acknowledge conflict and give it some respect."

"Yes. The alternative is to declare conflict unacceptable. That's what we do in most organizations. I'm sure you've come across that yourself, Webster. Of course, that doesn't make conflict impossible, doesn't make it go away."

"It only drives the conflict underground."

"Exactly. We're far better off to acknowledge it up front, and to take the onus away from conflict."

"I'm having trouble with that. Part of me, at least, wants to believe that there is something reprehensible about conflict in the organization. Since we all work for the same organization, there should be no conflict."

"Yes, I know that line. Conflict is viewed as a kind of unprofessional behavior."

"That's it. That's just what I'm feeling. I think that is part of my upbringing as a corporate man."

"And you're certainly not the only one. When conflict arises, we tend to see it as a breakdown of corporate discipline. We'd like to draw lines up from the two people who have the conflict and find the first person above them on the org chart where the lines intersect. Then, we think, 'If only that manager would shake some sense into these two. . . .'"

"Well? Why isn't that the answer?"

"It would be if the entire organization had a single goal, and that goal was everybody's individual goal as well. But that's just not the case. Organizations are complex. They exist to serve a diversity of goals. The way an organization is set up, the goals are distributed differently among people. So, your goal may be to bring a project home by a given date, while mine is to meet a third-quarter sales quota. These two may be part of some larger goal, but we two probably aren't explicitly aware of it."

"Each one only aware, really, of his own designated goal."

"Just so."

Mr. Tompkins offered a second possibility: "It might happen, I suppose, that our two goals are themselves in conflict. Consider the example you just gave: Suppose my project completion requires you to hold off implementing some new promotion till the quarter is over."

Dr. Boheme was nodding energetically. "There you have it. In that case, our goals are in conflict, or at least in partial conflict. So, of course, you and I are in conflict. The key thing here is to understand that neither of us has acted unprofessionally. There is *real* conflict between us, and that conflict deserves respect. If we drive it underground, paper it over with corporate-speak about teamwork and professionalism, then we never get on with the difficult but doable task of conflict resolution."

"A 'doable task,' you say." Mr. Tompkins looked away, into the interior of the pub. There was a crowd of drinkers there, jostling around a dart board, but he barely saw them; he was thinking of the conflicts in his own life. Was it a doable task to resolve conflict with Belok, for example?

"That's not to say we'll always succeed," Dr. Boheme went on. "Nobody's claiming this is easy. But at least we can learn to avoid some of the approaches that almost guarantee we will fail. Declaring conflict to be unprofessional and therefore not allowed to exist is the most obvious of these. If we replace these hopeless losers with techniques that have at least a chance of succeeding . . ."

"I wonder."

"Webster, you're thinking of the most intractable cases of conflict now, aren't you?"

"I am."

"Well, just to get us off on the right foot, pick another conflict to concentrate on. Conflict is everywhere in our business. Pick an easier one. We'll begin with that."

"Fair enough." He had no trouble coming up with several good candidates.

"Could we agree that the conflict you are thinking of is respectable? That all parties are acting professionally and that any conflict that arises between them is okay? It may have to be resolved for the organization's best interests, but it is not in any way reprehensible?"

"Okay, I guess. I'm not used to thinking of it that way, but now that you put it in those terms, I can see the sense of it."

"Good. Now every time you come face to face with a conflict, I want you to school yourself to repeat the following little mantra: 'Negotiation is hard; mediation is easy.'"

"What does that mean?"

"Negotiation among interested parties is most often a zero-sum game," Dr. Boheme said. "If you and I are dickering over the price of a real-estate property, for example, you can see that anything I gain is offset by your loss."

"If I'm the seller, then giving you a discount comes right out of my proceeds."

"Exactly. Negotiation is difficult. Some people are better at it than others, but we can't realistically expect everyone to master the skills of negotiation. Mediation, on the other hand, is a much simpler matter."

"Mediation implies there is a disinterested third party helping us reach agreement?"

"Yes. When the conflicting parties accept mediation, the entire tone of the interaction is changed. Now, following a few simple rules and procedures and with a bit of luck, the mediator has a good chance of making meaningful agreement happen. The parties come to understand and respect each other's needs, they brainstorm to find options they hadn't considered before, they bargain a bit, and they trust a bit. This is a formula that at least has a chance."

"But how do we get them started? How do we get the warring parties ever to agree to mediation?"

Dr. Boheme tapped a finger on the table in emphasis. "Not at the moment of conflict; that is the key. We need to do it *before* the conflict is fully formed. That is the essence of 'Everybody Wins.' We make a formal declaration before the effort even begins that everybody's 'win conditions' will be respected. We put into place procedures to elicit win conditions at all levels. We agree before any conflict becomes evident that, when it arises, as it certainly will, we will move automatically into mediation mode. We set up a system with trained mediators ready to roll. And, we have a fairly mechanical way to spot the conflicts."

"That's when my win conditions and yours, for example, are mutually exclusive."

"Yes. Or, partly so. I stress the 'partly' here, because it is essential to realize that people in conflict may have win conditions that are ninety-five percent compatible. If they fail to note this, they will never understand how compromise can be in both their interests. It is the mediator's job to make sure both parties have a full understanding of the extent of their common interest."

"I can certainly see that negotiation is hard, as your mantra claims. But I think I'd have to be a mediator a few times before I'm ready to believe that mediation is easy."

"It's not trivial, of course."

"I wouldn't even know how to begin. What would I say, for example, if I were the mediator between two warring parties?" Mr. Tompkins conjured up two imaginary people sitting with them at their little pub table, "Warring parties, locked in combat over some problem. How would I begin to mediate between these two opposite sides?"

"You'd begin by helping them to see that they weren't exactly on opposite sides at all. You'd point out to them, 'You two are on the same side; it is the problem that is on the other side.'"

Mr. Tompkins caught the last British Air flight to Varsjop from Gatwick that night. He wasn't quite ready to swallow Dr. Boheme's prescription whole, but at least he could now see a few things he had to try: First, he needed to acknowledge the inherent respectability of conflict in his organization so as not to let it be driven underground. And second, he would have to set up ways for conflict to be mediated. With such a beginning, the conflicts that tended to arise at Aidrivoli from this point on would have a chance to be sensibly resolved. He still didn't have the foggiest notion of what any of this implied about his own conflict with Belok.

That conflict would have to be dealt with somehow, though. Unresolved conflict could be the death knell to any project. During coffee breaks at the London tutorial, he had picked up some scuttlebutt about the FAA NASPlan projects. The rumors confirmed, just as Belinda had speculated, that there had been serious conflict between the central authority in Washington and the regions, and that this conflict—never resolved and never even acknowledged—had led the projects to certain disaster.

Suppressing a yawn, he pulled his journal from his carry-on bag and opened it on the tray table before him.

From Mr. Tompkins' Journal:

Conflict

o   Whenever there are multiple parties to a development effort, there are bound to be conflicting interests.

o   The business of building and installing systems is particularly conflict-prone.

o   Most system development organizations have poor conflict-resolution skills.

o   Conflict deserves respect. Conflict is not a sign of unprofessional behavior.

o   Declare up front that everybody's win conditions will be respected. Make sure that win conditions are elicited at all levels.

o   Negotiation is hard; mediation is easy.

o   Arrange up front that when win conditions are mutually exclusive or partly so, the parties will be expected to move into mediation to resolve conflict.

o   Remember: We are both on the same side; it is the problem that's on the other side.

18

MAESTRO DIYENIAR

৵

*M*aestro Diyeniar had been on the PMill-A project for a little more than a month. Reports were mixed. Early on, his manager, Osmun Gradish, had confided in Tompkins that Diyeniar was "not an asset," and that, although his work was impeccable, "the fellow spends most of his time chatting people up. I never met anybody with so much to say." It was obvious that Gradish would have liked to contribute his newest staff member back to ex-General Markov's personnel pool, where he had come from, but Mr. Tompkins encouraged him to delay any decision on Diyeniar for a few months more.

Melissa Alber was of quite the opposite opinion on the Maestro: "He is the most extraordinary man, Webster. He talks your ear off, but it's rather wonderful." She shook her head in admiration. "I'm still wondering exactly how he makes you feel so good."

"I'd heard he talks a lot, but does he talk about the work?"

"In a way, he does. But not about the technology of the work. Mostly he is a storyteller. He tells stories about people—people he met a long time ago, in school or in the

Army or on other projects. The stories are delicious. But, of course, they usually have some relevance to what the project is up to. They give you insight."

If Gabriel was right, the particular magic that Diyeniar did was helpful to projects. Maybe the stories were his way of conveying useful insight. "You think he may be doing this on purpose? trying to give just the right insight by telling just the right story?"

Melissa shook her head. "I don't for a moment think that. The man is a natural-born storyteller. The reason that his stories tend to be germane at all is that he naturally connects what is happening in the present to stories from the past. The connection is always seamless. But it's not pointed. For Diyeniar, it's just good storytelling, pure and simple."

"I must meet him. I can see that."

"Allow a few hours. He is not a fellow to be dealt with in twenty minutes, no matter how simple the subject. It seems like anything you say or do reminds him of a story. Or a song. Sometimes both."

"I'll allow a bit of time."

"He is at his best over lunch. Lunch with Diyeniar is a movable feast. It goes on forever. You'll have to move quickly to get him to yourself. I can tell you that the young people on his project have quite adopted him. They have had to move the tables together in the cafeteria to make room for all the people who like to sit with him."

"If he ties up the whole project for two-hour lunches, then I wonder if he really can be doing any good for our schedule."

"Oh, I wouldn't worry about that. Our people are working too much anyway. They're all putting in tons of overtime on what we all know is a hopeless cause."

"That's true enough, I guess."

"At least we're not hemorrhaging people any more. The requests to transfer have gone to zero."

"That's an interesting trade-off. If we think of lunch with Diyeniar as a full hour lost to the project, beyond what a normal lunch would take, but we save turnover, is that a positive result?"

"We don't need your simulator to tell us that," Melissa observed. She affected a counting gesture, moving successively along the fingers of her right hand. "If it takes each new person three months or more to come up to speed, that's the equivalent of six hundred lunches with Diyeniar. The withdrawn transfer requests alone have offset more than that."

Mr. Tompkins nodded in agreement.

"But there is something else going on here, Webster. He is building a culture for the project. He is a catalyst for a kind of team phenomenon that I haven't seen before. I mentioned that he tells stories. But he listens to stories as well. And, sometimes, he retells them. When you tell Maestro Diyeniar a story, you are entering it into a kind of collection. He is the oral history of our project. He is the keeper of our lore."

As Mrs. Beerzig was away from her desk, Mr. Tompkins picked up his own phone when it rang.

"Tompkins, I want to see the screws applied to these projects. This is not an option. I'm not going to be 'Mister Nice Guy' even one more day. You've already used up your honeymoon with me."

"Oh, Allair, it's you, isn't it? How nice to hear from you."

"Damn right, it's me, Tompkins. Apply the screws. Do it now. It's time to start our sprint for the finish."

Mr. Tompkins glanced at the countdown display, which now, on this early November day, read:

ONLY $\boxed{211}$ DAYS TILL D-DAY!

Two hundred and eleven calendar days: He knew precisely what that corresponded to in workdays. "We still have one hundred fifty-one workdays till June first, Allair. Isn't that a bit early to 'start our sprint,' as you put it?"

"We should have started it on day one, as far as I'm concerned. Only I was trying to be a kinder, gentler me. Well, no more. And, by the way, there are two hundred eleven workdays between now and June first, not one fifty-one."

"Ah. We're switching to a seven-day week, I gather."

"You bet we are. Put that out in a memo. I expect to see a big bump in hours applied, starting this week."

That was the easy part, of course. All along, Mrs. Beerzig had been doctoring up the numbers each week before they went out to Belok. She would just doctor them a bit differently from now on. And, he himself would write a mandatory-seven-day-week memo and send it off to Belok and no one else. *Oh, what a tangled web we weave. . . .*

"Now, how is the schedule going, Tompkins?"

"On target for June first. With or without the overtime." Oops, that was a mistake.

"Aha. That's it. I'm changing the delivery date. I'm pushing it ahead to May first."

Mr. Tompkins repressed a sigh. Then, he said what he had to say, as though it were a line in a play. "Now, that will be a struggle. I don't know, Allair. I don't think we can make May first. We might, but I suspect not."

"Then, that is definitely the date."

"It's going to be tough. I might say impossible, or almost impossible."

There was a click on the other end.

Impossible or almost impossible, of course, was what Belok wanted to hear. That was the way the man set his dates. Mr. Tompkins allowed himself only the time for one tiny, slightly bitter reflection: So much bother could have been avoided if only I had convinced him from the beginning that the original date we were striving for was already impossible.

His first lunch with Diyeniar did indeed take two hours. The Maestro was a tall, somewhat gangly man with a long, fine-bridged nose. He appeared to be about sixty years old, but his hair, what there was of it, was still quite black. It fell in long plaits onto his shoulders from around a bald pate. Diyeniar's eyes were electric.

They opened their sandwiches on a wooden picnic table in the glade below Aidrivoli-1. "Well, Maestro. I am delighted you could make the time for me."

Diyeniar shook his head. "This 'Maestro' business, it makes me laugh. What exactly is it that Diyeniar is a maestro of? The Maestro of C Programming, perhaps? Or a maestro debugger? More likely, I am Maestro of None."

"Excuse me?"

"Jack of all trades, but maestro of none. Since you kindly offered me your first name, Webster, I return the favor: Kayo."

"Kayo, then. Anyway, I'm glad we could have this time together, Kayo. I've been hearing good things about you."

A big smile. "That reminds me of a story. . . ."

What followed was a long ramble about Kayo's grandfather who had owned a hotel in the mountains near Märkst.

By the time the story was done, Mr. Tompkins had finished his sandwich and his companion hadn't even had one bite. There was only one obvious way to give the man a chance to eat: "Well, since we're talking about grandfathers," Mr. Tompkins began, "there is rather a funny story about mine . . ."

Kayo picked up his sandwich.

At the end of two hours, it wasn't obvious what had happened over lunch. There had been some lovely tales exchanged, and that was certainly pleasant. And, as Melissa had foreseen, he felt good. Was that it, though? Was that Diyeniar's magic?

On the way back to Aidrivoli-1, Mr. Tompkins raised the subject of conflict, something that was on his mind much of the time these days.

"Oh, yes," Kayo nodded. "There is always a conflict here or there: Two people who get their backs up over some subject where they are mostly in agreement, but all they can see is what they don't agree upon."

"And what should we do about such a thing?"

"What does a mother do with a child who has skinned his knee? A kiss to make it better, and then she diverts the child's attention away from what hurts to something that doesn't hurt at all. Before he knows it, the hurt really *is* gone and forgotten."

"She diverts his attention by telling him a story, for example?"

"Maybe that. Or something else. But don't forget the kiss, a mother's special kiss, applied directly to the spot that hurts."

"What is the equivalent of that kiss in our business, do you suppose?"

"That is the question. It should be some kind of small ceremony. In general, I have no idea what kind of ceremony it should be. But, in the specific, it is often so obvious."

Ceremony, of course, is what the initiation of mediation would be. "I do have an idea, Kayo, that I'd like to try out." He gave a shortened version of Dr. Boheme's use of mediation to resolve conflict.

Kayo was nodding yes. "They teach mediation now in the schools, you know. Not in the kindergarten, but in the middle grades. They teach kids to be mediators for disputes that arise between their classmates. I have seen the student book for this course. The course takes up only two hours of classroom time. You understand, in two hours with children that age, you are only reaching them about ten minutes. So, the entire course on mediation is ten minutes of material. And the amazing thing is that the children then go out into the play-ground and successfully resolve disputes."

"Negotiation is hard but mediation is easy," Tompkins prompted.

"I guess," the Maestro said. "Well, I like your idea that the first steps toward mediation might be the ceremony we're looking for, the mother's special kiss."

"Look around, Kayo, and let me know when you see a conflict developing. I'd like to try this idea out."

Maestro Diyeniar soon spotted a conflict on the Quirk B-Team. The manager, Loren Apfels, and his chief designer, Norwood Bolix, had had a falling out, and now, interaction between them was increasingly painful. Mr. Tompkins arranged to have the two show up together in his office for the first attempt at applying the mediation "ceremony." He invited Maestro Diyeniar to attend. The three arrived together and were ushered in by Mrs. Beerzig.

"Now look," Mr. Tompkins told Apfels and Bolix, "you two have gotten off on the wrong foot with each other. I think we should acknowledge that and not try to cover it up." He looked at them for agreement.

At least they didn't disagree. They stared back at him silently, waiting to see what would come next.

"Conflict is not reprehensible, not in this organization," Mr. Tompkins told them. "It's often perfectly reasonable. I don't think there is anything here for either of you to be ashamed of. But conflict can often get in the way, and that's why we do need to address it." He paused, dramatically, and then dropped his trump card: "We all need to understand that the two of you are not on opposite sides, really. You are both on the same side. It is the problem that is on the other side."

This had seemed like a powerful formulation when Dr. Boheme first presented it, but now it fell perfectly flat. Apfels and Bolix just stared at him, not even nodding. He looked to Kayo for some help, but Kayo only shrugged. He was on his own.

Mr. Tompkins plowed on. "You two have been trying to negotiate your differences. But negotiation is hard. Mediation, on the other hand, is pretty easy. So, here's what we're going to do. I'm going to be the mediator. We'll apply a few basic conflict resolution techniques, and then I'm sure we'll reach a workable agreement for you two to interact more harmoniously in the future. Now, what seems to be the problem here?"

Bolix looked over uneasily at Apfels. "Well, since you ask, I don't trust Loren. I don't now, I never did, and I never will."

"Ditto," said Apfels.

A protracted silence as Tompkins considered what to do or say next. He came up with nothing. "Um, Kayo?"

Kayo shook his head sadly. "So much for the mother's kiss." He turned to Apfels and Bolix. "My friends, Loren and Norwood, I wish you could each see in the other what I see: good qualities, including great integrity. I know you both, and I know that about both of you, . . . but apparently you don't know that about each other. You have made that very clear. I believe you have now put the ball in Webster's court to do something beyond just mediation. He'll figure out something, I'm sure. For now, why don't you leave us to work out a solution? You can trust us to make some change that will be acceptable to you both and will relieve the tension."

Bolix and Apfels stood up and exited. As soon as the door was closed behind them, Mr. Tompkins looked over at the Maestro. "What did I do wrong?"

Diyeniar shook his head sadly. "Only everything. I brought you the book from the schools, Webster, the guide for twelve- to fourteen-year-old mediators. I hoped you might have left a bit of time for us to go over it, maybe to practice a bit before our two friends showed up." Kayo opened the slender paperback book to one of its middle pages and passed it over.

Mr. T. looked down at the selected page. It was headed, The Five Steps of Mediation. The first step read:

> ONE— Get consent. Ask both people if they will allow you to mediate for them.

"Oh," Mr. Tompkins said. "Consent. I didn't do that. That was perhaps an error."

Kayo rolled his eyes.

Mr. Tompkins put his hand to his forehead. "I should have done that. I should have asked their consent."

"The asking and giving of consent for mediation was the mother's kiss we were looking for. You skipped the ceremony entirely and got directly on with the rest."

"Mmm." Mr. Tompkins read through the subsequent four steps. They were obvious enough, now that he'd seen them in print, but the truth was that he'd had no idea of how to proceed, and he probably would have botched up steps two through five as much as he had step one. He looked up, ruefully. "What I've discovered is that mediation may be easy, but it is not trivial."

"So true. Like flipping a pancake: It can be made to look easy...."

"I didn't do my homework. What a dummy."

Kayo nodded gently. "You were also the wrong person to mediate here. You are hardly a *disinterested* party. And you have power over them. A mediator is someone who leads from a position of no power."

"I botched it. What do we do now?"

"Now they have forced the endgame. Each has taken a position from which he cannot back down. The role of the mediator, as I see it, is to dance the two parties around that possibility, to help them avoid taking fixed positions."

"Ah."

"But they did. Now you need to reassign one of them. Some damage has been done, but you cut your losses. At least, that is better than allowing the problem to fester."

That afternoon, Mr. Tompkins did his homework. He read *The Students' Guide to Mediation* cover to cover (it was only sixteen pages long). He asked Mrs. Beerzig to order enough copies to be distributed to the entire staff. Then, he wrote a memo for all, saying that the organization was committed to soliciting and respecting the win conditions of all parties, and to mediating differences when they arose. Finally, he arranged with Gabriel to put together a small task force to collect and document win conditions from people at all levels, and to analyze them for potential problems.

The failed mediation between Apfels and Bolix was particularly embarrassing because he'd had an obviously better approach staring him in the face from the beginning: He should have asked Diyeniar to mediate. The Maestro was disinterested and had no positional power, he knew something about mediation (you didn't spend all those years teaching kindergarten without learning a thing or two about how conflicts are resolved), and he was a natural people-person. Mr. Tompkins got off a quick e-mail message to the Maestro saying that he would like him to be available to serve as a mediator in the future. A few moments later, the response came back. "Happy to help," it said. Under the signature line was a short poem:

> The road to wisdom, well, it's plain
> and simple to express,
> Err and err and err again,
> but less and less and less.
> — Piet Hein

From Mr. Tompkins' Journal:

<u>Role of the Catalyst</u>

o   There is such a thing as a catalytic personality. Such people contribute to projects by helping teams to form and jell, and to remain healthy and productive. Even if our catalysts did nothing else (they usually do a lot else), their catalytic role is important and valuable.

o   Mediation is a special case of the catalytic role. Mediation is learnable with a small investment.

o   The small ceremony beginning, "May I help by trying to mediate for you?" can be an essential first step in conflict resolution.

Interlude

❧

This would be the first weekend since Belok's mandate on seven-day weeks. Of course, almost no one knew about the mandate, since Tompkins' New Working Hours memo, although it was addressed to all staff, had in fact been delivered only to Minister Belok himself.

Mr. Tompkins and Belinda were in his office with the door closed. "Belinda, I'm beginning to feel like a mental patient. I feel like a man living in his own lie. I'm losing track of what's real and what isn't. We doctor the hours we send up to Korsach, we set fictitious policies we have no intention of applying, we conceal the existence of our B and C projects, I am continually assuring Belok that schedules will be met when I know they won't. Something is awfully wrong here."

Belinda shrugged. "That's for sure. But it's not *your* something."

"Isn't it? What does a man of integrity do in such circumstances? The answer can't be that he lies through his teeth."

"You wouldn't think so. Webster, the obvious answer is that a person of integrity has to draw a line in the sand and stand by it. You did that. You told Belok to stuff it in his ear, as I remember."

"I did. But then . . ."

"Then, he chose deliberately not to hear you, and made it impossible for you to do anything but lie to him. So, now you lie to him. That's a problem, but it's his problem, not yours."

"It is effectively mine as well. I'm the one that has to do the lying. I should walk away, Belinda. I really should. That would be the honorable thing."

"There is a reason why we're here, Webster: the Project Management Laboratory. We set out to discover some of the causal effects that drive project work. And we're getting very close. We can't walk away now. We'd miss all the fun."

"Living the lie is not part of the fun."

"No. My sympathy for that. You're paying the price so the rest of us can have such interesting and involving work. But it's going to be worth it, Webster. We just have to hold on a little longer. There is another thing, too: You could walk away, as I could. Gabriel could. But there are lots of other people who can't. You're their buffer. If you leave, you'll be abandoning them to Belok."

"I know. I keep telling myself all that. Only, I still feel like I'm acting dishonorably. Telling all these lies . . ."

"Like the guy who lies to the mugger and says he doesn't have any money on him, when he knows full well there is a twenty-dollar bill stuffed into his key case."

"It's still a lie."

"It's still a mugger. Belok is a mugger."

"I'm thinking about this weekend, Belinda. I've given my word, in a sense, that people will work all weekend. Only, of course, they won't, because I haven't asked them to. I'm thinking that, at the very minimum, I have to be here myself Saturday and Sunday. That is the very least I can do to retain a bit of honor."

"Webster, you turkey! This is going to be the most beautiful weekend of the year. Perfect weather, changing colors, the last few days of Indian summer. You have *got* to get away. Dr. Belinda is prescribing a full weekend for you. This is not an option. No kidding."

"Thank you, Dr. Belinda, but I think I have to stay." He looked forlornly out the window at the splendid colors around Aidrivoli. It was indeed going to be a spectacular weekend. "I just wouldn't feel right getting away."

"Well, we have to take some steps to make it okay. Let's see." Belinda walked over to the window and stood there with her back to him. She dropped her shoulders slightly and sighed. Then nothing. She kept her silence for long enough to make him think her mind might have drifted. Maybe it had. He never knew for sure what was going on inside that mind. Sometimes, it was brilliant, and other times, merely kooky. He had come to depend on her judgment almost utterly, but he still had to wonder if she was completely cured of her devastating burnout, or ever would be. She looked the part of the ultimate business executive in her crisp blazer and skirt, but then there were those omnipresent bare feet. . . .

Finally, Belinda turned around to face him. "Here is the plan, Boss. This will work. We declare a three-day weekend and close the entire complex, lock it up, force everybody to take off three full days."

"Belinda!"

"It will do them a world of good."

"But, Belok—he's bound to find out."

"Of course. Then, we'll have Mrs. Beerzig fill out the time sheets showing one hundred sixty-eight hours per week for every single person on the staff."

"Why one hundred sixty-eight?"

"That's seven days times twenty-four hours a day."

"This is your solution? Instead of lying a little, we lie a lot? Belok will see through this in a minute."

"Of course, he will. But then what will he do? Nothing. The key thing is that we're throwing down the gauntlet, but not obliging him to pick it up. He has the option to ignore. He'll take that option, Webster, I guarantee it."

It seemed crazy, but the same Webster Tompkins who'd felt obliged to work through the entirety of a two-day weekend, for some reason, now felt free to take the three-day weekend, once he had declared it. There was no figuring out just why this was. It was. He decided not to worry about it anymore.

The Residence maintained an old black Russian-made Lada sedan for the use of guests. Mr. Tompkins found his name alone on the sign-up list for the weekend; the car was his. He packed a lunch and headed toward the northeast into Morovia's interior.

By now, he had heard so many stories from Maestro Diyeniar about his grandfather's hotel in the hilly region around Märkst that he almost felt the place was part of his own family history. The hotel was still run by Diyeniar cousins. Mr. Tompkins got the Maestro to scribble down some directions and then he headed off for a weekend at the hotel. If nothing else, he would have the pleasure of a long, leisurely drive through the countryside. The sky was clear, the weather cool and crisp, and the tree colors nothing short of stunning.

Kayo's instructions told him to proceed east from the port town of Onlijop and watch for Route 4 North just before entering Märkst. He saw a red–and–black sign for Route 4 South where it joined the Onlijop road. All he had to do, he thought, was turn off at the next sign. Kayo had assured him that Route 4 North would be clearly marked. He drove on, watching for the sign, but he didn't see it.

A few minutes later, he found himself caught in the snarl of traffic around Märkst's Saturday morning farmers' market. He had gone too far. He turned the little car around and retraced his path. On the way out of Märkst, he did see the sign for Route 4 North, but he carried on past it, turned around, and approached it again from the west, all to figure out why he had missed the turn before. It was just idle curiosity. Was the turn not properly marked in the other direction? Or, in spite of Kayo's assurance, was the sign not easily seen when approaching from the west? To his surprise, the answer was neither; the sign was as big as life, clearly visible, and unmistakably pointing him toward Route 4 North. Tompkins was baffled. Why had he missed it the first time?

Mr. Tompkins turned the car around yet again and drove all the way back to the point where the two roads first merged. The sign there for Morovian National Route 4 South was a shield divided diagonally into red and black zones, with the lettering in white. He reversed and continued driving to the sign for Route 4 North, and there was the explanation of why he'd been unable to see it before. The sign was not a red–and–black shield with white lettering, but a plain white circle with black lettering. Route 4 evidently changed its status here from a national to a county road. Since he had been looking for a red–and–black shield, he had been unable to see the other. With a chuckle, Mr. Tompkins turned and headed north.

You can't see what's as plain as the nose on your face if you're sufficiently persuaded that it isn't there, Tompkins thought. He had been utterly convinced that the sign would be a red-and-black shield. He simply knew it. So he was looking confidently for the shield and sailed by, entirely blind to the black-and-white sign that told him where to turn north with Route 4. The laugh was definitely on him. What a hoot. There was nothing funnier, really, than a joke on oneself.

And then, little by little, the incident began to seem less funny to him. Finally, it didn't seem funny at all. He let the car slow down and eventually drift to the side of the road, where he stopped it. He turned off the ignition. Mr. Tompkins just sat there in the driver's seat, staring off into the distant woods. The incident with the sign had not just been a little lapse of logic on his part; it was more than that. It was the essential human error. At least, it was the essential Tompkins error. As he thought back over some of the key missteps he'd made in his career, there began to emerge a common pattern among them. In each case, he had been aware of something important that he didn't know (such as, where the black-and-red shield indicating Route 4 North would turn up). In each case, he'd been unaware that something he "knew" would eventually turn out to be wrong (the sign marking the turn *must be* a black-and-red shield). And, in each case, all his attention had been focused on figuring out the answer to what he didn't know, rather than reconsidering what he did know.

"That's my flaw," he thought. "Maybe it's everybody else's flaw as well, but it is certainly mine. That's the essence of where I go wrong. I get so convinced of my knowledge that I blind myself to evidence proving that what I seem to 'know' is wrong."

Mr. T. rested his head on the back of the car seat, and stared up into the gray fabric above him. What was it now that he knew absolutely, but that was dead wrong? What was his present blind spot? He had a gut feeling that there was something there, something that could make a huge difference in the way the projects back at Aidrivoli were approached. If only he could figure it out. Somewhere among all his premises was one that was flawed. If he could trap it now, it might open his eyes to some possibility he'd been blind to before. He closed his eyes and looked inward, examining and making himself doubt even his most strongly held convictions. He could hear Aristotle's voice inside his head: 'Think not about adding, but about subtracting. . . .' What was there that could be subtracted from the projects to make them run more efficiently? What was the false belief he held that made it impossible for him to see the signs that he now suspected were staring him squarely in the face?

He sat up and looked around. The setting, chosen quite at random, was lovely. There was a gentle ridge running along-side the road. Spread out beneath him was a colorful valley, with a narrow-gauge rail line running along the side of a river. At the far end of the valley, the river widened into a pond, glistening now in the low sun. This would be a fine place for a picnic. He pulled his boxed lunch and a blanket out of the boot and set himself up on a slate outcropping where the ridge fell away into the valley. Even after an unhurried lunch and then a little nap on the grass beside the slate, he still hadn't discovered what the false premise was. But he knew that he would one day. Now that he was on the lookout for it, it could not evade him for long.

Before setting off again, he pulled his journal out of his case and made one quick note.

From Mr. Tompkins' Journal:

Human Error

> o   It's not what you <u>don't</u> know that kills you, . . . it's what you know that isn't so.

19

PART AND WHOLE

૨૦

*A*ristotle Kenoros was a morning person. If he was going to make an appearance, it was most often the first business of the day. This morning, Mr. Tompkins arrived at his office to be told by Mrs. Beerzig that Morovia's First Programmer was waiting for him inside. Mr. T. found him sitting on the desk, staring up at a matrix of letters he had drawn on the white board.

"A report card," Kenoros told him. "I have graded the teams on their internal design efforts. For the purposes of this grade, I did not consider so much the quality of their designs as whether they had produced a design at all. If you have a low-level modular design that serves the function of a blueprint—that is, it establishes what all the coded modules will be and what interfaces there will be among them—then Kenoros gives you an A. If you have none, you get an F. In between, you get an in-between grade. Look at the pattern."

Mr. Tompkins sat down, stirring his coffee, and studied the matrix.

PRODUCT	A-TEAM	B-TEAM	C-TEAM
NOTATE	F	A	A
PMILL	F	A	A
PAINT-IT	F	A	B
PSHOP	F	A	A
QUIRK	F	B	A
QUICKERSTILL	C	A	A

"Tell me again, Aristotle, what an F means."

"It usually means the project produced a political document and called it a design. The document is typically some sort of a textual description of early thinking about internal structure."

"Not really a design in your terms."

"No. Of course, there *is* a design that comes about later, as a by-product of coding. But the activity called 'design' produces no real design. That gets you an F."

"Mmm. All the small teams got A's and B's. The big teams got all the F's. What's going on?"

"I ask you. It is a puzzle."

"First of all, I note that the Oracle's concept of Last Minute Implementation is going to be impossible without a good design."

"Very good, Webster. You're getting warm."

"I'm still not sure why the A-Teams did so dismally. What I'm sure of is that they just can't hope to do many of the pre-coding steps we'd like them to do working with such designs."

"Exactly. In fact, they are not going to be doing Last Minute Implementation. The six A-Teams started coding long ago. I had no success persuading them to defer implementation. I tried, but I had no success."

"And the others?"

"To varying degrees, all the B- and C-Teams are trying out the Oracle's approach. They are all trying to push back implementation, and to do as much verification work as possible before a single line of code is written. Some of them are trying rigorously to defer coding until the last sixth of the project."

"And none of the A-Teams?"

"None."

"Okay, I give up. What gives?"

Kenoros plunked himself down in the easy chair across from Tompkins. He was grinning, but not answering.

Tompkins prodded him again. "Why didn't the A-Teams produce a design?"

"Too big."

"What?"

"This is my theory. The teams were too big. During the whole time that design should have been going on, they had too many people to involve in that activity. Design is a job for a small group. You can put three or four or maybe five people around a white board and they can do design together. But you can't put twenty people around a white board."

"I still don't see why that should inhibit design. You can put three or four or five to work on design and put the rest to work on something else. Why not? Why can't they do something else?"

"What is the something else?"

"I don't know. Something else."

"The design step is the critical act of dividing the whole into pieces. Once you've done that, then you have good opportunity to allocate these pieces to people to work on separately. But before you've done it, you don't have pieces. What you've got is a whole. As long as it is a whole, people can only work on it in an undivided group."

"That's still no excuse for skipping the design work. If it has to be done, it has to be done. The manager could always put a small team to work and tell everybody else to be patient, to just sit on their hands, if there is nothing else to do."

"True. I think this is what happened on QuickerStill-A," Kenoros said. "But now, consider this 'solution' of yours from the standpoint of the project manager. Suppose you are managing a big project yourself. You've got thirty people from day one. You have also got an aggressive schedule—that's why they have loaded you up with so many people. Now, are you going to tell twenty-five of your people to sit on their hands for the next two months?"

"I see what you mean. They would be ready for mutiny."

"Of course. Also, you would stand out like a sore thumb. Imagine how you look to your boss and your boss's boss. You've got all this work to do before June first and most of your people are goofing off."

"Mmm. I don't look like a real manager."

"You don't. So, what do you do?"

"Well, I have to get those people working," Tompkins said. "I guess I look for early opportunities to peel off parts of the whole so I can allocate it to them."

"Right. Since the design activity is, by definition, concerned with peeling off parts in a sensible manner, you short-circuit that process to get the dividing up done as early as possible."

"I see. My early dividing up for work-allocation purposes makes a mockery of design. Does that have to be so?"

"Not entirely, but largely. True, there are always a few marginal activities that can be spun off before the design is done. But if you have to put a huge staff to work, those few assignments are not going to be nearly enough."

"To get the staff to work on real critical-path matters, I have to divide up the design work itself."

"Now you are on the slippery slope that leads eventually to no design," Kenoros said. "You make a crude division of the whole into five or ten pieces so you can put five or ten design teams to work. That crude division is a design step, but you don't approach it as such. You approach it as an exercise in personnel allocation."

"And the initial crude division, as you call it, is the heart of the design."

"It is. And since there is no one directly responsible for revisiting its logic, it remains the heart of the design. The result is no design. To make matters worse, it is coding and testing that are the most efficient users of people, so there is always the temptation to start these tasks almost immediately, even though no design is complete."

Mr. Tompkins was still not convinced. "If it's true, what you say, then *most* projects are effectively overstaffed during the period when design should be done. So, most projects wouldn't get any real design done."

Kenoros smiled somewhat bitterly. "I'm afraid that is the sad truth. Somewhere, today, there is a new project beginning, overstaffed from day one. The project will go through all the steps, or at least seem to, but no design will be done. The internal structures will evolve without ever being exposed to real design thinking or review. And then, someday, years later,

251

when the product needs to be reworked, one of the new project's staff members will do a thorough re-engineering of the design. He or she will reconstruct the actual design. And what happens next is very sad."

"What is that sad thing?"

"That future reverse engineer will be the first human being ever to set eyes on the real design of the product."

For most of the rest of the day, Mr. Tompkins rehashed the notion that early overstaffing effectively precludes sensible design. To the extent that Kenoros was right about this, the ramifications went far beyond Aidrivoli. They suggested that the entire software industry might be suboptimized in this way, addicted to early staff buildup and thus making a sham of the key internal design activity.

When Belinda wandered in after lunch, Tompkins dumped the whole idea on her. She seemed unimpressed. "So, what else is new? Management is all about compromise. One of the things that gets compromised is the design. In order to get people assigned, you accept a less than perfect design."

"Less than perfect would be one thing. Suppose, though, you accept having no design at all?"

"There is always a design. It's just not as good as it ought to be. Even in the case where the design phase is a total fiction, there will be a design. Otherwise, your future project person would never be able to re-engineer it from the code."

"Okay, I buy that. We are not talking about a design versus no design. What we're really talking about is a quality design versus something that emerges on its own, and has no quality. Since nobody was doing any real design thinking when the dividing up was required, the division is badly sub-optimized."

Belinda cleared herself a section of white board. "Now, that is something we can get a handle on. Consider this." She began sketching rapidly. "This is the whole of our system, and these are its parts.

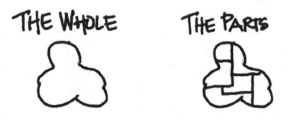

"This is only one way to divide the whole. There are infinitely many other ways as well. Here, for example, is another." She sketched a second partitioning next to the first. "In order to judge which is the better way to divide the whole into pieces, we need to consider the resultant interfaces. Without getting too formal about it, the more interfaces you have and the more complex they are, the worse the partitioning."

"That's true, of course," Mr. Tompkins added, "no matter what it is you're dividing; whether you're dividing the system or dividing work among your people."

Belinda nodded. "I'll get to that. Now let's fill in the interfaces among the pieces. What we're doing here is 'design evaluation,' since we're going to choose the partitioning that has the cleaner pattern of interfaces."

"So, we pick the version on the right," Mr. Tompkins spoke up like an overeager kid in class.

"Right. We choose it because it has fewer and thinner interfaces among its pieces. Now, we allocate the pieces to members of the team. The result is that partitioning of the work among people is isomorphic to partitioning of the system into its parts." She drew some more.

"The interfaces among the people on the team are isomorphic to the interfaces among the pieces of the whole that they've been allocated. So, . . ." Belinda pointed to pairs of corresponding interface sets from the two sides of the diagram, " . . . the interface between persons 3 and 4 of the project, for example, is isomorphic to the interface between parts 3 and 4 of the product."

She sat down and looked back at her diagram. "Now I'm getting depressed. When the work partitioning gets done in advance of the design, we guarantee that the interfaces among people are more complex than they really need to be."

"Exactly," Webster confirmed. "The total information shared by any two people to get their work done is larger than if the design had preceded the work allocation. People are forced to interact with more of their teammates in order to get anything done, and the interactions are more complex. The result is, less possibility of independent work, more telephone tag, more meetings, and more frustration."

She made a face. "Ick. I think that's the story of our early lives up there on the board, Webster. Ugly interfaces, frustration, too many meetings. Can it all be because of early over-staffing?"

"I'm beginning to think so."

There was a knock at the door, and Mrs. Beerzig announced the arrival of Avril Alterbek, manager of PShop-C. Mr. Tompkins quickly beckoned Avril into the office.

"Hi, folks. Any chance of a moment for me?"

"Always," Mr. Tompkins told her. He gestured to the chair opposite Belinda. "What's up?"

Avril sat down. "Management intervention is required. This is going to cost you."

"Oh, well, what do you need?" Anything but time, he was thinking.

"A ton of people."

"Ah." Mr. Tompkins paused a moment, recollecting his rationale for keeping the B- and C-projects leanly staffed. "We are not trying to run your project thin, Avril, just to save money. We were worried about getting you overstaffed. Why, just as you came in, we were talking about some of the unfortunate results of . . ." He stood up and walked over to the board, ready to begin his lecture.

"I know all that, Webster," Avril stopped him. "I know what the reasoning was. But things are changing on my project. We've got a breathtaking design done. It's a thing of beauty. Even Aristotle says it's about as pretty an internal design as he's ever seen. Of course, he gave us a lot of help making it so elegant and complete. Over the last few weeks, we've been inspecting it and testing it out on paper and proving it to ourselves. Of course, we're not done yet with any of those tasks, but we're getting close. We can see the work that lies ahead in very substantial detail. That's what we need the people for, Webster. There are seven in staff now, and that's just right for the moment: five designers and two in support staff. But two months from now, we're going to have work for another twenty people."

Belinda leaned toward him, excited. "Don't you see, Webster, this is the other side of the coin. What we've been talking about for the last hour is the disaster of overstaffing prior to design. But their design is nearly done. If we think of design as the critical partitioning act, they've done it. Now Avril's saying that she needs people to assign the pieces to."

"Exactly. I just wanted to give you some notice. . . ."

Belinda couldn't contain herself. "How many pieces, Avril?"

"Um, 1677 modules, some 1300 data items, 18 file structures, 20 builds . . ."

"Sounds like you could use even more than twenty additional people."

"I could. I didn't want to be greedy, but I could use as many as thirty-five. We've got blocks of modules to assign for coding, acceptance test suites to construct for all the builds, code inspections, some documentation cleanup tasks. All this work is almost completely spec'ed and ready to assign. As I say, within six or eight weeks . . ."

Belinda was on her feet. "Give them to her, Webster, the whole thirty-five. This is it. This is where we go for broke."

"Now wait a minute. We can't just dump thirty-five people on Avril in February. We'd stop her progress dead. She'd have to spend all her time bringing the new people up to speed."

"Give her thirty-five people who know her application cold."

Mr. Tompkins was baffled. "Where the hell are we going to come up with thirty-five people who know the ins and outs of PShop?"

"Raid the A-Team," Belinda said.

After Avril was gone, Belinda and Webster stayed on, mulling over the politics of the matter.

"I have no doubt you're right, Belinda, no doubt at all. If we were unconstrained, that is just what we would do. But with the situation as it is, I don't see how . . ."

"'What does the person of principle do?' Wasn't that the question you were asking earlier? And the answer you seemed to come up with was, Put the interests of the projects first; do what you can to help them produce good work and get their jobs done expeditiously. That is the principle that has guided you so far. Now it is telling you to raid the A-Teams and put their people to work for the B- and C-Teams, as their needs become clear."

Mr. Tompkins tried to keep his voice steady. "Belok would eat us alive. Before the weekend, you gave me a plan to throw the gauntlet down to Belok but give him the option to ignore it. If we throw this gauntlet down, he can't ignore it. He'll have to act. We'd be forcing him to act."

"Eventually that's what we're going to have to do."

"Eventually, yes. Just not this week. Avril says she can wait two months. Give me two months and then I'll raid the A-Team, I promise."

"She asked for people in two months, but the truth is that it would be better to give her a core of four or five now to form the nucleus of the expanded group."

"I know, but we'll have to wait. I have great hopes that if we can only wait a month or two . . ." He let his voice trail off. In a month or two, Lahksa would be back, that's what he was hoping. Or maybe NNL would be in charge again and would put Belok back in the cage where the man had been kept before.

Belinda frowned. "Avril's project is not the problem here. PShop is a relatively big effort. If she will be ready for thirty-five people in February, what state do you suppose Quicker-Still-B and -C and PMill-B and -C are in today? Those smaller projects are probably further along than Avril's. And they're going to need expanded staff almost immediately. We have to raid all the A-Teams, Webster, and we've got to begin it now."

He stared down at his hands for a long moment. "I know," he said softly.

Belinda was at the board again. "When the detailed, low-level modular design is done, opportunities for splitting up the work explode. That's not just true for our projects, but for all projects. That's telling us something that we've missed all these years, something the whole industry has missed. Look, we've been accustomed to staff projects like this." She drew swiftly on the board. "But the ideal staffing curve is entirely different."

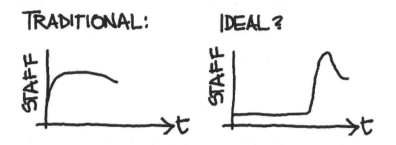

Mr. Tompkins tried to focus on her drawing rather than on the political dilemma of diverting people from the A-Teams. "Um, . . . ideal staffing. Yes, I think you're right. That is what the evidence is telling us and it certainly is at odds with convention. I admit that I never staffed a project that way. Not until now, anyway."

"I have, now that I think about it. But the projects that I kept thin until late and then added lots of people to were typically the more casual ones. I'd never have done it on a mission-critical development. Maybe I should have."

"Mmm."

"Webster, this may be the explanation for something that I've always wondered about. It's been my private—maybe highly jaded—suspicion that whenever projects were scheduled aggressively, they were doomed. I mean those projects where people are talking frankly about an aggressive schedule, I've always felt that those projects probably finished about two months to a year later than they would have if they'd been started off with a schedule that wasn't aggressive."

Mr. Tompkins was smiling. "That's the experiment we really should have run: two projects building the exact same product, one on an aggressive schedule and the other on a sensible schedule."

"The sensible schedule project would have finished earlier, I'm sure of it."

From Mr. Tompkins' Journal:

Staff Level

o   Early overstaffing tends to force projects into shortcutting the key design activity (to give all those people something to do).

o   When work is divided over a large staff prior to completion of design, the interfaces among people and among work groups are not minimized.

o   This leads to increased interdependence, meeting time, rework, and frustration.

o   Ideal staffing requires a small core team for most of the project, and then significant numbers of people added late in the process (as late as the last sixth of scheduled time).

o   Awful suspicion: Projects that set out to achieve 'aggressive' schedules probably take longer to complete than they would have if started with more reasonable schedules.

20

STANDING ON CEREMONY

ॐ

$\mathcal{P}$assing through the reception area first thing in the morning, Mr. Tompkins noticed that a fax was coming in. He looked at the partial page that was already printed and saw that it began "My dear Webster." His heart skipped a beat. There was only one person who addressed him that way. He collected a cup of coffee for himself and came back just as the full sheet was released. With the fax in hand, he repaired to his office, closing the door behind him. Maybe it would say when she was coming home.

> My dear Webster,
>
> Well, I found you another good one. Consultant, I mean. I just put him on the corporate jet this afternoon. Be a dear, and pick him up around 9 tomorrow.
>
> Don't worry about me, as I am having a lovely time and not getting into too much trouble (for me, anyway). And don't worry about you, either. I'll take care of everything as soon as I get back.
>
> Fondly,
> Lahksa

Wonder what that meant? Oh, well, there was no figuring out a complicated creature like Lahksa. It would all become clear in time. At least, it seemed like she might be coming home soon.

Not a word about where she was, but there was one tiny clue: The sending fax machine had time-stamped her message on the way out. It was marked 11:58 P.M. The time in Morovia was just shy of 8 A.M., which meant it was nearly 2 A.M. in New York. So, Lahksa's fax must have come from two time zones west of New York, in Mountain Time. He got out his day-planner and turned to its little map of time zones to double-check that the Mountain Time region included Alberta, Saskatchewan, Montana, Idaho, Wyoming, Colorado, Arizona, and New Mexico. He closed his eyes and tried to imagine Lahksa's presence in one of those locations. . . . He decided after a moment that she might be in New Mexico.

If she'd put her new recruit on a jet in the Mountain Time zone yesterday afternoon, local time, then why would it take the guy until nine this evening to arrive? Whoops. She must have meant 9 A.M., this morning. He jumped up, looking at his watch. He would have to round up a ride to take him out to the airport—pronto.

Only one person stepped from the jet—a tall, somewhat dazed-looking man with a red-tinged beard. He stumbled over to Mr. Tompkins and asked, "Where am I?"

"Morovia."

"My goodness." He stared around him in surprise and observed, as much to himself as to anyone else, "I've just met the most extraordinary woman. She attended my class in Santa Fe and we had a bite to eat after it was over. She asked me if I'd consider doing a day of consulting in Morovia. I said I'd love to—except for the fact that I had sworn off air travel.

262

She told me that modern travel in a corporate jet could be almost painless: The first thing you know you're there. Then she proposed a toast with her water glass, said 'drink up,' and I drank up and . . ."

". . . and the first thing you knew, you were here."

"Exactly. Amazing."

"How is she, by the way?"

"Oh, fine. Lovely, fascinating, full of beans. I get the feeling there is even more to her than meets the eye."

"You don't know the half of it."

"She said 'drink up' and then the steward was shaking me and saying it was time to de-plane. Say, you don't suppose she . . . ?"

"I do." Mr. Tompkins held out his hand. "Webster Tompkins, by the way. I'm your client."

"Oh. Pleased to meet you. Harry Winnipeg."

Mr. Tompkins was impressed. "Harry Winnipeg, the author? You've written a lot of books, if I'm not mistaken."

"Yes, tons."

"How is that? I mean, how is having all those books out there with your name on them?"

"Awful. There are so many that every time I think up a good idea for a new book, I've got to wonder whether I've already used it in one of my other books."

"You don't remember?"

"No, actually not, not every point. Sometimes, I pick up one of my books from twenty years ago or so and read it; it might as well be by someone else." And then, with a modest smile, he added: "It's usually pretty good stuff, though."

"So, what do you do? To make sure you're not repeating yourself, I mean."

"I have a full-time researcher who does nothing but read my own books. Say, is there breakfast in our future?"

"Yes. Coming up." Mr. Tompkins piled with his new consultant into the back of the Institute's ancient Buick and told the driver to head toward the old town of Varsjop, where there were some nice little coffee shops. He turned back to his new guest. "Tell me, Dr. Winnipeg, how do you do your consulting? I mean, What are your specialty areas?"

"You know, I often wonder that myself. Mostly, I just sniff around and look for problems." He looked across the car at Mr. Tompkins. "But I have a hunch you're going to tell me you don't really have any problems. Oh, just some little minor annoyances maybe, but nothing significant."

"Well, funny you should say that. That's rather perceptive of you. In fact, that's exactly what I was going to say. How did you know that?"

Dr. Winnipeg looked amused. "That's what people always say when they have a lot of problems."

"Oh."

They rode along for a short spell in silence.

"Since you seem to have us typed so well, Dr. Winnipeg, maybe you could predict what kind of problems we might have."

A wide yawn. The man was still waking up. "Oh, sure. People problems, I guess. That would be the most common."

Mr. Tompkins thought for a while. "What would you say if I told you that one of my project managers is curiously angry?"

"I would say you've got a people problem."

Mr. Tompkins introduced Dr. Winnipeg to Melissa Alber, who led him away to take part in the weekly PMill-A staff meeting. It was not until just before noon that his new consultant showed up again.

"Angry manager all taken care of, Webster. You needn't worry about it anymore."

"I needn't?"

"Nope. I demoted him."

"You did?"

"I did."

"Did he accept that? I mean, he doesn't exactly work for you."

"He not only accepted it, he grabbed onto it like a drowning man grabs a life jacket. I figure you and Melissa can work out the details. Anyway, Osmun is demoted."

"Well . . ."

"It's not clear exactly what he's demoted to. But he's not running the PMill-A project anymore."

"Oh. Well, I shall have to give some thought to finding a replacement. I don't doubt that there are some good possibilities from within the project itself. I'll have to talk to Melissa about that."

Dr. Winnipeg looked at him sharply. It was as if he were puzzled that Mr. Tompkins hadn't seen something obvious. "Why don't you bag the project, Webster? PMill-B and -C seem to be in pretty good shape. The A project has just been through too much. Progress has come to a grinding halt; nobody has any idea of what to do next; the design is a botch; the implementation effort is, as you'd expect, totally misdi-rected. All that's required now is an act of mercy by you to free those people to get started on something else. Time to cut your losses. I'm sure you know this already."

"Yes, well—but there are political considerations here. It's important to keep the project alive."

"Too late for that, I'm afraid. It's already dead."

"Propped up, then, to look alive."

"Ah, a zombie. When you prop up a dead project to make it look alive for political reasons, you're creating a zombie. I figure about ten percent of all projects worldwide are probably zombies. PMill-A is yours. Or one of yours. I don't doubt there are others."

Mr. Tompkins changed the subject. "What shall we do with Osmun?"

"He says that there is no staff group ready to take on the problems of configuration management for the products as they near completion. He'd like to have that job."

"Hmm. Well, he's certainly right that we've let that go for too long. And, nobody else is clamoring for the position. Why not? I suspect that he's got something to prove now, and he'll do it well."

Dr. Winnipeg had a faraway look. "I wish you could have seen his face when I told him he didn't have to be the manager anymore. It was as though the years were being stripped away. Didn't it ever occur to you before to let him off the hook?"

"Let him off the hook?" What a curious way to phrase it, thought Webster. "It certainly occurred to me to replace him, if that's what you mean. I knew I would have to do something. I had been dreading it."

"The poor man was begging for relief. All you had to do was give him permission to step down."

Mr. Tompkins shook his head. "I never thought of it that way."

Apparently, resolution of the Osmun Gradish affair had taken only a few minutes. As soon as the staff meeting was adjourned, Dr. Winnipeg and Osmun had repaired to his office. After a very short conversation, they came out, both looking pleased. They explained to the staff that Osmun was being transferred to a new responsibility. Then, Osmun went back into his office to pack. Dr. Winnipeg spent the rest of the morning wandering around the Aidrivoli complex, looking for anything else that might benefit from a fresh perspective.

One thing that he found was on the Air Traffic Control project. He happened upon a working meeting mid-morning and sat in for an hour and a half, not saying much of anything. After lunch, he took Mr. Tompkins back to the meeting.

On the way in, he counseled Mr. T. "Don't pay too much attention to what's going on. What I want you to do most of all is observe who is there."

The meeting was in the largest conference room in Aidrivoli-3. The tables had been arranged in a huge oval with Gulliver Menendez, the project leader, sitting at the head. Mr. Tompkins caught his eye and nodded to him before sitting with Dr. Winnipeg quietly in the back. The first thing he did was to count the people present. There were thirty-one, not including themselves.

Dr. Winnipeg leaned his head toward Webster and whispered: "Seven in staff, plus three consultants," and then, pointing his way around the oval, "the Ministers of Transport, Tourism, Harbors, and Airports, and their technical aides; three representatives of the European Air Traffic Control Task Force; two MSEI counselors; ATC technical personnel on loan from the Spanish government; the military air-traffic coordinator; four people from the Korsach airport staff; the Commissioner of General Aviation; the Commissioner of Communications and Telecommunications plus her aides; the head of the Morovian Olympic Committee; a representative of the International Olympic Committee; and the Minister of Fairs and Congresses."

"What on earth are they discussing?" Mr. Tompkins whispered back.

"Signaling protocol between aircraft and the towers."

Mr. Tompkins sighed. "How long have they been at it?"

"Gulliver told me at the break that this was the sixth day of the meeting."

"God."

They watched without comment for an hour. It was dreadful. Clearly, everyone in the room was finding the meeting unbearable. Finally, Dr. Winnipeg leaned in again to whisper, "Put me in, coach."

Mr. Tompkins stood and made his way to the head of the room. "Um, Gulliver, if you would permit . . ."

Gulliver looked relieved. "Oh, please. Thank you, Webster. Thank you." He loosened his tie and popped open the top button of his shirt. "Ladies and Gentlemen, this is Mr. Tompkins, the head of development here and manager of all activities at Aidrivoli."

"Thank you, Gulliver. Ladies and Gentlemen, I have been observing only for a short time. But even in this short time, I sense a good measure of frustration in the room."

There were loud groans of agreement from all sides.

"I thought so. Just this morning, I was leafing through an old book by the American writer Harry Winnipeg that I happened to have on my bookshelf. In this book, he talks a bit about frustration. I thought of that passage almost from the first moment I entered this room. The passage suggests that frustration is a kind of gold that you can mine to find out more about what makes you tick: you as an individual or, in this case, you as a working group. I think I know a way to help you mine some of this frustration, to help you out of your present morass. Are you game?"

There was a chorus of agreement.

"Very well then. I'd like to introduce formally the gentleman who has been observing your meeting for much of the day. Ladies and Gentlemen, Dr. Harry Winnipeg."

Dr. Winnipeg took his position at the front. He sat down comfortably on the edge of the head table. "You don't need me to tell you what the problem is. You all know what it is. Somebody say it."

"Too many people," one of Gulliver's staff members spoke up.

"Whatever we're discussing, it's only of interest to a handful of us," someone else shouted from the back.

"Too many people, most of them not involved in any given matter," Dr. Winnipeg summed up. He turned to Gulliver. "How bad is it? If we were to take a census of all the people involved in any way in this project, what percent of them are here in this room today?"

Gulliver looked around. "A hundred percent, or very close. A hundred percent minus two who are sick."

"I see. Now, how could that have happened? Gulliver, could you just hand me the agenda, just to check something out?"

"Um, well, the agenda is sort of informal. By that I mean, we're here to get the project going, you could say. That is the agenda."

"There is no published agenda, then. Well, you're not the first person to run a meeting with no published agenda, Gulliver. Don't feel alone in that. But it does have some consequences. To understand clearly, put yourself in the position of this gentleman," he strolled over to stand beside the Minister of Fairs and Congresses, "this gentleman whose name is . . . ?"

"Horsjuk," the man supplied.

"Minister Horsjuk. If Minister Horsjuk was wondering, just before the start of this meeting, whether he ought to attend or not, what did he have to go on? Nothing. How could he know that it would be entirely *safe* for him not to attend? Well, he had no way to know that.

"Now, that might not have mattered if, in general, he felt pretty safe about this project. But, frankly, nobody feels very safe about this project. We all understand that the project is up against some very serious challenges. There is also the uneasy feeling in the air that if it fails—and projects do sometimes fail—there might be some blame to be apportioned. So, the general sense of safety is not high. If people are feeling a little unsafe and a meeting is called with no agenda, they have to attend. Do you see that?"

"I should have published an agenda," Gulliver conceded ruefully. "Sorry, people. I won't make that mistake again."

"No great harm done," Dr. Winnipeg told him gently. "The beginnings of projects are often a bit disorganized. The hidden agenda of early meetings is always to figure out who all the key players are. So, even if you had published an agenda, you might have had too many people show up."

"Ah. But they wouldn't have had to stay all this time," the young project manager pointed out.

"True. As soon as they got the flavor of the people involved, they could leave as long as there was nothing specific on the agenda that required them to stay. Well, that's almost the whole truth. To make it whole you'd have to satisfy them on one key matter. Any idea what that would be?"

Gulliver considered for a moment. "I guess they'd have to be sure that I was going to run the meeting according to the agenda."

"Exactly. If you satisfied them on that score, then they'd look down over the remaining agenda items and excuse themselves if they felt safe not being present for those discussions." He turned back to the assembled group. "How would you all feel about that?"

The entire group signaled approval Morovian-style by knocking their knuckles on the table.

"Good. So, a published agenda for each meeting; short meetings so that they can each be dedicated to a small enough subject, likely to require the attendance of only a small subset of the whole working group; and meetings conducted exactly according to the agenda so people feel safe that there won't be extra topics addressed. Easy enough?"

Gulliver Menendez nodded. "Easy enough."

"That will go a long way toward making your meetings smaller and less frustrating. But there will still be some that are just too full. That will happen when the subject is likely to be particularly amusing, or the fireworks particularly grand. What are you going to do about those cases?"

"Uh . . . I don't know."

"Let me suggest a ceremony to begin each and every meeting. If you use this ceremony properly, it will trim all your meetings and, best of all, focus everyone's attention on the value of keeping meetings small. Will you try out this ceremony with me?" He addressed the question to the whole group. There were nods around the room.

Dr. Winnipeg raised Gulliver Menendez to his feet and positioned him at the front of the room. "The ceremony has five parts. One, you declare, Gulliver, the value of releasing even one person from the meeting and your intention to do so. Two, the group gives you its consent. Three, you select and release at least one person based on the critical nature of work

271

that he or she could do if released. Four, that person makes a parting statement to the group about what he or she would like to see happen at the meeting. Five, the group signals approval as the person leaves."

"Okay," Gulliver nodded.

"Let's begin. Part one, you look around at the size of the group and declare your intentions. Go ahead."

"Um." Gulliver looked around. "Well, there are a lot of us here today, aren't there? Too many. I, uh, I think I'd be inclined to release someone, just to trim the group a bit."

"Part two: The rest of you signal agreement."

Laughter around the room. "Go for it, Gulliver," someone shouted out. There were calls of "Yes!" and "How about me?"

Dr. Winnipeg raised one hand to quiet the group. "Good. Part three: You pick someone and . . ."

Gulliver pointed toward one of his lieutenants. "You, Konrad. Pack it up. You're out of here."

"Whoa," Dr. Winnipeg said. "Careful that you don't cause him to lose face. Remember, you have to release the person or persons whose time you value most. You have to be utterly honest about this and you have to make sure everyone knows it. Now tell me, honestly, whose time have you been most upset about tying up in this meeting?"

"Ah." Gulliver walked over to one of the Spanish ATC consultants, a member of the project's technical staff, and one of the Korsach new-tower personnel, who happened to be sitting together. "That would be these three. They could be meeting alone to work out some of our key protocols. Freeing them from this meeting would be invaluable." He looked back at Dr. Winnipeg for approval. "So, I am releasing the three of you from this meeting."

"Good. Part four: The selected people gather their things together, stand up, and make a parting statement."

They stood. One of them, with a glance at the others, spoke up. "I think I could speak for the group. What we'd like to see you do in our absence is firm up who will be the Euro ATC liaison, and appoint a working group to be responsible for 'passing' aircraft into Morovian airspace. Anything else?" He looked at his colleagues on either side. They both shook their heads. Then, all three gathered their materials and started toward the door.

"Part five," Dr. Winnipeg told the room, "the rest of you signal approval as they leave."

There was a thunder of knuckles knocking on the tables as the three selected people made their way out.

"That's your ceremony. Projects have need of ceremony, you know; projects are living things, sociological organisms. I advise you to perform this particular ceremony at the beginning of every meeting. Make it part of your routine so everyone learns the drill." Dr. Winnipeg sat down.

Gulliver remained standing. He paused a moment. "Given what we've just learned, I think the only remaining order of business for today is to adjourn. Our next meeting, I assure you, will be announced with a very carefully crafted agenda." He paused again. "I'm just waiting for those three to come back, before I adjourn."

"Oh, I don't think they're coming back," Mr. Tompkins laughed. "Not a chance."

At the end of the day, Mr. Tompkins took Dr. Winnipeg back to the airport.

"Well," he said, as they waited for the plane to taxi up to the airport door, "this has been quite an experience. I learned about zombie projects and some of the reasons for over-full meetings and how to correct them. I've been reading your

273

books all these years, but it was still an enlightening experience to see you work. And, I do thank you for resolving the problem of our angry manager. I think it was the right solution. I'm just a little embarrassed not to have seen it myself."

"It was a pleasure."

"Why was he so angry, by the way? Why was he so angry as to be abusive to his people, yelling and shouting at them in front of their peers and showing contempt? Did you ever figure that out?"

"Oh yes, that was the easy part. I knew the answer to that before I even met him."

The steward was at the door, beckoning to Dr. Winnipeg to board. Mr. Tompkins nodded at him and signaled for a minute or two of grace. He turned back to his companion. "I'd love to hear your take on that."

Dr. Winnipeg nodded. "It was fear, Webster. The man was scared to death. He was afraid he was going to fail, afraid he was going to let you down, afraid he was going to let his people down, afraid he was going to let his country down."

"He was angry because he was afraid?"

"He showed anger because he was afraid. Anger *is* fear. Fear is considered an unacceptable emotion in the workplace; you're not allowed to show it. But something needs to be let out. You have to pick a surrogate emotion or else you will pop. For some reason, anger is an acceptable emotion, so that is almost always the one you pick. Anger becomes the surrogate for fear. I don't mean to say there aren't other explanations for anger in the family or anger among friends, but in business, it's almost always fear."

From Mr. Tompkins' Journal:

<u>Project Sociology</u>

o   Keep meetings small by making it safe for unessential people not to attend. A published agenda, rigorously followed, is the easiest way to make nonattendance safe.

o   Projects have need of ceremony.

o   Use ceremony to focus attention on project goals and ideals: small meetings, zero-defect work, etc.

o   Take steps to protect people from abusive anger.

o   Remember: Anger = Fear. Managers who inflict abusive, angry behavior on their subordinates are almost always doing it because they're afraid.

o   Observation: If everybody understands that Anger = Fear, anger will be a transparent signal that the angry person is afraid; since there is an inclination not to reveal fear, he or she won't be able to vent the anger anymore. (This doesn't solve the angry person's problem, but it sure can make it easier on everyone else.)

21
ENDGAME BEGINS

৯৯

*S*he reappeared as mysteriously as she had left. The door to her office, which had been closed now for nearly ten months, was open. She was inside, sitting in her regular easy chair by the window, staring peacefully out at the rain.

His first impulse was . . . well, he wasn't quite sure what the first one was. His second impulse was to lash out, and it came almost immediately after the first. "Where the hell have you been?" His voice came out much louder than he had intended.

She looked up, smiling shyly. "Webster."

"Goddammit, Lahksa, you left us in the lurch. All these months without even a phone call . . ."

"I'm back, Webster." She stood and crossed the room to meet him at the door.

"Where the hell have you been?" he repeated.

"Bermuda. Or, at least, most recently. Do you like my tan?"

"I hate it. I am really annoyed, Lahksa. I really am."

"I think he missed me."

"I am disappointed and annoyed and irritated and angry and ticked off and let down and provoked and disturbed and . . ."

"He did miss me. I missed you too, Webster." She kissed him. He stepped back, unsure of himself. After a moment, he said, in a quieter voice, "Do you think that makes it all okay?" It did, of course.

"Webster."

His irritation welled up in him again. "We were worried sick about you. We didn't know . . . And, things have been going dreadfully here. We could have used a little help."

"Oh, dear, I do know about that. Belok?"

"Damn right, Belok. I could have used some advice, at the very least."

"Well, don't worry your head about it anymore, dear. I've taken care of Belok."

"You have?"

"I have. He's gone for the foreseeable future."

"And to what do we owe that good luck?"

"Well, the poor man has come down sick with something."

"Something serious, I hope."

"Not fatal, mind you, but nasty. He's got herpes."

"Erghhh. Not the kind that gets you right in the . . ."

"Yes, I'm afraid so. He's got a perfectly terrible case of it. Awfully painful, I understand. Anyway, he has gone off to a clinic in Atlanta that has a patented treatment for that kind of herpes."

"Oh, my. And you say he'll be gone for a while?" All that really mattered, of course, was for him to stay away another nine months or so, until Tompkins' contract was done.

"A year. He'll be out of pain as soon as they begin treatment, but he won't be able to leave. He's got to keep up with his daily treatments. I don't think we'll be seeing anymore of Allair."

Mr. Tompkins was struck by a horrible thought. "Wait a minute, how did he happen to come down with this affliction? And how did it happen to coincide so exactly with your return?"

She smiled her lopsided smile. "Dear me, how can I tell you this, Webster? There is something rather awful about me, I'm afraid. I have a terrible habit. I don't know what comes over me. I put things in people's drinks."

"You put herpes in his drink?"

"So to speak. He drinks Southern Comfort. I'd picked up a special little powder on my travels, just a pinch, and I emptied it all into his Southern Comfort. I did this Friday night in Korsach. By Saturday morning, he was in agony. I had picked up the phone number of the clinic in Georgia; actually, I got it from the same source who sold me the powder. Anyway, I made a call that morning, and by yesterday Allair was on his way in the corporate jet. I came here on the train as soon as that was taken care of."

"The six A-Team projects are all zombies," Mr. Tompkins told them. "They are long dead, only propped up to look alive for political reasons. With the unfortunate departure of our beloved Minister Belok, . . ."

An unseemly snicker from Kenoros.

" . . . the 'political reasons' cease to exist. So, I say we now do what Belinda has been urging for the last few weeks: Raid the A-Teams."

"I did use the term raid when I proposed that to you, Webster. But you can't use it; not when you announce what's going to happen. We have to think out very carefully how this is to be presented to the staff."

"Point taken, Belinda. We need to present it so no face is lost. The A-Team projects are zombies, but the people on them aren't. They have feelings. How shall we put it to them? Melissa?"

"You'll be rescuing them, Webster. They all know, they've known from the beginning, that only one product will go out the door. Two of the teams will not produce the winning version. PMill-A, for example, has known for a while now that they were not going to be the winner. I have a hunch the other A-Teams are similarly aware. We need to present this as a rescue of valuable resources. We're moving them out of a dead-end effort and back onto the critical path."

"Something like that," Gabriel agreed. "What we don't want to do now, however, is move the A-Team people directly onto the B- and C-Teams. If we do that, half of them will be set up for a second defeat." He crossed the room to the white board and began to draw. "What I propose instead is that we set up staff groups under each product manager, and use the A-Team personnel to populate these groups."

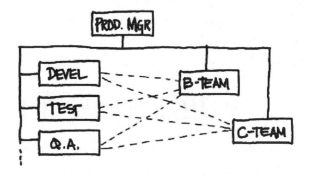

The assembled management team stared up at the ex-General's diagram.

"That's a beginning," Mr. Tompkins told them. "What you've just drawn, Gabriel, is a proposed *re*-design for our system. We design and build systems here, but we also *are* a system. You've just redesigned us. Before we move into implementation, I suggest we treat this like any other design, force it through the same process we've been using with software designs on the B- and C-Teams." He turned to Kenoros. "Aristotle, will you guide us?"

Kenoros stood up, smiling. "Okay, Boss." He addressed the group. "People, put your design hats on. Okay? Okay. Here we go."

With Belok out of the picture, no one could fault Mr. Tompkins for returning to the original schedule. He had done that promptly. There was a huge sense of relief around the complex. The new date was one that gave a good chance to all the B and C projects, even the largest of them The smaller ones, the QuickerStill projects, for example, were likely to finish well ahead of the new target. In fact, he had still not given up his hope that at least one of them would be able to deliver its product by June first. Belok was gone, but Tompkins was still focused on Belok's damn date. He had even instructed Mrs. Beerzig to maintain the countdown in his office for June first. On this mid-February day it read:

ONLY $\boxed{106}$ DAYS TILL D-DAY!

Once the groups had been successfully restructured, there was precious little for Mr. Tompkins to do. He wandered about most days, chatting with people, picking up scuttlebutt, expressing admiration for all the good work, and, most of all, looking for opportunities to lend a hand. There weren't many of these. The projects were proceeding smoothly, and he was beginning to feel extraneous.

Belinda, too, had the feeling. She was spending more and more time back in the harbor park, sitting under her palm tree, reading. She almost never came in anymore, unless the weather was dismal. Mr. Tompkins joined her in the park one afternoon, bringing along a box lunch for them both.

"Nothing to do," he told her.

She grinned. "Your job is done, Webster. This is the way the ends of projects are supposed to be, but almost never are. All you've got left to do now is pick up your binoculars and watch how it all turns out, just like General Patton."

When she had first recalled that scene from the film all those months ago, Webster had been rather charmed. From that early vantage point, he couldn't imagine a better ending than one that let him confidently observe the outcome, knowing full well that all his plans were about to succeed. But now that he was in just that position, he was going crazy. He wondered if Patton hadn't felt the same way.

After lunch, having left Belinda in the park, he stopped by the Residence library and found a copy of the film. He took the video upstairs to his suite and viewed just the beginning scene of Patton watching the battle through binoculars. To Webster's surprise, the scene unfolded slightly differently from what Belinda had remembered. True, Patton observed *almost* all the battle without doing a thing. He had indeed already done his part in planning the maneuvers, training the fighting divisions, securing supplies, and timing the initial attack. But, at the very end of the scene, he put his binoculars down for a moment and dispatched a courier to General Bradley with a minor change of plan. He had intervened. Now, that was *real* management. You train all the troops so that the battle is almost certain to unfold flawlessly. You watch quietly, just to be sure that it does. But when something goes even a little bit awry, you intervene.

"Things are going so smoothly I'm bored," Molly Makmora told him about the QuickerStill-C project. "That's good, mind you. A nice side effect of Kenoros's design scheme is that it provides us with excellent metrics to monitor this part of the project. We know exactly how many modules there are; and we can predict fairly precisely how many lines of code, how many expected defects, how much time per defect on average, how much work remains in each of the categories of work. . . ."

"How can you be sure that your projections for lines of code will be so good?"

"Well, we've got about half the modules coded already. We can see how our projection technique worked on the first four hundred or so modules, so we can feel pretty comfortable that it will work as well on the rest.

"What really gives us a sense of control is the build plan," she went on. "Here, look at this." She walked with him to the QuickerStill-C war room and then led him to one wall where there was a multicolored graph on display. "We originally planned to deliver the product in 60 builds. Each build is a subset of the whole, and each one adds incrementally to the one before. So, here we are today at Build Number 24. As you can see from this work sheet, Build 24 includes these 409 modules. Build 23, which we completed last week, . . ." she found the related work sheet for Build 23, ". . . had 392 modules. So, we're adding 17 modules in this new build. And, here, you see the module IDs and sizes of those 17 modules."

"Nice."

"More than nice. We have calibrated each build in terms of its percentage of the whole product. Remember that the whole product was originally sized at 1500 function points. We subsequently revised that upward to 1850. When we put Build Number 1 together, we observed that it implemented about 2 percent of the whole, or 37 function points. Build 2 added another 30, so when Build 2 was complete and proved out, we knew that we had successfully implemented 67 function points out of the whole of 1850, or 3.6 percent. We concluded from that that the integration work—that is, that portion of the project beginning with Build 1 and culminating in full-product delivery—was 3.6 percent done.

"Now, this graph shows the same kind of conclusions for each successful build."

Functionality Included in Successive Builds

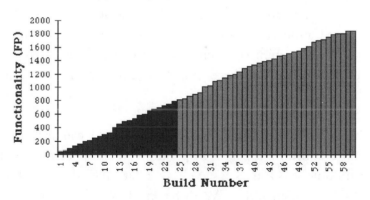

"Each bar on the graph is a build. The dark ones are completed. We have divided our full-product acceptance test into pieces so that we have an acceptance test for each build. We don't call the build complete until it has passed its acceptance test without flaw."

Mr. Tompkins put his finger on the bar for Build 24. "So, when Build 24 passes its test, you'll know you're 46 percent of the way home."

"Right. We're integrating builds at a present rate of about one every two or three days." She stepped to the right side of the graph. "So, now you know how we can be so confident that we'll be done by the last week in June. We're getting constant status information from the product itself. That's what each successful build is, the voice of the product announcing just how far along it is toward completion."

Mr. T. looked sadly at the date under her finger. He still would have liked to have a last laugh on Belok by bringing one project home by June first. "No chance of speeding that up a bit? I mean . . . not that I'm complaining. . . . This project is proceeding admirably. It's just that . . ."

She smiled. "I know what you're thinking, Webster. June first, right? It's still on my mind sometimes, too. Well, I don't see how we could, frankly. We have become very efficient at proving out the builds, so we could up the rate a bit, but our limiting factor is production time. Here, look." She pointed him toward another display on the war room wall. "This is how the time is spent on each module, getting it ready to be incorporated in its build: coding time, inspection time, unit test, documentation, et cetera."

"Nothing there you could subtract?"

She glanced at the table again. "Nothing I can see. The most time-consuming part is inspection. We inspect each and every module as soon as it's coded. That takes three people and usually lasts an hour. We don't know what we can subtract from the process, but one thing we know that we can't subtract is inspection."

There was something about the way she phrased this that jarred him. Take your eye off what you don't know, he told himself, and focus on what you do know. It's not what you don't know that kills you but what you know that isn't so. "How do we know that we can't eliminate inspection?" he asked.

"I think that has been the entire lesson of the last ten years, Webster. Inspections are the cheapest way to eliminate defects. If you don't eliminate them in inspections, you just have to take them out in testing. And that costs you more than what you'd save by eliminating code inspections."

Aristotle Kenoros happened by and joined the conversation. "Yup. That's what the evidence says," he chimed in. "Cheapest way to assure a quality product is code inspections."

"And we know we're getting a quality product. Look at this." She pointed proudly to a huge red display on the far wall that read "14 straight!"

"Fourteen straight whats?" Mr. Tompkins asked her.

"Fourteen straight inspections without a single defect detected." She looked extremely pleased.

"That is impressive," Mr. Tompkins allowed. "I guess, though, that we could have dispensed with those fourteen inspections and saved some forty-two person-hours and not hurt quality one whit, since they didn't find any defects."

Molly looked disappointed in him. "I think you miss the point, Webster. It's because of code inspections that we're getting such high quality."

"Not because of those last fourteen, however. Those we could have done without."

"Well, . . . the statistics on net benefit of inspections are pretty impressive, still. I'm not at all sure . . ."

"Kill them," Mr. Tompkins said. He was suddenly excited.

"Huh?"

"Kill the inspections. Stop all code inspections."

"Wait a minute," she wailed. "We can't do that. Aristotle, tell him. Tell him what you told us about the cost of removing defects in inspection. Tell him he's off the wall."

Kenoros made a strange face. "Off the wall, yes. But wrong, no. I hadn't thought of it till you brought it up, Webster, but if the inspections aren't detecting defects, we can't justify them on the basis of reduced cost per defect."

"Unless something has gone terribly wrong in the inspection process . . ."

"It hasn't," Molly answered him promptly. "We checked. The modules that sail through inspection without any defects are also sailing through testing. There just aren't any defects to detect."

"Then the inspection is useless and I say kill it."

She looked again to Kenoros for help.

"I don't know. . . ." he began.

Mr. Tompkins interrupted him. "Aristotle, the defects aren't there. There's a reason for that. The original code production is going much more smoothly than we would have expected."

"Mmm."

"Remember that you told me that defects, when they occur, are not exactly in the module, but on the 'edge' of the module?"

"Yes."

"They are interface flaws, most of them. So, they are really design errors. It's crazy to do a design analysis when you're looking at one piece of code. This is you speaking. You need to do that when you're looking at a design. The reason the statistics are so impressive on code inspections is that they are a slightly better way than testing to remove these design defects. But you've implemented a still better way, the more formal design. And you've already inspected the design. I declare that all these modules have already been inspected, not at code time, but at design time. And so, further inspection is superfluous."

"You may be right," Kenoros allowed. He was beginning to convince himself. "If you are right, it suggests that the code inspections that the rest of the world is so enamored over are just a remedial design technique. If we do a proper and complete design before coding, and we inspect the design, we shouldn't need code inspection. I don't know if that's one hundred percent true or not, but I do know one thing."

"What's that?"

"We need to find out. We're not running much of a Project Management Laboratory if we don't find the answer to this one."

Mr. Tompkins was sitting at his desk, staring down baffled at an empty journal page, when Lahksa showed up at his door.

He looked up. "Oh. It's you, Lahksa." He blushed slightly, as he often did when she stopped by. Then, with a glance down at the accusingly empty page, "You gave me this journal," he told her, "all those months ago. You told me to write something in it every day. Write whatever it was that I learned that day. And I have, most days. But now I haven't written a thing in it for weeks. Do you know why that is?"

"No." She sat down on the edge of his desk. "Tell me."

"Because I don't know what I learned from the Belok affair. If I had resolved it myself, somehow, I could take a lesson from that. Whatever I did to get him off my back, I could write that down as a lesson learned. But I didn't resolve it. You did."

"And you can't write that down."

"No. It's too dumb. From my point of view, you descended like a passing angel and solved my problem for me. It was more or less a miracle. I can hardly write that. I can hardly write, 'If you work for a jerk, wait for a miracle to occur.'"

"What would you rather write?"

"Something that a person could do. After all, the world is full of people who have horrid forms of pathology above them on the org chart, some as bad as Belok or worse. The lesson I'd like to write down is what they should do about that."

"Maybe there is nothing they can do, Webster. There often isn't. Did you, honestly, have any hope of dealing with the pathology of Belok by yourself?"

"It hadn't come to me yet, but maybe there was something I could have done."

"I don't think so. I don't think you can 'cure' pathology from beneath. I honestly don't, Webster. I don't think there is any way to do that."

He sighed. "Maybe you're right. Maybe there is no way."

"Maybe that's your lesson learned."

With that, she ruffled his hair affectionately and left him to write his entry.

From Mr. Tompkins' Journal:

Pathological Politics (Again)

o   You can't expect to cure pathology from beneath.

o   Don't waste your time or jeopardize your position by trying.

o   Sometimes, your only option is to bide your time, waiting for the problem to resolve itself, or for a good opportunity for you to move on.

o   Miracles may happen (but don't count on them).

22

THE YEAR'S HOTTEST IPO

ào

On May 24th, the QuickerStill B-Team delivered its
product. On May 29th, QuickerStill-C delivered. On May
30th, PMill-C delivered.

Mr. Tompkins was exultant. "Can you believe this,
Belinda? We actually pulled off three deliveries, all before
Belok's idiotic date."

"Does that mean it wasn't an idiotic date after all?"

"Of course it was an idiotic date," he bristled. "It would
have been a decent stretch goal for our two smallest products,
but as a planning date it was idiotic. Belok had actually committed to the distribution chain for all six products to begin
shipping starting tomorrow. June first wasn't even a sensible
stretch goal for any of the larger projects. And, as a planning
date, it was idiotic for any of them."

"Whoa. Are you suggesting that a project ought to have
both a schedule and a goal? and that they might even be different? That's rather radical of you, Webster."

"Well? Doesn't that make sense? A good *goal* is right on
the edge of possible. So, it makes a lousy scheduling date. A

good *schedule* is likely to be met, so it doesn't make much of a goal. Why shouldn't projects have both?"

"Oh, I'm not disagreeing. It's just that you are hardly standing with the crowd on this one."

"You're right. I'm all alone. Maybe that's a sign that I'm right."

On June 1st, word came that NNL was finally back. Mr. Tompkins was summoned with some urgency to see him.

The assistant who had made the appointment seemed almost breathless with excitement. She didn't give much away, but there was clearly something in the works. In his own experience, excitement in the Head Office was usually a bad sign. Head Office people tended to get excited when heads were rolling or work was about to be canceled. He took the morning train to Korsach with some trepidation. Oh, there really wasn't much anyone could do now to spoil his sense of achievement for projects that had already come home. But he was still mildly worried.

As it was during Webster's first visit those many months ago, NNL's office was again unlit but for the glow of his monitor. Again, it took a moment to locate the man, lost in the huge room. He was in a dark corner, Twinkie in hand. In mouth, actually. "Mordig, Tobkigs," he said around a mouthful of cake.

"Morning, Sir. Welcome back."

"Wade a minig," Himself said. He swallowed and wiped his mouth on a napkin. Then, he looked up at Tompkins with an enormous grin. "We did it, Tompkins! We pulled it off!"

"The projects? Well, yes, we did have a bit of . . ."

"No, not the projects. Although they certainly did help. Nice going, by the way. But no, that wasn't what I was talking about. I was talking about the offering."

"Offering?"

"We're going public, Tompkins. Morovia Inc. is going public. The IPO is scheduled for next week. This is a major coup. The underwriters say it's going to be the hottest IPO of the year."

"My goodness. Morovia going public. I think we're likely to be the world's first publicly traded country."

"I hadn't thought of that, but you may be right."

"Congratulations are in order, I guess. Well, congratulations, Sir. I hope you make a bundle of money on the offering. Another bundle, that is."

"Not just me, Tompkins. All of us. You, in particular."

"Me?"

"Yes. Don't you remember, you have got stock. You own half a percent of the outstanding stock."

"I do?" Mr. Tompkins' interest was suddenly piqued.

"Of course, you do. Fifty thousand shares."

"Um, is there any estimate yet about what the offering price will be?"

NNL was having trouble containing his glee. "Fourteen dollars! Can you believe it? They thought at first it would be eleven, but the issue was so oversubscribed that they had to bump up the price. It could go even higher by next week. And god-knows-what it will open at. It's not crazy to think about twenty dollars or even twenty-four by end of the first day." He put his head back and crowed. "We're rich!"

"Um, you were always rich."

"Richer, then. Much richer. Wow. Hooray for capitalism. I feel like Scrooge McDuck, just about to start burrowing in his money."

Mr. Tompkins, still in a bit of a daze, did the arithmetic on his own holdings. At $14 a share, he would be worth . . . Wow.

And at $24 . . . Hooray for capitalism, indeed. "Well, this is decidedly good news," he said, with as much restraint as he could muster.

"Everybody is getting some of the action," NNL told him. "We're distributing small amounts of stock to all employees. And I've made a pool of some thirty thousand extra shares available to you to distribute among those of your people whom you select . . ."

"My goodness. Well, I will certainly know where to place that," Mr. Tompkins told him fervidly. He was thinking of Belinda, Gabriel, Aristotle. . . .

"I thought you would." NNL's face was alive with the ebb and flow of emotion. He would seem to have himself calmed down, and then it would all erupt again. "Hooooheeeeeeeee!" he yelped.

"Yes."

NNL calmed himself abruptly. "Oh, one slightly complicated thing, Tompkins. The underwriters inform us that we have to terminate your contract before the offering. That means you get paid off, but have no further obligation to us as of the offering date. Legal reasons, apparently. Of course, the new management will be after you to sign on for another contract. I don't doubt you can stick it to them. They're all quite aware of the wonders you've accomplished."

That put a slightly different light on matters. "Hmm," Mr. Tompkins began. "Well, I will certainly listen. You know, though, my work here really is done. The rest of the projects are on track. I have no doubt they'll come home in fine shape. The major data from our experiments is all collected now, though we'll certainly be interested to observe completion of the larger projects. I don't have to be boss, however, to make sure the final data is recorded and published. That work is already under way." He paused for a moment to consider. "I think I might just move on."

"Oh, dear. The new directors will be distressed. Any idea who should be your replacement?"

"Melissa Alber," Tompkins answered without hesitation. "She is ripe for the job, talented, gutsy, capable, charismatic. She is so right for my job that I've begun to feel that I was just in the way of her career. I would be delighted to step aside and let her have it."

"Well, as I say, the directors will be upset about losing you. But, what the hell? Melissa sounds like a perfect replacement, and maybe you do need to move on. I'm certainly not going to spend the rest of my life here, either. I wish you well, Tompkins, whatever you decide to do."

"Well, thank you. I'm not at all sure what it will be, but I'm looking forward to it. How about yourself, Sir? Any idea what you'll be taking on next?"

"Mmph." A cloud of annoyance came over NNL's boyish features. "I had a lovely idea, but it hasn't panned out." He shook his head in irritation. "I thought I'd look around for another country to buy up, another leveraged stock deal. I thought I'd look for a situation similar to Morovia, you know, an ex-East Bloc country now up for grabs, poor but well-educated, eager to move more quickly into the developed world."

"Bulgaria, perhaps?" Mr. Tompkins offered.

"That's just what I thought. No deal, though. Somebody else has already picked it up. Just my luck. You invent a better mousetrap and somebody steals it from you and cleans up big time."

"Oh, well, something else will turn up."

"Any ideas?"

A moment of reflection. "How about the U.S.?" Mr. T. suggested.

"Ooooh."

"Of course, it's a bit more ambitious."

"Of course. But still, who would do it if not myself?"

"Who indeed?" Tompkins echoed.

Himself probably could pull it off, given enough time. Tompkins started to have second thoughts about his suggestion. Oh, dear. Maybe he should have kept his mouth shut. Maybe a leveraged buyout of the United States by NNL would not be the best thing for the country. Mr. Tompkins still had patriotic feelings. "Um, if you did acquire the U.S., you wouldn't interfere, would you, with civil rights?"

"Oh, goodness, no. I'd only run the business part."

"No interfering in government?"

"Well, not much anyway. I would have the right, wouldn't I, to make one tiny change?"

"Well, I suppose, if it were just one. What are you thinking?"

"I think I'd move the Anti-Trust Division to Nome, Alaska."

"Ah. Well, I expect the American people could live with that."

A pause. This was it, then. Mr. Tompkins had come abruptly to the end of his time in Morovia. He'd stay on a month or so to bring Melissa up to speed, and then he'd be gone. This interview was clearly over. In a few moments, he'd leave and probably would never see NNL again.

NNL was thinking the same thing. He stood and shoved his hand awkwardly toward Mr. Tompkins. "Here now. Thank you for what you've done, Tompkins," he said gruffly.

Mr. Tompkins stood to shake his hand somberly.

"Thank you, Tompkins. . . . um, Webster. It was a job well done."

"And thank you, Sir."

"Bill. Please call me Bill."

"Thank you, Bill."

As soon as Mr. Tompkins was back in his Aidrivoli office, there was a telephone call from NNL. "Webster, have you any idea where What's-his-name is? You know, the greasy little man. My Minister of Internal Affairs. I haven't seen him since I got back."

"Belok."

"Yes, that's the guy. Belok."

"I hear he is on extended sick leave, actually. He's been gone about four months."

"Oh. Really?" There was a silent moment. "Well, that's a great loss, I guess. I mean, I think I guess that."

Mr. Tompkins kept his face a blank. "We've all done our best to make do in Allair's absence."

"Yes, well, the little problem I have is that I had sort of proposed to the new board that my Minister of Internal Affairs would take over for me as CEO. And now I don't seem to have a Minister of Internal Affairs. They're sure to notice. Damn. I'm feeling quite keen to be out of here, and on to some new adventure. But, with nobody to pass the helm to . . ."

"So, . . . could you appoint a new Minister? What's the fun of having the title of Tyrant if you don't get to do stuff?"

"Are you asking for the job?"

"No way. I'm off to spend my new-found wealth."

"Who, then?"

"Um, let me think. Your prior Minister of Internal Affairs was a bit of a hatchet man. Does the new one have to be the same sort?"

"Actually, no. I'd rather have someone more like me. You know: brilliant, but sort of a nice fellow. Or a nice fellow and brilliant. Something like that."

A half-second delay, while the brilliant but nice fellow on the other end of the line considered. "You're good, Webster. That's an inspired suggestion. People love him and he's as savvy as they come."

"And a natural leader."

"Good choice."

"It is, rather, isn't it. I've got a natural flair for this sort of thing."

Mr. T. was just settling down to think of something to write in his journal when the phone rang again. Mrs. Beerzig had left, so he picked it up himself. The voice on the other end was one that he might have thought he'd never hear again.

"Tompkins. Look alive there. This is Minister Belok."

The phone connection was crystal clear. Did that mean that Belok was calling from close by? Could he be back in his office in Korsach and about to consolidate his crumbling position? Tompkins might have guessed just that. But now he didn't have to guess where the call was coming from: A little white caller-ID box had just been installed beside his phone, and it even worked on international calls. He looked down at its tiny screen. The caller identity shown there was GEN-HERP CLINIC: OSIMEE, GA (USA). Belok was still taking the treatment. The fact that he referred to himself as 'Minister,' meant that he hadn't heard about the changes that were in the works.

"Hello, Allair. How are you?"

"Cut the crap. Tompkins, I want you to move everybody out of Aidrivoli-1, -5, -6, and -7. I'm renting the space. I've got a terrific tenant. I've arranged it all by phone this morning."

"Gee, what will we do with all those people?"

"What do I care? Squeeze them into the other buildings. Tear down the interior walls and build big bull pens. Fire a few of them; you've got way too many people anyway."

"Golly, I shouldn't think that would make anybody too happy."

A chuckle on the other end. "I guess not. Well, tough noogies. We're not running a popularity contest here. Every day they use up all that space is costing me seven thousand two hundred twenty-three dollars of lost rent. That's what I'll be getting from the new tenants. So, get your people out of there by Friday."

"Let's see, fourteen hundred people in our three remaining buildings. That's going to work out to less than forty square feet per person."

"Right."

"Less than in a prison."

"Right. And listen, don't move out the furniture or the computers or anything. I'm selling it all to the new tenants."

"Oh, dear. This *is* upsetting news. What will my people do?"

"Have them share. They've been living in the lap of luxury for too damn long. I'm turning over a new leaf: From now on, this organization is going to become *lean and mean.*"

"Oh, no."

"Yes! I've been reading about 'lean and mean' in the business press. It's sweeping the whole country. The whole goddamn U.S. It's the new big thing: layoffs, salary cuts, tighter workspace, spartan conditions."

"But I don't much want my organization to become 'lean and mean,' Allair. No, I don't think I want that at all. I think what I want is quite the opposite: prosperous and caring."

"Don't jerk me around, Tompkins!"

"Yes, prosperous and caring. That's the thing. We are a class operation, and we ought to look and feel like one."

Belok screeched into the phone. "You are on thin ice, Tompkins. Don't take me lightly. Just do as you're told."

"No, I don't think I will, Allair. Tell your tenants to kiss off."

A short silence. Then, the voice on the other end of the line hissed, "Let me recall to you a few facts, you dunderhead. You are powerless and afraid, and I am one mean and dangerous man. You don't dare trifle with me. You haven't got the guts."

Mr. Tompkins looked at his watch. There was a lecture in fifteen minutes at the Institute. If he left now, he could pass through the newly blooming rose gardens on his way. Nothing left to do here but get this time-waster out of his hair. Nothing left but the coup de grace: "Allair, if I am such a pushover and you are such a dangerous fellow, how come I am sitting here on top of the world and you're stuck in a clinic in Georgia with blisters on your pecker?"

There was a soft gasp on the line. Tompkins didn't wait for any further response. He hung up the phone and headed out into the pleasant Morovian afternoon, taking his journal with him.

From Mr. Tompkins' Journal:

<u>Lean and Mean</u>

     o   Lean and Mean is a formula developed in failing companies by the people responsible for the failure.

     o   It is the opposite of any organization's natural goal: to be prosperous and caring.

     o   Whenever you hear the phrase "lean and mean," replace it with what it really connotes: failing and frightened.

23

PASSING THROUGH
RIGA ON THE WAY HOME

ॐ

*M*r. Tompkins was dreaming. This was to be his last night
in Morovia. The party that evening at the Residence had
gone on forever, with a huge, celebratory crowd present.
Everyone was there. Frankly, he'd had too much to eat and far
too much to drink. That was probably the reason for this
dream, in which he saw a swirl of smoke with a light inside
and something else there, too. It was a giant head. No body,
just a head. The face was slightly cherubic, but huge, and on
top of the head was an immense turban. The face glowed,
alive, its eyes and features animated, and out of its mouth came
a deep, rumbling voice:

"I am Yordini!" it said, grandly.

"Yordini," Tompkins replied in shock. "The Yordini?"

"The Yordini," the head confirmed.

"The fortune teller?"

There was an angry thunder clap. "The *futurist,* dammit!"

"That's what I meant."

"The Great Yordini."

"Gee."

"You are one lucky fellow, Tompkins. You are to be given a glimpse into the future."

"Wow."

"Ask your questions and I will give you answers. The future is as clear to me as the past is to others."

Tompkins thought rapidly: There were so many things that he needed to know. He was leaving a lot of loose ends. "Tell me . . ." he considered briefly, "tell me what will happen to the ATC project. Will Gulliver Menendez and his people deliver the system on time for the Summer Games?"

Yordini closed his eyes. A disconnected hand appeared and rubbed his chin thoughtfully. "Yes," he said at last. "Not perfect and not without operational problems, but they will make the date. There will be some delays on incoming flights, but no crashes."

"Well, that's a relief. Tell me what's going to happen to Belinda Binda? Will she be okay? Will she be able to get back on track again?"

Again, the closed eyes. "Yes. In a manner of speaking."

"What does that mean?"

"She will have a career again, but it won't be one hundred percent respectable."

"Oh, dear. What will she become?"

"U.S. Senator from the State of California."

"Oh. Well, I think that is a good thing for her. And a good thing for the rest of us, as well."

"What else?"

"Allair Belok. What will happen to him?"

"A life of great portent. He will become comptroller of a public company, an investment banker, a captain of industry, and finally, a special assistant in the White House."

"And then?"

"Then to the Federal Prison at Danbury."

"Yes, I thought so."

"And finally, he will find religion and have his own radio talk show."

"As you would expect."

"What else?"

The head was beginning to rise slowly and the smoke to swirl more heavily.

"Wait. Wait. What will happen to the American software industry? Will all the jobs be lost to third-world countries as some have feared?"

The head was almost gone now. And then it was gone. All that was left behind was the disembodied voice. "Read my book on the subject," it said.

The journal that had been his companion for the whole adventure was open on his desk before him. It was turned to page 102, the first blank page. He would have liked to make a final entry, but there was really nothing he could think of that would sum up his Morovian experience. Maybe the journal in its entirety was the summing up. He turned back one page to see what he'd written in what he now knew would be the last entry. It was one he'd thought of often but only committed to paper a few days ago.

Radical Common Sense

o   A project needs to have both goals and estimates.

o   They should be different.

There was a knock at the door. Mrs. Beerzig stuck her head in. "Webster, would you have time for an interview? There is a gentleman here from the press."

"Sure, why not?" he said cheerfully.

The man who was ushered in by Mrs. Beerzig was not a stranger as Mr. Tompkins had expected. It was Alonzo Davici, one of ex-General Markov's star managers.

"Alonzo—well, this is a surprise." He shook Alonzo's big hand. Alonzo had a walrus mustache and an amused glint in his eye. "This is a new role for you, I think. Journalist?"

"I've been promoted. Perhaps you hadn't heard. I went to work for the Institute. They made me editor-in-chief of the new journal we're publishing. It's to be called *Aidrivoli Software Magazine.*"

"Oh, yes. I had heard that. Well, congratulations."

"Thank you. For our first issue, I thought we'd do a feature on none other than yourself, about your experience here in Morovia."

"Why not? Why not, indeed? I'd be delighted. Tell me, what would you like to know? Ask away."

"Well, just any lessons you might have learned in the long trip up to your recent success. I mean, you seem to have done some things right along the way. What were they?"

"More important, I should think, is what were the things I did wrong, and what did I learn from them?"

"That was to be my next question," Alonzo conceded.

"What did I do right and wrong, and what did I learn?" He thought for a moment. "It's funny you should ask that. It's a question I've asked myself almost every day since I first came here. I would ask myself that question each evening, and if anything occurred to me, I would write it down."

Alonzo raised his eyebrows. "I haven't been in the magazine business very long, but I'm already attuned to the possibility that something the interviewee has written down could save the interviewer a lot of time. I don't suppose you could give me a copy of what you've written?"

Mr. Tompkins looked down at his journal on the desk in front of him. "I'll do better than that. I'll give you the original. I can't think of a better person to have it." He passed the journal over.

Alonzo took the book in surprise. "Well . . ." He opened it and thumbed through a few pages. "Why, this is just what we're looking for. I suspect this is what managers have been looking for for years. How many of these entries are there?"

"One hundred and one," Mr. Tompkins told him.

"And you're willing to give this up? I mean, we could have a copy made and get the original back to you."

Mr. Tompkins shook his head. "No need, really. I hope the contents may be of some use to you, and your readers. But the journal can be of no further use to me, ever. I can never imagine opening it again. I don't need to. I carry those hundred and one principles everywhere I go. They're carved directly into my hide."

There was one more thing that wasn't resolved, and apparently it wasn't going to be. He hadn't seen Lahksa since the party last night. She hadn't turned up at the airport with all the others to see him off and when he had called her, there had been no answer. Not only was there not to be a discussion, as he had hoped, of what might lie ahead for them; there wasn't even going to be a good-bye.

He settled dejectedly into his seat in the corporate jet. Seafood was already asleep on the seat beside him, knocked out by his pill. Mr. Tompkins was just strapping himself in when the steward came back to check.

"Well, then, Mr. Tompkins. Just relax now and have a good flight. The next stop will be ..."

"Boston," Mr. Tompkins finished for him.

"That's the second stop. We have one stop in between."

"Oh? Where will that be?"

"Riga, Latvia. I know, I know, it's off the beaten track a bit. The truth is that not all countries will let us enter their airspace, coming as we do from a state with no modern air traffic control."

"Ah, but all that will change, my friend. By the summer of 2000. Morovia is going to have a first-class air control system. Take my word for it."

"I look forward to it. How about some champagne, sir?"

Mr. Tompkins accepted a glass and tipped back its contents. He was asleep before the plane even took off.

There was a hand pushing against his shoulder. "Mr. Tompkins. Wake up, sir. We're in Riga."

Mr. T. looked up at the steward sleepily. "We are?"

"Yes, sir. As we'll be here several hours, we've engaged a local man with a car to show you around." The steward promised to keep an eye on Seafood.

"Oh. Well. That's nice, I guess. I've never been to Latvia. Why not?"

He stood up, stretching, and allowed himself to be guided down the stairs to the tarmac where there was a taxi waiting for him.

"No customs?" he asked the driver.

The man shook his head.

Tompkins looked around. The airport seemed to be in the middle of a wide, pleasant meadow. There were palm trees beside the runway. "Gee, I never thought there would be palm trees here."

The driver grunted. He opened the door, and Mr. Tompkins got in. Within ten minutes, they were in the outskirts of a pleasant city, mostly in sand colors and pastels. It did not look at all like the kind of northern place he would have expected Riga to be. Riga, he would have thought, would be ...Then he knew, of course, that this wasn't Riga after all.

"What is this city called?" he asked the taxi driver.

The answer, when it came back, was exactly what he'd been expecting: "Sofia."

"Ah."

It was so obvious, now that he thought about it. Whoever it was that now ran Bulgaria wanted to have a little chat with Tompkins. They wanted to suggest that he do the same thing for them that he'd done for Morovia. This was to be an employment interview. And, like the last one, it was to be an interview with a certain troubling aspect about it: He would be offered a job, but it wasn't at all clear that he could say no. Well, this time, he told himself, he was going to say no.

The cab pulled up to a vast rococo palace. "What is this?" he asked.

"It was the ancient seat of the King," the driver told him. "It's here where the Nation's Noble Leader now lives and rules from."

"Bulgaria has its own NNL?"

"Yes," the man smiled. "Bulgaria's NNL. We call him BNNL."

Tompkins rolled his eyes. Oh, well. Might as well see what the fellow had in mind. Get it over with.

Two footmen in elaborate dress escorted him through the palace. He followed them up a vast circular stairway that formed an entry into a part of the palace that, judged by a glance into its interior, was even more palatial than what he had passed through already. Someone was waiting for him at the top of the stairs, a small figure almost lost in the grandeur of the place.

"Lahksa!"

"Hullo, Webster."

"Lahksa. I thought . . . Oh, I should have known. You're up to your old tricks again."

She gave him the lopsided smile, but didn't say anything.

"Well. I'll listen to what you've got to say, but don't expect me to be so easy as last time."

"Thank you, Webster. I'm glad you're not angry."

"Not angry. It's just that I had hoped . . ." No need to go into that. "So you are Bulgaria's NNL. Well, I should have guessed. Himself told me that someone had gotten in and arranged a buyout ahead of him. Who else but you? Well, you'll probably make a fine BNNL. . . ."

"But Webster, it isn't I who bought Bulgaria."

"It isn't?"

"No. How could I? Oh, I did come away with a nice bit of stock from the IPO, I'm not complaining. But it would never have been enough to pull off this deal. No, I am not the new owner here."

"Well, who is, then?"

"You are, Webster."

"What?!?"

"You are the new owner, at least the majority owner. You are BNNL."

"How could that be? Now, don't give me that grin of yours. How did you do this?"

"Your various holdings, your stock certificates, I'm afraid, were no match for my sneaky little fingers. I sort of picked them up."

"You are incorrigible."

"Probably so."

"But I still wouldn't have thought that my small number of shares would be enough to buy a whole country."

"Well, we did add in Belinda's shares and those of Aristotle, and my own as well. . . ."

He knew from the prospectus exactly how many shares each person had. "That still doesn't seem like enough. Sixty thousand shares from the three of you, and then my own fifty thousand. . . ."

She looked at him, startled. "You had options, Webster."

"I did?"

"Of course. Don't you remember? I handed them over to you myself when you signed your contract."

"I . . . I honestly never looked. They're probably still there where I put them in my document box."

"I don't think so," Lahksa said, smirking.

"Oh. How many options did I have, by the way?"

"Three hundred thousand shares. Worth about $7.2 million at today's price."

"Oh."

"A bit of leverage here and there, and voilá. I learned the formula from Himself. He was quite adroit at that sort of thing."

Mr. Tompkins' head was swimming. "I don't know what to say."

"Belinda and Aristotle have signed on to help you get started. It looks like we may be able to pinch a few key people from your old staff, all without getting Melissa too upset. And I've been tracking down those four key managers you so respected back in New Jersey. I'll bet we'll get at least two of them to come. The Morovia IPO has made such ventures look pretty good."

"Well . . . "

"Say you'll do it, Webster. Please do. I'd be so pleased."

He stopped, staring at her. "Now just wait a minute." This time he was not going to capitulate without getting what he really wanted. He put on his most severe expression. "Tell me, Lahksa, exactly what role you've picked out for yourself."

For the first time that he had ever noticed, she looked unsure of herself. She bit her lip. "I . . ."

"Tell me, Lahksa."

She looked down at the floor. "I hadn't thought," she said softly.

"Well, then, I'll tell you. I'm offering a role to you. You'll take it—or I'll turn on my heel and walk out of here."

She still wouldn't look at him. "What role are you offering me, Webster?"

He waited a moment before telling her, "Co-NNL and wife."

"Oh, Webster. I thought you'd never ask."

"Well?"

"I do. I will. I take it."

"Good." He looked around. "So. Where do we go from here?"

"The royal apartments," she said, nodding toward an ornate portal. "Through there."

He lifted her into his arms and carried her across the threshold.